PRAISE FOR MIC]

"Thrilling entertainment."

— *PUBLISHERS WEEKLY* ON
MUTATION

"McBride writes with the perfect mixture of suspense and horror that keeps the reader on edge."

— EXAMINER

"McBride's style brings to mind both James Rollins and Michael Crichton."

— SCI-FI & SCARY

"Highly recommended for fans of creature horror and the thrillers of Michael Crichton."

— *THE HORROR REVIEW*

"Michael McBride literally stunned me with his enigmatic talent and kept me hanging on right up until the end."

— *MIDWEST BOOK REVIEW*

ALSO BY MICHAEL MCBRIDE

THE UNIT 51 TRILOGY

*Subhuman * Forsaken * Mutation*

THE VIRAL APOCALYPSE SERIES

*Contagion * Ruination * Extinction*

STANDALONE SCI-FI/HORROR

*Ancient Enemy * Burial Ground * Chimera * Extant * Fearful Symmetry * Innocents Lost * Predatory Instinct * Remains * Subterrestrial * Sunblind * Unidentified * Vector Borne*

THE SNOWBLIND SERIES

*Snowblind * Snowblind: The Killing Grounds*

STANDALONE SUSPENSE THRILLERS

*Bloodletting * Condemned * Immun3 * The Coyote * The Event*

THE EXTINCTION AGENDA SERIES

(Written as Michael Laurence)

*The Extinction Agenda * The Annihilation Protocol * The Elimination Threat*

THE CREATURE FILES

SPORES

MICHAEL MCBRIDE

PRETERNATURAL PRESS
DENVER, COLORADO

First paperback edition published by Preternatural Press

www.michaelmcbride.net

Cover Design by Deranged Doctor Design

Site plan, Historic American Engineering Record, U.S. Army; U.S. National Park Service, Rocky Mountain Regional Office, 1995. From Prints & Photographs Division, Library of Congress (HEAR COLO, Reproduction 1-COMCI, 1- (image 9 of 13); https://www.loc.gov/resource/hhh.co0168.sheet/?sp=1 accessed January 23, 2025)

ISBN 979-8-308-04339-3 (hardcover)

ISBN 979-8-308-04320-1 (trade paperback)

First Edition: January 2025

10 9 8 7 6 5 4 3 2 1

For all of my friends, family, and readers, without whom this book wouldn't exist

U.S. ARMY AIR FORCES NEWSREELS
REEL 2, 1942

A country at war!

The Army Chemical Corps is in double-step to provide the armaments of war an embattled world must have to ensure democracy's survival. America's vast resources are being harnessed to produce chemical and incendiary munitions for our boys overseas. With construction completed on the Rocky Mountain Arsenal in Denver, Colorado, chemistry genius joins with the muscle of thousands of patriotic men and women to win for the ways of freedom. Its present-day production of chlorine and mustard gas, lewisite and white phosphorous is but a mere fraction of the job that lies ahead. As cluster bombs and loaded shells roll off the assembly line and begin their journey around the globe, the forces of liberty can rest assured that the Chemical Corps will meet the demands of the war efforts and bring victory to the side of the right.

Take that, Hitler!

PRODUCTION END - 1982

ROCKY MOUNTAIN ARSENAL

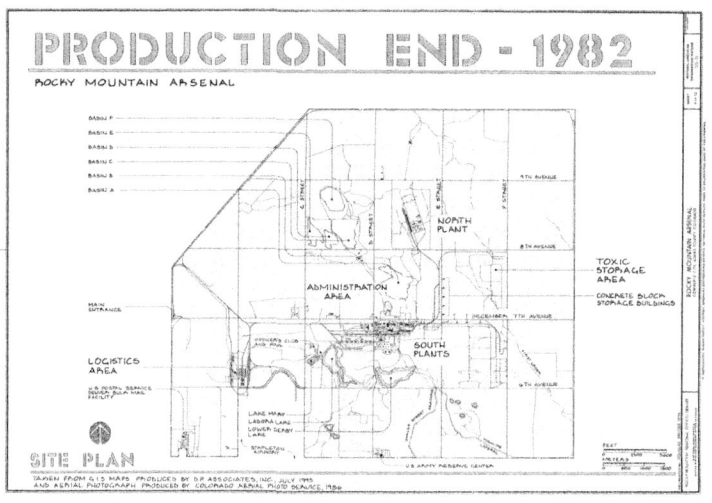

SITE PLAN

TAKEN FROM G.I.S MAPS PRODUCED BY D.P. ASSOCIATES, INC., JULY 1993.
AND AERIAL PHOTOGRAPH PRODUCED BY COLORADO AERIAL PHOTO SERVICE, 1986.

PROLOGUE

The Ford F-150 sped east on the narrow two-lane highway, the peripheral glow of its headlights illuminating barren grasslands from which an occasional oil derrick materialized, its hammerlike pump rising and falling against the dark horizon. Silhouetted cattle dotted the fields, their monotonous lowing punctuated by the rattle of the horse trailer juddering over every crack in the weathered asphalt.

Dayna Raines lay on the back seat of the extended cab, watching the world pass through the side window. She was still too wound up from the show to close her eyes, let alone sleep. Second place. She simply couldn't believe it. Sure, she'd been practicing every day since she was old enough to sit in a saddle, but never in her wildest dreams had she thought she'd place so high, especially with this year's competition. Yet she had. She and Thunder had pulled off the performance of a lifetime and qualified for regionals. In Houston! And if she somehow managed to reach the winner's circle there, then this time next year she'd be on her way to Lexington for the National Horse Show.

"Try to get some shuteye back there," her dad said. "Even red ribbon winners have to go to school in the morning."

The dashboard lights limned her parents' contented faces with an almost ethereal light. Her dad lowered his hand from the wheel and rested it on her mom's knee. She merely smiled at him and resumed humming along to the music.

They could be so corny.

"Can't I stay home, just this once?" Dayna asked.

"Not if you expect to miss a whole week in May," Mom said.

"I'll be worthless tomorrow on so little sleep."

"How is that different from any other day?" Dad asked.

"Oh, ha-ha. You're a riot."

Thunder whinnied from the trailer.

Dayna met her father's eyes in the rearview mirror. Her Thoroughbred gelding never raised a fuss.

"Can I at least drive myself?" Dayna asked.

"Not until you have your license."

"But I've been driving on the ranch since I was—"

Thunder screamed and kicked the dropdown back door, causing the entire trailer to swing. Dad's eyes crinkled with concern when he glanced at the rearview mirror again.

"You don't think a rattlesnake got in there with him, do you?" Mom asked.

"It's too late in the season for—"

Thunder screamed and kicked again. And again and again. The force of the repeated impacts made the entire truck swerve into the oncoming lane.

Dad's eyes widened in panic. Mom braced herself against the dashboard.

A roaring sound arose, drowning out even Thunder's frightened cries.

The road in front of the F-150 rose, as though a hill had suddenly appeared where there hadn't been one before. It rolled toward them like a wave, breaking apart as it advanced. The truck plummeted into the Earth as the ground simply vanished beneath it. Rocks and fractured asphalt slammed against the hood and dented the roof. The grill struck first, hurling Dayna between the front seats, past her parents, and through the shattered windshield.

She struck something hard, her breath bursting from her lips, freckling her chin with blood. Ribs cracked and bones snapped. Something sharp poked her from the inside. She couldn't see her parents. Where were they? She caught a fleeting glimpse of her mom, her head forced back by the airbag—

An avalanche of rubble eclipsed the sky. It buried the truck and pinned Dayna, leaving her barely enough space to turn her head. Her breath returned with a gasp. She tried to cry out. To move. She could barely . . . inhale. Dust . . . in her lungs.

Pain.

There was so much pain.

From somewhere far away, she heard a horse bleating in agony.

Its tortured screams followed her into the darkness.

1

Denver International Airport
12:06 a.m.

Today

Mateo Ramos tossed the last suitcase into the baggage cart and closed the curtain. He lowered his head against the deluge and climbed behind the wheel of the tug. The sheeting rain beat a drumroll on the roof of the ground support vehicle, its lone wiper overwhelmed by the sheer volume of water. He accelerated across the tarmac toward the entrance to the service tunnel, beckoned by the pale amber glow.

His shift had ended more than an hour ago. Not that anyone cared. Pretty much everyone else had already taken off for the night, including his supervisor. Thanks to the weather system rolling in from the west, every incoming flight had been either canceled or postponed until the morning. All except for Flight 2213 out of Albuquerque anyway, which had been delayed for more than two hours before finally taking off. At least it was an Embraer 175, not a Boeing 737, and the seventy-eight-seater had been practically empty to boot. He hadn't even needed the second cart, which was fine by him. His back was killing him, his clothes were soaked underneath his slicker, and he couldn't have been in a worse mood. He was tired of always getting the short end of the stick and had half a mind to tell Mr. Pritchard exactly where he could stick this job, but Isabella would kill him if he lost his health insurance this close to her due date.

The tug descended the ramp into the underground tunnel, which was barely wide enough for two absurdly narrow lanes. A bare concrete wall passed on one side, while chain-link fencing had been strung between the support columns on the other, barring access to the fat pipes behind it. Stairways to maintenance rooms and fire escapes appeared in his peripheral vision, only to disappear just as quickly. Ordinarily, these underground warrens were a beehive of activity, with tugs and baggage carts racing at breakneck speeds from the concourses to the terminal and back again. There were often so many that accidents and gridlock occurred, necessitating traffic cops and emergency medical personnel during peak hours.

In many ways, Denver International Airport was its own little city. With a total land mass of nearly fifty-three square miles, it was larger than both Boston and San Francisco. Nearly forty thousand employees were required to handle the quarter of a million travelers who passed through the terminal and rode the train to the three remote concourses every day, the majority of them with checked baggage that needed to be transported through a million square feet of subterranean passages to the 7000-foot-long tunnels connecting them to the runways. There were so many side corridors and alleys that it was easy to see how countless workers had gotten lost through the years. Easier still to see why there were so many conspiracy theories about what went on down here, although in his three years as a baggage handler, he had yet to stumble upon the headquarters of the Illuminati or any little green men.

Chuckling, he accelerated through the tunnel.

BRITTANY BLOOM STRODE past one closed restaurant and shop after another, long blond hair flowing behind her and the clicking of heels echoing from the empty concourse. Her carry-on bag's wheels squeaked on the polished tile, which only served to amplify her already rotten mood. She'd intended to grab something to eat at Albuquerque International Sunport, but everyplace had been closed by the time she arrived, and her flight had been delayed for so long that now nothing was open here, either. With seemingly every other incoming flight delayed or canceled, she could only pray the car rental counter would still be open by the time she caught the bus there, assuming it was even running.

She needed to take a deep breath and clear her mind of all this negativity, which only hammered home the message that she shouldn't have had to be here in the first place. It wasn't like the client's group was going to prescribe a competing pharmaceutical, not while her employer had the market for his medical specialty cornered. He just wanted to see her again and, like most young doctors, wasn't accustomed to being told "no." She'd just have to wear a skirt that was a little looser than this one, a blouse that wasn't quite as sheer, and a professional smile she hoped wouldn't wither under his advances.

But that was tomorrow's problem. Tonight, she just needed to find anyplace serving actual food and pass out in the hotel bed for a few blissful hours.

Brittany mounted the escalator and rode all the way down to the train platform, where a few other passengers she recognized from her flight waited. The digital signs above the sliding access doors let her know that it would be five minutes before the train arrived.

"Perfect," she whispered. "Just perfect."

She should have used the restroom when she'd had the chance, but she'd decided to hold off in hopes of avoiding this exact situation. Now, unless she wanted to wait another ten minutes for the next train, there wasn't enough time to ride the escalator up to the concourse and get back down here again.

A clump of flight attendants and pilots descended the escalator. Despite suffering through the same turbulence and screaming baby for an hour and a half straight, they appeared to be in much higher spirits than she was. They shouldered right up to her in front of the door to the lead car and kept on talking and laughing like she wasn't even there. She contemplated moving to a different car's entrance, but she was exhausted and her feet were killing her, so she just tuned them out and alternately stared at her phone and the empty transit tunnel on the other side of the glass.

A computerized voice announced the train's arrival.

Lighted cars blurred past the window and screeched to a halt. The doors whooshed open. She stepped inside, grabbed the nearest metal pole, and braced her feet. With a hydraulic hiss, the doors closed, and the vehicle slowly started to move.

GERRY DRAKE SHOULDERED through the flimsy plywood door, removed his hardhat, and rode the escalator up to the main level. The Jeppesen Terminal renovation project had already been months behind schedule when he took the job, and there was nothing he could do to change that. Good luck finding skilled construction workers in this market, let alone any willing to work overnights at an airport where they had to park their cars twenty minutes away and take a routinely delayed shuttle. Heck, there wasn't even any food available. And while the city's pay and benefits were decent, it did have that pesky rule requiring citizenship or a green card, and he'd found very few people with either who were willing to work as hard as the day laborers he was accustomed to hiring.

At least his guys weren't tripping over travelers all

night. Crews from the first and second shifts received countless complaints about everything from construction noise and the volume of their voices to their lack of uniforms and inability to answer questions about flight times and gates, for which the oblivious executive management team continually reprimanded them. And while it felt like this place was slowly sucking the life out of him, there were also nights like this, when the terminal was practically empty and he could come up to the Great Hall, grab a seat wherever he wanted, and enjoy his lunch while marveling at the architectural ingenuity.

The place really was a masterpiece of design and engineering, assuming anyone ever bothered to notice. From the peaked roof designed to look like snowcapped mountains to the soaring windows offering views of the entire Front Range of the Rockies, it was a work of art at peace with its environment, or at least as much as a facility of its nature could be. And while his contribution might have been merely expanding and modernizing the train platforms, it meant something to be a part of this place's storied history.

Drake leaned back in the chair and surveyed the vast space, where a single maintenance worker drove his floor polisher across the glimmering granite tiles. A pair of TSA officers walked along the second-story balcony, closed storefronts passing beside them. Despite the clamor of hammers and the clanging of ductwork reverberating from the level below him, it was a strangely serene moment, as though the Earth had stopped turning and time itself held its breath.

A distant rumble made the ground tremble. The sound grew to a roar and the entire airport shook.

Potted plants toppled over. Chairs clattered to the floor. Glass shattered. Signage fell. The maintenance worker removed his headphones and looked curiously at all of the work he'd suddenly inherited.

Bleating alarms and shouting voices filled the air.

Drake struggled to his feet and staggered across the bucking ground toward the escalator.

THE OVERHEAD LIGHTS flickered and died. Ramos slammed the brakes as the entire world shook. Debris rained from the ceiling. Chain-link fencing fell onto his skidding vehicle, raking the hood and windshield. The bumper clipped a support column. He felt the tug threatening to roll, the weight of the full cart lifting its outside tires from the ground. Overcorrecting, he slammed into the opposite wall and struck his forehead against the steering wheel. Luggage tumbled from the cart and scattered across the concrete.

THE ENTIRE TRAIN LURCHED. With a scream of shearing metal, it jumped the track and slammed back and forth between the retaining walls, filling the air with sparks. The ground opened in front of the lead vehicle, swallowing chunks of concrete and lengths of rail. The

front end abruptly dipped and slammed into the far lip of
the crater, shattering the windshield.

Brittany lost her grip on the post and slid down the
slanted floor in the darkness, colliding with rolling bags
and the airplane crew. A cry burst from her lips, but a blow
to the back of her head cut it short. The seamless black
sparkled with stars and she tasted blood in the back of her
throat.

Emergency lights snapped on, filling the tunnel with
an eerie crimson glow. Warning beacons flashed and
bleeped. One of the flight attendants sobbed, the awful
sound hanging in the stillness.

DRAKE BOUNDED down the steps of the stalled escalator
and ran toward the construction barrier. He'd heard a
resounding crash from deeper in the tunnel, one far louder
than the fallen plywood walls could have made. His crew
backed away from their abandoned equipment as beams
and conduits fell from the partially finished ceiling and
crashed to the floor where they'd been standing mere
seconds prior.

The shaking abruptly ceased, leaving them staring at
each other in shock.

Running footsteps and crackling walkie-talkies
emanated from the Great Hall above them. The reserve
generator kicked in and restored power to the terminal,
which only served to add countless more alarms to the
chorus.

"Is everyone all right?" he asked.

"What the hell was that?" one of his men asked. "It felt like the whole place got hit by a giant truck."

Drake's mind raced through the possibilities. There were redundancies upon redundancies outside the airport boundaries to ensure the uninterrupted flow of electricity, which meant the disruption had to have occurred within the facility itself. Was this a terrorist attack? Had someone detonated a bomb? No . . . that had most definitely been an earthquake. He'd experienced enough of them growing up in California, but he'd never heard of one hitting this area.

Faint screams echoed from the tunnel.

The men all looked at one another to see if the others had heard it, too.

Drake shouldered past them and took off at a sprint along the narrow walkway beside the track.

RAMOS DABBED the bridge of his nose and glanced at his bloody fingertips. His vision swam as he took in his surroundings. The suitcases scattered across the floor. The smoke trickling from underneath the hood. The twinkling glass from the shattered headlight.

Everything had happened so fast that he couldn't wrap his head around it.

The tug's engine rattled and died. He tried starting it again, but the blasted thing wouldn't turn over. With a groan, he opened the door and fell to the ground. He struggled to his feet and leaned against the little vehicle while he rode out a wave of dizziness.

At a guess, he was maybe halfway between C Con and B Con, and with the way he felt right now, he wasn't about to make the trek on foot. He hesitated to call in the accident — there'd be incident reports and investigations, worker's comp and medical exams — but he couldn't see how he had a choice in the matter.

He unholstered the transceiver from his hip and dialed in dispatch, but there wasn't so much as a buzz of static. A glance at the unit revealed its broken casing and cracked screen. He must have landed on it when he fell from the tug.

Ramos swore and hurled the useless device against the wall. If he hadn't gotten stuck waiting for that stupid flight, he'd be sound asleep in his bed and not staring down the barrel of a termination hearing. This wasn't his fault, though. He clearly remembered the ground shuddering and—

Something bad had happened. There must have been a plane crash or an explosion. Maybe even a terrorist attack, in which case he sure as hell didn't want to be standing around with his thumb up his butt.

He took off at a jog, his head clearing a little more with every step. There were maintenance exits all through these tunnels, and while he'd never bothered to find out where they went, he knew there were landlines hardwired to the communications center inside of each.

It didn't take long to reach the ramp leading up to the nearest door, above which were signs indicating there was a fire extinguisher and an AED inside. The doorknob turned easily in his hand, but the door must have shifted in its frame. He repeatedly threw his shoulder into it until it finally opened and sent him stumbling into a dimly lit corridor. The staircase to his left granted access to the electrical, ventilation, and long-abandoned baggage conveyor systems, while the door straight ahead serviced the eastern tracks of the automated train. And there, on the wall to his right, was a yellow emergency phone with a direct line to the comm center.

Ramos snatched it from the cradle, brought it to his ear, and listened to the open line ring as he waited for the operator to pick up. Three rings. Four. Five. For the comm center to be so overwhelmed that they couldn't answer an emergency line, something really terrible must have—

A scream echoed from the other side of the door to the eastern tracks. He set down the handset, the tinny ringing sound reverberating in the short corridor as he slowly approached the metal slab. More screams erupted, from seemingly mere feet away. He jerked open the door and stepped into a nightmare.

The narrow walkway beside the tracks was riddled with cracks and simply ended about fifty feet away, where a giant sinkhole appeared to have opened up beneath the train. The lead car stood at a thirty-degree angle from the pit, its front end crumpled around the jagged ledge. Panicked cries and pained sobs emanated from inside the vehicle. A man wearing a pilot's uniform forced the side doors open and squeezed between them—

A chunk of concrete broke from the lip, dropping the nose of the first car and raising the second from the ground by its coupling. The pilot tumbled through the gap and plummeted into the depths, his startled shout ending with a sickening *thuck*.

Ramos worked his way as close to the edge as he dared. He lowered himself to the ground so he could look into the car through the slender gap between the upper rim of the windshield and the concrete. There were at least four or five people still trapped inside, looking up at him through wide, frightened eyes.

"Grab my hand!" he shouted, thrusting his arm through the opening.

———

THE FLOOR BUCKLED and groaned as Brittany scooted closer to the front, broken glass crunching underfoot. Fractured concrete filled the opening where the windshield had been, save for the foot-wide gap above it through which a baggage handler leaned. Even if she managed to reach his hand, there was barely enough space for her to squeeze through, and if the car shifted at all . . .

Blood trickled down her forehead and into her eye. She wiped it away and forced down the memory of the pilot falling from the open doorway. A sharp cracking sound echoed from the depths, eliciting shrieks of terror from the trailing vehicles.

"Hurry up!" the baggage handler shouted.

One of the stewardesses elbowed her aside and grasped the man's hand. Baring his teeth, he pulled until her entire torso was through the opening, then reached back for Brittany. This time, she didn't hesitate. She grabbed his hand, braced her foot against the concrete, and climbed—

With a metallic screech, the car dropped several feet, tipping forward in the process.

The baggage handler shrieked in agony. Bones snapped. Warmth spattered Brittany's face. She experienced a sensation of weightlessness as the car inverted. The other passengers tumbled past her through the gaping hole where the windshield had been and careened, screaming, into the darkness in a tangle of severed limbs. She caught the frame as she fell and hung on for dear life.

———

DRAKE RACED ALONG THE TRACKS, his chest aching from the exertion. His transceiver crackled with the staccato voices of emergency personnel responding to disasters all over the airport. The comm center was down, leaving panicked dispatchers coordinating their movements by radio alone. A section of the parking structure had collapsed, dropping chunks of concrete onto parked cars. There was an electrical fire somewhere and equipment failures all over the place. A car rental agency bus had struck a support post on the arrivals level. Goods had fallen from store shelves, including duty free shops, from which flammable pools of alcohol seeped. Alarms and sirens blared. Officers from all levels of law enforcement converged on the airport from seemingly everywhere at once.

The screams grew louder with every step. Emergency lights glinted from the train's roof as it slowly came into view. His subconscious picked up on a snippet of conversation from his walkie-talkie.

"*. . .magnitude five-point-eight . . . epicenter seven miles west. . .*"

Fine cracks marred the walkway and the concrete wall

beside him. None of them appeared structurally significant, but if there was another quake or the aftershocks were powerful enough—

The ground shivered, knocking him off stride. This wasn't right. These things didn't happen here. The airport hadn't been designed to handle any sort of seismic activity.

An eyewatering chemical scent struck him as he approached. The ground had collapsed, taking an enormous section of the track with it. A baggage handler lay at the edge of the broken concrete, staring blankly at the ground, blood flowing from his shoulder. The woman beside him was in even worse shape.

With a resounding *crack*, the entire train lurched forward. The front car dropped several feet, its weight dragging the second car to its tipping point and lifting the front end of the third. Shadows moved behind their windows. Shouts echoed from inside. A woman screamed from directly below him. He glanced down—

"Oh, my God."

The woman dangled from the front of the vehicle, her feet swinging over the nothingness. He could barely see the rubble, maybe fifty feet below her, and the broken bodies draped over it. His mind reeled with the impossibility of it all. The concourse had been built on solid bedrock . . . hadn't it?

"Help!" she screamed.

A high-heeled shoe fell from her foot and tumbled into the pit. There was no way she'd be able to hang on until help arrived.

He had to do something.

A sliver of the walkway clung to the wall. He scooted

along it until he was even with the car's open side door, maybe four feet away. Heart pounding, he lunged across the gap, flattened himself against the inverted vehicle, and carefully lowered himself inside. He slid down the wall and balanced on the deformed windshield frame, one foot on either side of the woman's hands. She looked up at him through wide, terrified eyes.

"Please don't let me fall."

Drake transferred all of his weight to his heels as he slowly squatted and reached down between his knees. He grasped her wrists and pulled—

The concrete supporting the train broke with a thunderous boom. Drake shouted as the car dropped straight down into the earth. He drew the woman to his chest and braced for—

Impact.

He absorbed the woman's weight, his back folding over a jagged mound of concrete, his ribs snapping like kindling. Her forehead struck the ground with an awful thump. The other cars came crashing down right on top of theirs, one after another, crushing each other, trapping the two of them inside the wreckage.

Smoke and dust flooded the cab. Pitiful cries drifted from somewhere above him. The woman made no attempt to move.

Drake sputtered and tried to roll over, but he could barely turn his head far enough to let the blood drain from his mouth. It dribbled down the rubble and dripped into a puddle of shimmering fluid.

Something moved in his peripheral vision. Small. Low to the ground.

A wolf spider crawled from a crevice, its long spindly legs rippling toward him. Wiry filaments grew from its head and back. A reddish-brown fuzz framed its sickly black eyes. It seemed to swell, as though inflating—

A powdery mist burst from its back and swirled into the air.

2

5,000 Feet Above Eastern Colorado
1:16 a.m.

G eneral Jack Randall unconsciously traced the weblike scarring covering the right half of his face while he watched the dark prairie streaking past below the Sikorsky UH-60 Black Hawk, but he saw none of it. In his mind, he'd been transported to another time, one long removed, but never far from his thoughts. He'd spent all of the intervening years preparing for this eventuality, as he'd always feared he'd one day return to this place, the site of his greatest achievement . . . and his most catastrophic failure.

"ETA five minutes, sir," the pilot said, his voice made tinny by the headset.

Randall merely nodded. While it had been decades since his last field operation, the men seated beside and behind him in the helicopter needed no last-minute instructions. They'd done this same thing dozens of times and in as many locations, albeit none of them this close to a population center. And that was what worried him. If they were indeed dealing with what he feared, then they couldn't have been headed into a worse setting. Containment inside an airport through which nearly eighty million travelers passed every year posed challenges beyond any they'd ever faced and there was no room for mistakes.

A great shining beacon of light emerged from the darkness and slowly resolved into the telltale mustache-shaped hotel, multi-peaked terminal, and remote concourses of Denver International Airport. The chopper banked around the perimeter and descended toward the northernmost gates, where the tarmac had been cleared of all planes, support vehicles, and personnel to ensure there were no witnesses to his team's arrival. If anyone were to notice five men entering the building wearing isolation gear resembling spacesuits, there would be questions that neither he nor the men higher up the chain of command were prepared to answer.

"I'll get you as close to the building as I can," the pilot said.

Randall didn't respond. He might have been creeping into his mid-eighties and long past his physical prime, but he needed no concessions or special treatment beyond those afforded by his rank. The day he couldn't perform his duties at the level he demanded of himself, he'd put a gun in his mouth.

"Codenames only from this point on," he said.

"Yes, sir," his men answered as one.

A lone transport vehicle trailing a pair of open baggage

carts emerged from the tunnel below the wall of windows lining the gates. The driver climbed out and strode across the wet pavement to greet the new arrivals, the rotor wash making her baggy yellow hazmat suit flap as though preparing to take flight. The chopper's flashing red and green running lights reflected from her visor as it settled to the ground a dozen feet away.

Randall looked past her into the dimly lit tunnel and couldn't help but think of the inscription above the gates to hell in Dante's Inferno.

Abandon all hope, ye who enter here.

RANDALL PULLED ASIDE the driver while his men loaded their gear into the rearmost cart. Despite her diminutive frame and dainty features, U.S. Air Force Lt. Colonel Tanja Malikov radiated an aura of authority. Under FEMA's direction, the Medical Element Commander of the Colorado Chemical Biological Rapid Response Team — CCB-RRT — had assumed control of the situation within minutes of the discovery of the bodies. She was undoubtedly bitter about being ordered to stand down, move her men outside the cordon, and, worse, play chauffer for the unit usurping her command, but Randall didn't care in the slightest. The U.S. Army CBRNE Enhanced Response Force — CERF — might fall under the auspices of the Department of Defense and function outside of the traditional emergency response framework with which she was familiar, but make no mistake . . .

He was in charge now.

"Status update," Randall shouted over the chopper's roar.

"The entire concourse . . . " Malikov's words dried up when she noticed his hideously disfigured face, but she recovered quickly enough. " . . . has been evacuated and the eastern tunnels quarantined."

"What about the remains?"

"Undisturbed, as ordered, although their condition appears to have . . . degenerated."

Randall recalled the initial imagery he'd received. Any appreciable progression of the physical symptoms over such a short period of time was cause for alarm.

"You've been able to contain the warm zone to the subterranean levels of the concourse, correct?"

"My men are exceptionally good at what they do. We've detected zero chemical or biological contaminants outside of the exclusion zone."

"And you've been able to keep a lid on it?"

"So far, but even with changing gates and rerouting all incoming and outgoing flights through the other two concourses, it's only a matter of time before the cancelations start piling up and the sky overhead becomes a parking lot. Blaming the concourse's closure on earthquake damage will buy us some time, but based on the condition of the other buildings, that excuse won't hold up to scrutiny for very long."

Randall froze and stared at Malikov.

"You haven't halted airport operations?"

"That's a decision for the FAA and DOT," she said. "They're concerned that shutting this place down would disrupt the entire global airline industry and create conditions ripe for societal unrest."

Randall ground his teeth so hard he thought he heard a molar crack.

"I appreciate your concern, but my team has this place locked down tight," Malikov said, discreetly watching him from the corner of her eye. "And you did say you've never seen anything like this before, right?"

Randall didn't dignify her insinuation with a response. He waved off the Black Hawk and rounded on his men, who'd taken seats on the first baggage cart, legs hanging over the sides and heads lowered against the rotor wash.

"Helmets and comms on at all times," he said. "And no direct physical contact."

"What are those suits anyway?" Malikov asked.

"They're pretty much just like the one you're wearing," Alpha said, "only they cost about a million dollars more."

Colonel Aaron Massie had been with CERF for nearly twenty years, far longer than any of the others. The special tactics officer was an expert on assault zone assessment, fire support, battlefield trauma care, and combat search and rescue. He was also accustomed to having unquestioned command of field operations and resented being forced to play second fiddle, but considering the situation's catastrophic potential, Randall needed to handle this one personally. And he sure as hell didn't have to justify his rationale for doing so to a subordinate, no matter how suspicious his motives might be.

"They're tactical CBRNE suits made of Kevlar-reinforced Tyvek material," Gamma said, offering a wink and a roguish smile. Randall had wrenched Lieutenant Colonel Gavin Robbins from the clutches of DEVCOM, the Army Futures Command's cutting-edge research laboratory, where his technological talents were wasted. "They utilize both long- and short-range comms with individual frequencies so we can communicate directly with one another or with the team as a whole using these forearm control panels. In addition to custom features like airtight seals and self-cooling zones, the primary life support subsystem, or PLiSS, we all wear on our backs is equipped with an advanced oxygen delivery unit, plus carbon dioxide, trace contaminant, and waste elimination systems."

"Waste elimination?" Malikov said.

Beta chuckled and clapped Delta on the shoulder. While Captain Brett Feldman, who'd served tours of duty in both Afghanistan and Syria, was six years older than his brother, the two could have passed for twins. He'd started lobbying for Brian's recruitment before he'd even made it through basic training.

"You wouldn't believe what this guy's doing in his suit right now," he said.

Malikov merely rolled her eyes and headed for the tug.

Randall climbed into the vehicle beside her and seated his helmet over his head. He latched the airtight collar and dialed up the flow of oxygen from his PLiSS as the vehicle accelerated into the tunnel. The emergency lighting cast a harsh red glare on the exhaust-stained concrete walls and dusty pipes blurring past in his peripheral vision. He needed to absorb every last detail if he was going to figure out how the contaminant had gotten into the airport and, if it truly was what he thought it was, how he was going to prevent it from wiping out every living organism with which it came into contact.

A NEGATIVE PRESSURE chamber had been erected in the middle of the tunnel, spanning its entire width. Randall passed through the plastic sheeting and found a dozen body bags spread out on the ground, already unzipped and ready for the human remains awaiting him down in the sinkhole, from which the back end of the train stood.

He walked right up to the edge and looked down. The pit had to be nearly a hundred feet deep and twenty-five feet across, at least at the top. It widened significantly toward the bottom, where standing fluid reflected the portable stadium lights shining down from the rim. The train cars rested at odd angles on top of one another, making it difficult to see the bodies trapped inside and strewn across the rubble below them.

The earth shuddered, causing the wreckage to groan and a powdery residue to billow into the air. Particulate matter glimmered in the haze, which swirled and eddied like smoke as it slowly dissipated.

Randall rode out the aftershock and crouched to get a better look at the remains. Even from this height, he could tell that not only were they dealing with exactly what he feared, but its reproductive rate was beyond any theoretical worst-case scenario.

He clenched his fists so none of the others would see his hands shaking when he turned to face them.

"I need twelve portable patient isolation units," he said.

"We have three-layer CDC Hot Zone body bags," Malikov said. "There's no need for PIUs unless these people aren't actually. . . "

Her voice trailed off as the implications of his words stuck her.

Randall merely stared at her until she reluctantly nodded and ducked out of sight to make the call.

3
_____

Pasadena, California
1:38 a.m.

The ringing phone roused Dayna from a deep sleep, Thunder's screams reverberating in her subconscious. She could still feel the pain in her chest, taste the dust in her mouth. It was the dream. The same dream she had every night. Buried beneath the rubble. Praying for a merciful God to save her, to put her poor horse out of his misery, to make her parents breathe again.

She wiped the cold sweat from her brow, grabbed her cellphone from the nightstand, and answered without looking at the number of the incoming call.

"Dr. Raines? This is Dr. Cassandra Dobbs at USGS."

Dayna sat up and hit the bedside lamp, all vestiges of sleep now gone. She'd known the Emergency Management Coordinator of the United States Geological Survey since grad school, but not once in the intervening decade had she called her this late at night, let alone referred to herself in such a formal manner, which could only mean only one thing: she was calling in a professional capacity.

Something terrible must have happened.

"What's going on, Cassie?"

"Approximately thirty minutes ago, seismic monitoring stations detected a magnitude five-point-eight earthquake in Colorado. Its epicenter is roughly eight miles northeast of downtown Denver."

"That can't be right. There hasn't been an earthquake that far east of the Trans-Rocky Mountain Fault System in more than fifty years, and that one was . . ."

Dayna's words died on her lips.

"That's why we're calling you. As one of the world's foremost authorities on non-tectonic seismic activity and predictive modeling, you're in a position to offer insight we desperately need."

"You're worried about spontaneous regeneration of that specific seismographic process?"

"We're worried that we don't have the slightest idea what might have caused it. There are too many variables unique to this situation for accurate seismic forecasting."

"Wait . . . are you suggesting you want me on the ground?"

"I'm afraid we might require more than that."

It took Dayna a moment to comprehend the implications. Her mouth instantly dried out and her stomach twisted into a knot.

"You can't be serious."

"That's worst-case scenario," Cassie said. "Look . . . we

need to figure out what's going on down there and if we should be concerned about future activity of even greater severity. There are three million people in the Denver metro area, none of whose homes were designed to withstand any kind of tectonic activity. Nearly a fifth of them live within a ten-mile radius of the epicenter. We could very well be looking at another Mexico City."

Dayna sighed and swung her bare legs over the side of the bed. It looked like she was done sleeping for the foreseeable future.

"What do you need from me?"

"Go to your lab and gather whatever equipment you need. A car will pick you up there in forty-five minutes and take you to John Wayne, where a plane bound for DIA will be waiting." Cassie paused. "This is the real deal, Dayna. Some very powerful people have taken an acute interest in this situation, so be extremely careful."

THE BLACK CHEVY TAHOE drove right out onto the tarmac at John Wayne Orange County Airport, where men wearing drab military fatigues transferred the cargo from a matching government vehicle to the waiting Gulfstream G150 charter plane. As soon as they finished, the vehicle sped away and Dayna's driver pulled into the vacated gap. The men opened the trunk behind her and started unloading her gear.

"Careful with those cases," she called back to them. "That equipment is extremely fragile."

A man wearing a flight suit opened her door and offered his hand.

"Captain Ryan Christensen, United States Navy," he said, helping her from the vehicle and guiding her toward the lowered boarding stairs. "If you'll please come with me, ma'am . . ."

Dayna bounded up into a cabin where four others already waited. They looked expectantly at her as the pilot raised the stairs behind her and hustled into the cockpit, from which she heard the copilot already coordinating takeoff with the tower.

A young man with shaggy chestnut hair and a wispy chin beard lounged on the leather sofa to her right. He inclined his chin in greeting, pulled the hood of his sweatshirt over his head, and closed his eyes. A heap of neon-colored bags covered with patches and logos filled the seat across the aisle from him. A diminutive man with short dark hair sat in the rear-facing seat behind him, across the retractable table from a woman with olive skin and messy ebon hair. A burly man wearing a flannel shirt and khaki work pants sat across the aisle from her. He glanced up from his tablet, offered a wan smile, and returned his attention to the screen.

Dayna stuffed her bag under the rear-facing seat opposite him and stumbled into the table when the plane abruptly started moving. She buckled herself into the plush chair and watched the asphalt race past in the darkness. The turbines screamed and the nose rose so sharply that the lap belt bit into her hips. She yawned to release the pressure in her ears and watched Hollywood fall away below her.

"You must be our mysterious leader." The man across the table from her set down his tablet and proffered his hand. "I'm Avery Stephens. Urban Search and Rescue, California Task Force Five. Chemical Engineer and civilian WMD specialist."

"WMD?" the woman across the aisle said. "Why on earth would we need a weapons of mass destruction specialist?"

"All I know is we're going to be potentially dealing with some pretty nasty chemicals under unknown conditions."

"There must be some sort of mistake. I'm a medical mycologist. I specialize in fungal pathologies and the development of antifungal treatments."

"I've seen you on campus," Dayna said. "Doctor . . . "

"Partridge. Sydney Partridge. Affiliate faculty. I teach a graduate-level class in biomedical engineering. You're from Caltech, too?"

"Yeah. Dayna Raines. Seismological Laboratory."

"I'm starting to sense a pattern here," the man across the aisle from her said. "My name's Tim Telford. I teach courses in geological and environmental engineering at USC and consult on mining closure and reclamation projects for both the National Park Service and the State of California." He shifted in his seat so he could see the guy sprawled on the couch behind him. "What kind of specialist are you, my slumbering friend?"

The young man cracked an eye, then slowly closed it again.

"Craig Preston," he said, "but I'm known professionally as BlitzCraig. I'm the reigning Drone Racing League

Champion. You've probably seen me on NBC or Fox Sports."

Dayna felt a sinking sensation in the pit of her stomach as the pieces started to fit together. She wished to God she'd never answered her phone.

"SO WHAT, exactly, are we dealing with?" Sydney asked.

Dayna swiveled her laptop on the small table so everyone could see the screen. Everyone except for Craig anyway, who'd plugged in a pair of earbuds and stared at his phone. She brought up a satellite image with an enormous red bull's-eye overlaid on it.

"This map shows the epicenter and range of the earthquake superimposed over a one-hundred-square-mile grid. That's downtown Denver in the bottom left corner of the screen. I-25 heads due north from there through Commerce City and Northglenn, at the top left. The more sparsely populated suburbs of Reunion and Henderson are at the top, while Aurora is at the bottom. Denver International Airport and the surrounding acreage fill the majority of the right side of the screen. That conspicuous polygon-shaped gap of undeveloped land right in the middle is the Rocky Mountain Arsenal National Wildlife Refuge, where, from 1942 to 1982, the Army Chemical Corps produced incendiary munitions and chemical warfare agents."

"Chief among them sarin and VX, which were originally developed by the Nazis," Stephens said. "They formed the backbone of our post-World War Two chemical arsenal."

"Active production was halted more than forty years ago, and the bombs were dismantled, but the entire area remained severely contaminated, thanks in large part to methods of disposal that were questionable at best, even for the time."

"How questionable?" Telford asked.

Dayna switched to another tab, which contained an old black-and-white aerial photograph of the site before the military base had been demolished. It showed facilities identified as North and South Plants, Toxic Storage Yard, and chemical evaporation basins A through F. She clicked on a dot labeled "Injection Disposal Well," and a page filled with detailed schematics opened.

"This is a deep injection well," Dayna said. "The shaft is just over twelve thousand feet long. It passes through sixteen distinct layers of sedimentary rock and shale and terminates below a stratum of Precambrian granite. While we might not have possessed the same level of geological knowledge half a century ago, one could argue that forcing a hundred-and-sixty-five million gallons of chemicals into the ground over a four-year span wasn't necessarily the brightest idea. In fact, it resulted in a swarm of earthquakes greater than five-point-three magnitude on the Richter scale, necessitating its permanent decommissioning." She opened another page displaying a map of those earthquakes, along with amoeboid shapes marking their "felt" range. "Now, if you compare the epicenter of those quakes to today's . . ."

She overlaid the graphic on top of the satellite map. The epicenters aligned perfectly.

"The area's been stable for over fifty years," Telford said. "What changed?"

"That's what they need us to figure out."

"You'll have to forgive me," Sydney said, "but I don't understand what any of this has to do with me. All I was told was that they needed someone with extensive biomedical expertise to help qualify a potentially novel extremophilic species."

"Extremophilic?" Stephens said.

"It means they're able to survive in some of the harshest conditions on the planet," Telford said. "Like the bacteria that live in those brightly colored hot springs in Yellowstone and the hydrothermal vents on the bottom of the ocean."

"Fungi are capable of surviving in similar environments," Sydney said. "We're talking about a broad kingdom of eukaryotic organisms, which, in addition to mushrooms, includes molds, yeasts, and numerous species that have adapted to survive extreme temperatures, pressures, salinity, desiccation, and pH. Many of them are capable of producing compounds with antimicrobial properties and groundbreaking medical applications. In fact, we've been able to synthesize promising anti-inflammatory drugs from fungi living beneath the oceanic crust and cancer treatments from a toxic species of mold that thrives in Death Valley. We've even found species capable of breaking down hazardous chemicals into their inert organic constituents, but there aren't any capable of causing earthquakes. And none that couldn't be more quickly and easily classified using the equipment in my lab."

"All of this brainpower and none of you have figured it out yet?" Craig piped up. "They're worried those chemicals just kept on eating through the ground and they've destabilized the region. It's Lady Earthquake's job to figure out if the whole area's going to collapse and swallow downtown Denver. Mr. Weapons of Mass Destruction needs to determine which chemicals are still active down there and how to neutralize them. It's my job to pilot some fancy camera straight down a two-mile-long shaft and explore the cavity at the bottom, and Mine Guy's to figure out how to seal it back up. And you, Miss Shroom? You get to identify whatever's got these super-secret government types all hot and bothered."

"They think this species has military applications?"

"Ding-ding-ding. Tell her what she's won, Johnny."

Everyone turned and looked at Dayna.

"Is that true?" Sydney asked.

"I was given just as little information as the rest of you, but his logic stands to reason."

"I didn't sign on for this."

"That makes two of us, but, at this point, I don't see how any of us has much of a choice in the matter. Whatever happened back then . . . it's our problem now."

4

Rocky Mountain Arsenal

1966

"How did it happen?" *Major Jack Randall asked.*

"We're still trying to figure that out," Dr. James Thompson said.

The two men were diametric opposites. Where Randall was broad and muscular, Thompson was narrow and soft. They made for an unusual pairing as they strode down the corridor toward the laboratory known as The Warren. The soldiers guarding the door saluted and parted to make way for their commanding officer and the chief civilian scientist.

"Well, you'd better do so in a hurry."

Chemsuits and gas masks hung from hooks on the wall beside the chemical showers. An observation window granted

Randall an unobstructed view of the sealed lab on the other side of the wall. He watched the scientists inside through the tempered glass while he donned his protective gear. A hatch reminiscent of the watertight bulkhead door on a submarine separated the two rooms. He spun the wheel, stepped into the airlock, and waited for Thompson to close the door behind them. The electromagnetic lock disengaged with a thud, allowing him to open the inner door and enter the lab.

Racks upon racks of wire cages covered the wall to his right. The rabbits housed here were designated for the nerve gas program, which had been established in response to the Army arriving in Germany with chlorine and mustard gasses, only to find itself confronted with an array of chemical weapons, which, by comparison, made theirs look like novelty itching powders.

While Allied forces had been resting on their laurels, Nazi scientists had used Germany's defeat in the First World War as motivation to build an arsenal against which no enemy could stand. The G-agents — tabun (GA), sarin (GB), soman (GD), and cyclosarin (GF) — were colorless, tasteless, and lethal in minuscule concentrations, both in liquid and gaseous states. By the time a victim noticed his runny nose, constricted pupils, and the tightness in his chest, it was too late to stop the inevitable. He quickly developed blisters on his eyes and in his lungs, lost control of his bodily functions, and succumbed to uncontrollable muscle contractions, which progressed into unrelenting seizures and, finally, death. These nerve agents had the potential to wipe out armies with a single warhead and, worse, entire cities with a barrage of intercontinental ballistic missiles.

Thus, the plants at the RMA had transitioned from the production of lewisite to sarin, the deadliest of the G-agents, and the race to stockpile as much as humanly possible had commenced. Of course, doing so posed a significant risk not only to the men and women of the U.S. Army Chemical Corps, but also to the surrounding communities. An inadvertent mixing of chemicals or ruptured artillery shell could prove catastrophic. Even a slow leak could wipe out the entire base, necessitating the installation of an early detection system . . . a job perfect for these rabbits.

Had any of them still been alive.

Randall opened one of the cage doors, grabbed the lifeless ball of fur, and lifted it from the litter. Its tongue protruded from between its long, hooked teeth. The glimmer of life had faded from its waxen eyes, but it showed no signs of rigor mortis.

"This couldn't have happened more than a few hours ago," he said.

"3:56 a.m., to be precise," Thompson said. "The men were alerted by the screaming."

"Screaming?"

"That's how they described it. They were just down the hall. By the time they got in here, all of the rabbits were dead."

Randall set the limp animal on a stainless-steel examination tray and reached back into the cage. The rubber gloves minimized his sensitivity, forcing him to grab handfuls of the litter and sift it through his fingers until he found what he was told would be there. Even then, he was surprised to find the locust carcasses.

"How did they get in here?" he asked.

"We believe through the ventilation ducts."

"How in God's name did they get out of their cage in the first place?"

"You wouldn't believe me if I told you. It's one of those things you're just going to have to see for yourself."

"Wasn't someone supposed to be monitoring them?"

"According to the logs, the sentry rounded right on schedule."

Randall manipulated one of the dead insects into his gloved palm. The African desert locust — schistocerca gregaria *— looked like the ordinary grasshoppers in the surrounding plains, only larger and reddish-brown, with a black face and scarlet eyes. Its entire body was riddled with holes, as though someone had repeatedly punctured its carapace and abdomen with a pin.*

He turned around to qualify his discovery with the doctor, only to find him intently studying the rabbit on the examination tray. Thompson parted the animal's fur, revealing fresh pinprick lesions inflicted so close to its time of death that minimal bleeding had occurred.

"It looks like the locusts attacked it," Randall said.

"That's how it appears, although these injuries resemble puncture wounds, not bites."

"That shouldn't have killed them."

"You're right, but, for the life of me, I can't tell you what did."

WHILE UNCLE SAM considered the chemical warfare program one of his main priorities, he invested heavily in the burgeoning field of biological weaponry. Four square miles of arsenal land had been devoted to growing grain infected with a fungal disease called wheat stem rust. Puccinia graminis tritici, *known as Agent TX, was more than a mere nuisance species. Infection not only decreased a crop's yield by more than twenty percent, but it also increased the risk of contracting mycotoxicosis — a potentially fatal gastrointestinal disease — from ingesting tainted grain, effectively wiping out entire harvests. This one anticrop agent had the potential to economically cripple the mighty Soviet Union and starve its people, ending the threat of a third world war before the first shots were even fired.*

This particular fungus also had an added benefit with extraordinary military applications: it could be used to harvest deoxynivalenol, *a mycotoxin that could be used to both incapacitate and kill, depending upon the concentration.*

Randall supervised both the facility responsible for the purification, storage, and shipment of TX to Beale Air Force Base in California and the laboratory where they tested experimental methods of dispersal. The bioagent couldn't simply be loaded into a bomb and dropped on a field without serving as a declaration of war. He had an entire team dedicated to researching stealthier means of weaponization, chief among them the use of insects as vectors.

The Japanese had successfully spread the plague via infected fleas, but their plan to disperse millions by high-altitude balloon had been riddled with flaws. Even if the insects managed to survive the fall, once they were free to roam the streets, the efficacy of the plan was under the direct control of so many mindless creatures. There was no doubt the plague would eventually take root, yet as a weapon it lacked the immediacy necessary during times of war, which were won in the here and now, not some number of months into the unknown future. Plus, there was no means of containing the spread. Had the Japanese set Operation Cherry Blossoms at Night into motion, the American military personnel infected during the planned assault on San Diego would have carried the disease right back across the Pacific with them on the naval vessels stationed there. An effective bioweapon required both immediacy and containment, which was where Randall's hand-selected team of scientists came in.

It wasn't enough for a wheat stem rust infection to trigger a series of events that would slowly lead to economic ruin and starvation; it needed to do so in a fast and predictable manner. African desert locusts were the swarming variety, the kind that descended as a cloud and reduced entire fields to inedible stalks. This particular species could be counted on to lay siege to the targeted area, but the problem quickly became one of containment. An aggressive swarm could potentially follow the grain belt west through the Ukraine and cut a swath across Eastern Europe, leaving behind worthless acres infected with wheat stem rust to such an extent that nothing would grow there for years to come, but if his scientific team's theory was correct, they'd finally found a solution.

Or at least they'd thought they had.

Randall stood in the center of the entomology lab, surrounded by six-foot-tall aquariums swarming with *locusts. All except for one, anyway. The glass was cracked, and one corner of the lid was raised ever so slightly. It took him a moment to realize that the damage had been inflicted from the inside, where, unlike the other cages, a cluster of wheat plants grew largely unmolested. The soil, however, was littered with small bones, feathers, and scavenged carcasses.*

"What the hell happened here?"

"Show him what you showed me," Thompson said.

Like all of the civilian scientists, Dr. Calvin Waller wore black-rimmed glasses, a white lab coat, and an ID badge clipped to his breast pocket. He was their resident entomologist, a field Randall suspected he'd chosen for his physical resemblance to his subjects. He was tall and slender and moved as though he possessed joints where others didn't.

"If you'll follow me, Major," he said, guiding them around the back of the aquarium.

Randall climbed onto the waiting ladder and scrutinized the lid. It was immediately apparent what had happened. Hundreds of locusts had crammed their bodies into the seam, one on top the other, using the crushed carcasses of their brethren to raise the lid high enough for the remainder to squeeze out.

"Extraordinary," he whispered.

Cattail-like spines protruded from the carcasses. They were actually the stalks of a fungus called Ophiocordyceps unilateralis, *an entomopathogenic species from Thailand that infected ants, causing them to climb a specific plant to a predetermined height, bite onto the underside of a leaf, and cling there until the fungus consumed its body and produced an explosion of spores from its fruiting bodies. The locusts had been suitable vectors for the wheat stem rust bacterium, but the* unilateralis *had only infected one of the twelve groups exposed to it — the one bred for aggressiveness toward avian predators, a flock of which could end their infestation before it began — and even then, only a small number had survived to repopulate the swarm.*

"*We suspect the fungus orchestrated the locusts' behavior using the same combination of neuromodulator chemicals — specifically* guanobutyric *acid and* sphingosine *— that it utilizes to compel ants to initiate their mandibular 'death grip.' Or at least that's our working theory.*"

"*You're suggesting the fungus made hundreds of locusts cram themselves into a tiny crack until there were enough dead bodies to raise the lid,*" Randall said. "*That implies a level of coordination beyond anything we've ever seen.*"

"*Not even honeybees exhibit such extreme hive-mind behavior. These individuals willingly sacrificed themselves so the others could escape. That's higher-level thinking not traditionally associated with so-called lower life forms.*"

"*A fungus can't think.*"

"*It can in the sense that the ant — or, in this case, the locust — is able to. Its sole biological imperative is the perpetuation of its species, which means that it will do everything in its power to achieve its reproductive potential.*"

Randall plucked one of the dead insects from the breach and inspected its carapace. It looked like it had been stomped by a shoe. Several other carcasses came away with it, all of them tangled together by snarls of stalks and some kind of reddish fuzz.

"*What's this furry stuff?*"

"*Hyphae. They're thin filaments that spread throughout the host's body while the fungus consumes it. They help maintain structural integrity and form a network not unlike our own circulatory or nervous systems."*

Randall recalled the holes in the exoskeletons of the locusts he'd sifted from the litter in the rabbit's cage.

"So where are all of these growths on the ones that escaped?"

5

Dayna leaned back in her seat and rubbed her weary eyes. She'd gone through the entire list of more than six hundred chemicals used and manufactured on the Rocky Mountain Arsenal three times now. It was impossible to predict how any of them would have reacted to the different layers of strata, let alone what toxic stews might have formed from the myriad combinations of volatile organic compounds, heavy metals, pesticides, and nerve agents. The mere thought of forcing all of them down into the ground was both irresponsible and absurd. How anyone could have proposed such a foolhardy and shortsighted method of disposal was beyond her. It was like injecting toxins underneath the skin and hoping they didn't interact with the rest of the body. Well, here were the inevitable consequences of their folly, and she could only pray things didn't get worse.

Of course, modern engineers were still doing the exact same thing. Fracking involved forcing fluid into shale formations to cause localized earthquakes under 2.0 on the Richter scale, which broke up the layers of overlying rock so gas could be extracted through production wells. The same oil exploration companies generated even more seismic activity, and of considerably greater magnitude, by injecting the wastewater from the process back into the ground through deep-injection wells similar to the one the Chemical Corps had used, kicking the seismic can down the road for future generations. With nowhere to go and little chance of evaporation, that fluid continued to sink and apply pressure on the bedrock, creating new faults and stimulating existing ones, triggering earthquakes for generations to come.

"So far there aren't any confirmed casualties," Stephens said, "but if you look at these pictures, it's only a matter of time before there are."

He turned his laptop so the others could see the screen, which displayed aerial images of downtown Denver. Spotlights slashed through the pall of smoke hanging over the entire area. Red and blue emergency lights flooded the streets, where sporadic fires still burned. Several buildings appeared to have at least partially collapsed, dropping mounds of bricks and rubble onto parked cars and intersections. The surrounding suburbs appeared to have fared better, although footage showed collapsed roofs, massive cracks in residential streets, and geysers firing from toppled fire hydrants, all set to a soundtrack of whupping rotors and blaring car alarms.

Dayna merely nodded. She'd seen similar scenes from different angles on as many local TV stations, but the national and cable news networks had yet to descend in force. Once they did, however, it was only a matter of time before someone connected the dots to the previous earthquakes at the RMA and made her job infinitely more difficult. They needed to get out there first and establish a perimeter . . . but around what? She didn't have any idea what they'd find when they got there. All she'd been able to learn about the deep injection well was that the aboveground assembly had been removed in 1966 and the hole permanently sealed in 1985. Even the Superfund site contained little detail beyond noting that the top ten feet of contaminated soil had been relocated to a landfill on the northern edge of the acreage and some amount of toxic waste had been interred beneath "large, engineered covers" to prevent further poisoning of the groundwater.

She brought up a satellite map of the area and stared at the long-decommissioned well's GPS coordinates. The surrounding land was permanently scarred by the dirt roads that once serviced the razed production and assembly plants, chemical evaporation basins originally lined with a paltry layer of asphalt, and barren patches where so many toxins had seeped into the earth that nothing would ever grow again. All of this within a couple thousand feet of walking trails, recreation areas, and brand-new homes.

This was a situation unlike any the world had ever

known. Lord only knew how many toxic chemicals were seeping into the drinking water or being released into the air at that very moment, let alone what unknown biological processes were transpiring in the subterranean reservoir that the Earth was no longer able to contain.

DAYNA FURROWED her brow as she watched the gray clouds billow against the dark sky, snuffing out all but the most ambitious stars. Flashing red, green, and white lights appeared from their roiling black bellies, only to vanish again. She couldn't recall ever seeing so many planes this close together.

The pilot's voice emerged from the overhead speakers.

"We'll be landing on the south cargo runway. Ground transportation is already waiting for you there."

"Does anyone else think that's kind of strange?" Sydney asked.

"Landing on a cargo runway?" Telford said. "It's better than endlessly circling up here with all of these other planes."

Dayna leaned closer to the window. The ground intermittently materialized from the clouds below her. She caught occasional glimpses of the serrated peaks of the Rocky Mountains and the urban sprawl stretching from the foothills all the way across the eastern plains. The flashing lights of emergency vehicles raced through neighborhoods filled with panicked residents unceremoniously awakened by the quake. News helicopters circled the downtown area through the lingering smoke, their spotlights slashing across skyscrapers still without power and streets clogged with traffic that wouldn't be breaking up anytime soon.

A dark swatch of land to the northwest, fringed by streetlights to the west and I-70 to the south, marked their ultimate destination. Somewhere down there, more than two miles below those barren fields, was the unknown source of seismic activity responsible for an earthquake that never should have happened . . . a source she needed to make sure wouldn't further destabilize and cause a mass casualty event.

DIA's main terminal rose from the plains as they descended, its tentlike spines illuminated from within. Strings of white and red runway lights welcomed one plane after another, while green and blue beacons guided them through a maze of taxiways toward concourses ensconced in glowing golden auras. Seemingly every gate of the two innermost was occupied, while the outermost sat alone in a sea of black, cut off from the rest of the facilities, almost as though it had been quarantined. She could only speculate as to the reason why, but the airport was so close to the epicenter of the earthquake that it was probably a small miracle the whole place hadn't been shut down.

Or worse.

The plane rapidly descended and touched down on the landing strip farthest from the airport itself. They passed an unlabeled warehouse surrounded by fuel trucks and maintenance vehicles and veered onto a tarmac servicing luxury and charter aviation companies. All of the hangar doors were closed, and the private planes and vehicles on the south side of the facilities sat cold and dark. A trio of white Chevy Tahoes adorned with FEMA logos emerged from between the buildings and streaked across the apron to meet them, red lights flashing.

As soon as the plane stopped, the copilot bounded from the cockpit and opened the side door. An agent wearing a navy-blue windbreaker jumped from the lead vehicle and jogged to greet Dayna as she stepped down to the asphalt.

"Dr. Raines?" he shouted over the whine of turbines. "Carl Travis. FEMA Emergency Response Team Lead. If you'll come with me . . . "

He ushered her to the first SUV, while his men commenced transferring the equipment from the cargo hold of the plane to the trunks of the other two. Everything happened so fast that she barely had time to nervously glance back at her new teammates from the plane, who squeezed into the rows of seats behind her, before the vehicle sped past the hangars and down a back road, dodging the main thoroughfare, where the headlights of early morning travelers filled all four lanes and lighted signs warned of potential extended delays.

THE TAHOE SPED west on 56th Avenue, flashing red lights illuminating the towering powerlines and vast stretches of wild grasses blurring past in the darkness. It slewed around the corner onto Havana and blew through an access-controlled gate manned by a single patrolman, who closed it behind them and returned to his vehicle. Houses in varying stages of completion streaked past on the left, their yards separated from the wildlife refuge by a single road and a simple chain-link fence. Civilization fell away behind the vehicle as it crossed East 64th and rocketed past road signs directing them toward trails, lakes, and a fishing fee station.

Travis handed Dayna a tablet with a black-and-white map of the Rocky Mountain Arsenal on the screen. It was nearly identical to the one she and her team had studied on the plane, only it had been divided into thirty-five numbered units, each of which encompassed 640 square acres.

"That's Lake Mary to your right," he said, gesturing toward clumps of deciduous trees, through which Dayna caught a glimpse of moonlight reflecting from water. "And Lake Ladora beyond that. The South Plants, commissioned in 1942 for the production of primitive chemical weapons and incendiary munitions, used to be just on the other side of them. After the Army built the North Plants and transitioned to the production of more advanced chemical weaponry, it was leased to a private company for the production of pesticides." The trees vanished behind them, leaving nothing but uninterrupted fields and barbed-wire fences on either side of the cracked asphalt. "Chemical Basins C, D, and E were over there. They were filled sequentially. As one overflowed, engineers dug the next to accommodate the increased volume."

"They just let the chemicals sit out there?" Sydney said.

"This was a different era. You have to look at it from a historical perspective: World War Two posed an existential threat the likes of which this country had never experienced before. The Japanese struck an American naval base, albeit across the Pacific Ocean, and intelligence confirmed the Nazis had developed rockets capable of hitting the mainland. Chemical engineers were forced to throw caution to the wind for the sake of the country's survival, although, in all fairness, they lacked our modern scientific understanding and likely didn't consider, let alone appreciate, the long-term consequences of their actions."

A police cruiser blocked the intersection ahead, its lightbar dark. It backed out of the way long enough for the convoy make a right turn.

"Chemical Basin F was the largest of all," Travis said. "All ninety-three acres filled so fast that they had to install spray nozzles to accelerate evaporation, which only served to contaminate miles of land downwind, principally used to bury containers of off-spec sulfur mustard and lewisite. Granted, the government's spent hundreds of millions of dollars decontaminating this place, but you couldn't pay me enough to live anywhere near here, let alone drink the water."

"Surely they didn't allow nerve agents or any of their precursor chemicals to mix in those ponds," Stephens said.

"Those were housed in the North Plants, about a mile northeast of here, pretty much right at the center of the property. They manufactured sarin there until the late fifties, when they transitioned to the production of rocket fuels and an anti-crop agent called TX."

A golden aura materialized to the east. It grew brighter as they approached and resolved into an array of stadium lights shining onto the field north of the road. A FEMA Mobile Emergency Response Support Vehicle that looked like an ambulance crossed with a motorhome was parked off in the weeds. Several figures wearing hazmat gear picked their way through knee-high blue grama and cheatgrass toward a jagged black hole in the earth.

"Is that where the deep injection well used to be?" Dayna asked, triangulating their location on the map.

"Technically, the well's still there," Travis said. "Only the aboveground rigging was removed. All but the final seventy feet of the shaft were encased in concrete to ensure stability and prevent chemicals from inadvertently contaminating the more permeable layers of strata and groundwater above the toxic aquifer."

"They used concrete for chemicals capable of eating through asphalt and expected a porous geologic formation to hold them?" Dayna suppressed her revulsion, took a deep breath, and approached the scenario from an unemotional, rational perspective. "A million gallons of fluid would fill a football stadium to a depth of just under three feet. A hundred and sixty-five million would fill two to overflowing. Now imagine what that volume of toxic chemicals could do to a permeable layer of strata over a duration of roughly sixty years."

"It would be like fracking with nitroglycerine," Stephens said.

"Or fast-forwarding eons of patient erosion through karst topography," Telford said.

"You think caverns formed under the granite?" Travis said.

"There's no way of knowing. At least not until we get a camera down there."

"We'll find out soon enough," Dayna said, watching

the men in isolation suits take readings of the air and soil with portable gas analyzers.

She glanced in the opposite direction — toward the spotlights of news choppers knifing through the smoke over downtown — and hoped to God the chemicals hadn't destabilized the area as badly as she feared.

6

Denver International Airport
5:29 a.m.

Randall clung to the cable as the winch slowly lowered him into the sinkhole. The powerful beam from the spotlight mounted to the primary life support subsystem on his back shone over his left shoulder, dissolving shadows and laying bare everything in its path. He passed five feet of solid concrete, the underside of which was heavily scalloped. The bedrock and deeper strata had fared even worse. Between the erosion and the fractures caused by the earthquake, it was hard to imagine what this must have looked like beforehand. Certainly not the almost pyramidal, rubble-filled cavity into which he descended.

His light passed through the windows of the inverted train cars, casting shadows from the vertical posts metering the inner space. While the rear vehicle had been empty, two people had been inside the third. They lay crumpled on the spiderwebbed front windshield, flat against the glass, which appeared to have collected a patina of red dust. He had to wait until he'd been lowered past them to look up at their faces—

His pulse rushed in his ears.

To say their condition had degenerated was an understatement. Where initial photographs had shown rings of a grainy substance around their eyes, nostrils, and mouths, there were now furry rust-colored growths. They protruded from the corners of the decedents' eyes and underneath their lids, making the cloudy irises appear to stare in horror into the depths. The protrusions from their noses resembled the tentacles of so many jellyfish, while those in their mouths parted their teeth and peeled back their lips.

The proliferation on the men in the second vehicle was even more advanced, although it was hard to tell where the growths on their faces ended and those arising from the blood they'd spilled upon impact with the cracked windshield began.

Alpha glanced up, his beam swinging wildly across the wreckage. His voice crackled from the speaker inside Randall's helmet.

"You have to see this."

Randall alighted on the uneven rubble and stepped out of his harness. Particulate matter sparkled in his light like motes of dust, a trace layer of which had settled on the jagged rocks and concrete chunks around him. It came away on the bottoms of Alpha's boots as he led Randall over the treacherous mound to the other side of the crumpled train car, where he crouched and looked through a narrow gap between the front end and the ground.

A blond woman lay on top of the man who'd broken her fall, although not well enough to save her life. Her hair largely concealed the growths on her ruined face, although more of the furry biofilm covered the rock upon which she'd smashed it. The man underneath her, however . . . the protuberances on his face were so advanced that his cloudy eyes appeared to stare up at them from behind a spiked mask. Wiry strands resembling antlers jutted from underneath his eyelids and lips.

"These two were exposed to a greater extent than the others," Randall said. "The source must be somewhere nearby."

"That's what I wanted to show you," Alpha said, aiming his beam at something on the rocks several feet downhill from the bodies.

Randall furrowed his brow and leaned closer. It looked like a vegetal husk covered with long reddish stalactites . . . until he recognized the spindly legs, hairy little thorax, and pincer-like mandibles. The spider appeared to have burst, as though someone had stuffed a firecracker inside it.

He glanced at Alpha, who carefully gauged his reaction when he spoke.

"What aren't you telling us, Chief?"

Randall merely stood and turned in a circle, scouring the eroded earthen walls with his beam.

"Find out where that spider came from," he said. "Now."

He struck off toward the other men, leaving Alpha staring at his back.

RANDALL SIDESTEPPED the flight attendant's torso and strode right up to Beta, who walked a circuit of cavern, slowly waving the probe wand of a portable gas chromatograph-mass spectrometer. The machine was designed to detect and identify trace amounts of explosive compounds, chemical agents, and environmental contaminants in their solid, liquid, and vapor states.

"What have you found?"

Beta set down the device and scrolled through the readout on the screen while he spoke.

"Pretty much exactly what we expected," he said. "Nearly indetectable levels of various chlorinated ethers, organochlorides, and aromatic hydrocarbons, but only in the immediate vicinity."

"DIMP?"

Beta met his stare and nodded.

Diisopropyl methylphosphonate was an exclusive byproduct of sarin production, which proved that some amount of chemical waste from the RMA had worked its way through two vertical and seven horizontal miles of porous rock and shale. Of course, Randall had known as much the moment he'd seen the bodies. The higher-ups must have recognized it as well, although they couldn't possibly know the true nature of the threat they now faced. Neither did his subordinates, although it was only a matter of time before they found out.

Randall scrutinized the residual puddles of shimmering liquid on the ground. His scientific team at the RMA had assured him that the chemicals would be injected well below the water table, preventing the fluoride-based precursors from hydrolyzing and producing hydrofluoric acid, a corrosive so powerful that it could eat straight through solid rock. They'd obviously been wrong, and while the resultant acid must have been severely diluted for the process of erosion to have taken this long, it had obviously infiltrated the groundwater and now flowed wherever the subterranean aquifer did, potentially creating an entire network of caverns where none had existed before.

"Three-dimensional rendering should be finished any second now," Gamma said from behind him.

Randall picked his way down the rugged slope to where the tech specialist crouched, his laptop perched on a concrete slab. He'd used a light detection and ranging — LiDAR — scanner to take readings of the sinkhole. The unit used a laser beam to measure distances and angles and record those measurements in a way that allowed the reconstruction algorithms to create an identical digital 3-D replica, right down to the smallest fissure or crack in the wall. The data could then be manipulated to view the individual human remains, the train cars, or the cavern itself from every conceivable angle, memorializing the scene more precisely than any number of photographs. More importantly, the laser was powerful enough to penetrate and reveal crevices they might have missed with the naked eye.

"Right there," the tech specialist said, zooming in on the multicolored image to reveal a tiny red triangle, nearly concealed by the rubble, at the base of the arched wall.

Randall glanced over his shoulder, but despite knowing the crevice was there, he still couldn't see it.

"Get a drone in there. I want to know how deep it goes and how far it reaches."

"I'm on it."

Randall headed back toward the wreckage and stared down at the body of a pilot, whose injuries suggested a fall from significant height. He knelt to get a better look. Pinprick lesions the size of pores covered the man's skin. They were so small that Randall hadn't been able to appreciate them while standing. He'd seen similar wounds before, a long time ago, only they'd been on rabbits, not on a human being.

The memory of what he'd done years ago rose unbidden. He stuffed it down and focused on the task at hand. There would be plenty of time for recriminations after the truth came out. And considering the team from the USGS had already arrived at the site, it wouldn't be much longer now.

RANDALL'S MEN worked at a breakneck pace. Word had come down through official channels that the powers that be had delayed the national media for as long as possible. He and his team needed to clean up this mess and get the hell out of there before word of what they were doing here leaked, as though somehow that was their biggest concern. If they didn't figure out where that spider had come from and how it had been exposed to the organism, then a little bad PR would be the least of their worries.

Delta had gone outside to scan the surrounding area with a drone specially equipped with ground penetrating radar, which allowed him to map subsurface features by continuously firing electromagnetic impulses straight down into the earth and collecting those signals again when they rebounded from buried objects or strata of different densities, like topsoil, limestone, and bedrock. More importantly, it helped visualize any negative spaces, specifically subterranean cavities, tunnels, and caves.

His older brother sat at the edge of the pit, video screen on his lap and legs dangling over the nothingness. He piloted a spherical amphibious vehicle with continuous LiDAR capabilities through the narrow opening in the cavern wall, freeing Gamma to manage the monitors displaying the live imagery and the algorithmic reconstructions in real time.

The raw GPR data on the left screen featured wavy black, white, and gray horizontal bands that marked the layers of earth beneath the tarmac, as though poorly photographed in cross-section, like an ultrasound. While Randall was by no means an expert interpreter, it was readily apparent that there were no other subterranean cavities within thirty feet of the surface on the airport grounds. Of course, that didn't mean there weren't others, farther down, capable of causing significant damage with another earthquake, but it was good to know there was no imminent risk of collapse or potential source of exposure to chemicals.

Or worse.

The LiDAR imagery on the right screen resembled a wire-frame reconstruction of the interior of the rocky crevice, one that only hinted at its true size and shape. The passage fluctuated between six and eight inches wide, but never rose above five inches in height. Although the drone encountered dozens of side passages, none of them were large enough to accommodate even its diminutive size. It had fallen down numerous deep chutes, where the chemicals appeared to have been abruptly channeled upward through less dense strata, but that didn't matter in the slightest; the drone wouldn't be making the return trip. Either they'd end up abandoning it in the subterranean tunnel or utilizing the gumball-sized Semtex charge to collapse it.

"Passing a thousand feet," Gamma said. "We're nearly beyond the westernmost runway."

"How far down?" Randall asked.

"Three hundred thirty feet. We're tracking at an average descent of roughly thirty-two degrees, which, if you extrapolate the drone's current course, places us at just under twelve thousand feet at the seven-mile mark."

Randall nodded. That was exactly what he'd expected.

"Reconstruct what you have so far," he said. "I want to see those side passages."

Gamma flashed through a series of prompts and a three-dimensional recreation of the cavern and narrow tunnel appeared. The tech specialist zoomed in until the lateral passageways appeared, almost like randomly spaced legs from a centipede's body. Several extended more than twenty feet into the surrounding earth, and while many widened into fluid-filled reservoirs, none of them extended beyond the laser's range.

"Can any of those passages reach the surface?" Randall asked.

"It's impossible to say for sure, but it's highly unlikely."

Randall allowed himself the hint of a smile. They'd gotten off easy.

"Then tell Delta to expand aerial reconnaissance into the fields to the west of the airport." He walked over to where Beta sat, controlling the drone while he watched the dark imagery from the camera inside the sphere. "As soon as that drone's comfortably beyond the airport's perimeter, detonate it."

"Yes, sir," Beta said. "What about the bodies?"

Randall looked down into the pit, where Alpha had nearly finished stuffing the remains into portable isolation units. From here, they'd be winched to the surface, loaded into an armored military vehicle, and transported to a secure location for observation. At least until he triggered the incendiary devices his special tactics officer had covertly wired into the units to prevent some black budget biowarfare research program from making them disappear.

"They're taken care of," Randall said. "You just focus on sealing that tunnel. I don't want so much as an earthworm to be able to get through there."

7

Rocky Mountain Arsenal National Wildlife Refuge
6:18 a.m.

D ayna climbed into the mobile emergency response support vehicle, which was considerably larger on the inside than it had looked from the road. The interior had been divided roughly in half, with a scientific suite in back and a command center in front. The former housed humming lab equipment, cabinets overflowing with supplies and gear, and individual changing stalls for the hazmat suits hanging beside them, while the latter contained racks upon racks of communications systems and digital displays. Black boxes with flashing lights and bristling cables covered every available inch of the walls and workstations. A man sat with his back to her, seemingly oblivious to her presence as he looked from one monitor to the next and coordinated the movements of various agencies through his headset.

Several of the screens displayed black-and-white live feeds of the surrounding area: the men taking readings in the field, the gaping wound in the earth where the deep injection well had been, and the inflatable decontamination chamber. Others showed the surrounding police barricades and teams of agents in matching windbreakers at remote sites, both inside and out. Local and national news broadcasts, all of which featured images of Denver International Airport, played on even more. Half a dozen remote transceivers, attuned to as many radio frequencies, crackled from the charging ports mounted in between.

"I don't have time to hold your hand," the man said, without so much as glancing in her direction. "Suits are in the back. I assume you know how to dress yourself."

The truth was Dayna had never had cause to wear protective gear before. Surely she could figure it out, though. She was already kicking off her shoes when the others joined her. They selected their suits, sat down on the benches, and slipped their legs into the baggy orange getups in silence. Everyone looked as nervous as she felt; even Stephens, who'd obviously done this before. Craig, on the other hand, was positively giddy.

"This is just like *Lethal Company*," he said, glancing from one blank face to the next. "You know . . . the survival game? It's an online horror co-op where you have to scavenge scrap from these abandoned moons—"

"This is no game," Stephens said. "These suits will protect you from chemicals that can kill you in any number of horrific ways, including rupturing the vessels in your lungs and causing you to drown in your own blood, but only if properly worn."

Craig grumbled under his breath, but he kept his thoughts to himself.

"You want to slip on these silicon socks before the rubber boots," Stephens said. "Same with these inner gloves, or you'll never get your hands out again."

Dayna watched him and mimicked his movements, her heart beating faster and faster as she shouldered the harness for the SCBA tank, seated the mask over her face, and dialed up the airflow.

"What's wrong?" Telford asked.

Her expression must have betrayed her dawning panic.

"Just a little claustrophobic is all."

She forced a smile as she donned her safety helmet, plugged the ventilation hose into the regulator valve, and raised the hood.

"Are you going to be all right?" Stephens asked, his voice emerging from the inset speaker by her ear. She nodded as he zipped up her suit and helped her into thick black gloves that latched onto the couplings on her wrists. "The microphones built into these oxygen masks allow all of us to remain in constant contact via a common short-range channel with a range of just under a mile, so I suggest limiting conversation to avoid driving each other crazy."

Sydney squeezed Dayna's gloved hand.

"We'll all be right here with you the whole time," she said.

"I appreciate your concern, but I'll be fine," Dayna said, brushing past the others and descending the steps. "Let's just get this over with. The sooner we're done, the sooner we can go home."

DAYNA LED her team into the field, the damp weeds swishing against their suits. The air positively shivered with the roar of planes endlessly circling against the pale blue sky as they awaited their turn to land at DIA, mere miles to the east. It was strange to think that this sanctuary populated by bison and ferrets, deer and bald eagles, had not so long ago been a toxic swamp unsuitable for habitation.

The rising sun cast their elongated shadows onto the dead earth as they approached their destination. Jagged chunks of concrete and granite stood at steep angles from the ground, encircling the gaping hole like a crown. A tremor passed beneath their feet, one so faint that none of the others appeared to notice. The aftershocks were diminishing in both frequency and intensity. While this was by no means an indication that seismic activity had abated, it was at least a step in the right direction.

She cautiously tested her footing on a slanted chunk of rubble and leaned out over the pit. It was maybe eight feet wide at the surface, where the containment shell had once been. The stadium lights ringing the orifice illuminated the crater to a depth of roughly twenty feet, where the chute abruptly narrowed to four feet in width, beyond which darkness extended into the fathomless depths.

As she'd expected, the chemicals had eroded the original pipe, concrete casing, and adjacent rock. This much damage two miles above the actual well suggested the erosion at the bottom was likely far more extensive than she'd initially suspected and potentially destabilized the entire area. With any luck, the earthquake was simply a call to action, but she feared it was more than that. If they didn't neutralize the chemicals and backfill the well soon, the seismic activity would continue to intensify until the ground collapsed, taking everything for miles in every direction with it.

"Readings show dramatically elevated levels of chemical contamination in the air and soil," Stephens said through the headset.

"What's the significance?" Sydney asked.

"Some amount of aerosolized waste was forced up from the well."

"Twelve thousand feet?"

"Subterranean faults are under extreme pressure," Dayna said. "There's no way of accurately predicting where they are, let alone how far or how deep they run. That's why forcing any amount of fluid into the ground is a bad idea. It increases the pressure and accelerates erosion, destabilizing those fractures and inducing earthquakes, which release tremendous amounts of heat and energy, vaporizing liquids and blowing the caps off wells like these."

"If that's the case, then why aren't there earthquakes like this happening everywhere?" Sydney asked.

"There are. Earthquake frequency has risen exponentially since natural gas and petroleum drilling operations started disposing of wastewater through deep injection wells. The state of Oklahoma averaged fewer than two earthquakes per year before the practice started in 2009. It's now on pace to average several thousand a year."

Dayna walked back to the stack of cases unloaded from

the vehicles and set to work assembling her digital seismograph, while Sydney unloaded a device resembling an extremely long endoscopist's scope with a fancy tissue collection tool. The medical mycologist carried it down to the crater and began feeding the snakelike device into the depths.

"I deal with induced earthquakes like this one on a daily basis," Dayna said, "although they're considerably smaller in magnitude and the result of injecting millions of gallons of brine and diluted chemicals, not hundreds of millions of gallons of straight toxic waste, which makes this site inherently unstable and unpredictable."

"Should we be worried?" Sydney asked.

Dayna chose her words carefully.

"While I don't believe we're in imminent danger, I won't feel comfortable until we determine the nature and extent of the damage beneath our feet."

"Which is where I come in," Telford said.

"All right then," Stephens said. "Time to get to work."

"I take it that's my cue," Craig said. He carefully lifted a quadcopter from the foam insert inside a hard-shell case and commenced attaching landing gear and an array of cameras and remote sensors. "She's a work of art. I'm going to have to take her home with me when we're done. Isn't that right, *My Precioussss?*"

Dayna allowed herself a half-smile, which quickly evaporated when she turned around and saw Sydney kneeling beside the hole, staring at the sample she'd collected from the shaft with a concerned expression on her face.

DAYNA TRIED to tune out the chaos around her while she finished networking her equipment to her field tablet. The digital seismograph utilized the probes she'd staked into the earth to detect even the most subtle vibrations, while the infrasonic array — which resembled a giant twenty-two-legged octopus with super-sensitive microphones and microbarographs attached to each appendage — detected soundwaves beneath not only the range of human hearing, but also instrumental and environmental floors. By integrating the incoming data from both devices, she'd be able to detect and analyze geophysical anomalies and isolate their source, create a dynamic model, and simulate the fault system behavior to determine just how worried they should be, although Sydney appeared to be worried enough for all of them.

The medical mycologists had set up her microbial identification system on a folding table beneath a neon green popup canopy tent in case it started to rain again. The unit, which looked like a vintage CRT monitor crossed with a mini refrigerator, hummed as she ran the samples she'd collected from the soil, air, and inside the pit. She hadn't spoken a word and refrained from so much as looking at any of the others.

Telford helped Craig connect the remote sensing devices to the drone and evaluate the quality of the feeds they broadcast to their corresponding monitors. The night vision cameras would allow them to see everything directly below and in front of the drone, while the LiDAR scanner would survey the surrounding area to create a 3-D model of the cavity two miles down, should there actually be one.

Stephens broke away from the pair of men from the rapid response team, who resumed watching the screens on their devices while waving the attached wands. He strode toward Dayna through the weeds, his voice emerging from the speaker before he was even halfway there.

"Photoionization detectors show the concentrations of aromatic hydrocarbons rising from the well have diminished dramatically, but I'm afraid we're going to have to continue wearing these suits while we're within a quarter-mile radius. And unless you want to turn that shaft into a giant Bunsen burner, I wouldn't suggest lighting a match."

"I'll try to resist the urge," Dayna said, returning her attention to her readouts.

The seismograph was so sensitive that it displayed every distinct vibration, from the air traffic overhead to the cars on the distant highway, but beneath them, she was picking up faint, irregular vibrations similar in amplitude to ripples lapping the bank of a placid body of water.

"There's definitely still fluid down there," she said. "And I'm picking up noises in the infrasonic range. Nothing I'd attribute to tectonic activity, though. More like the resonance of air flowing into an enclosed space."

"You're saying there's a cavern down there," Telford said.

"There's one way to know for sure . . . " She looked up from her instrumentation and turned in a circle. "Someone, do me a favor? Grab a rock and toss it down the well."

"I'm on it," Craig said.

He rushed right up to the edge of the unstable pit, grabbed the largest stone he could lift, and hurled it into the shaft. The seismic and infrasonic readings spiked every time it rebounded from the walls, their intensity diminishing with each repetition. When it hit the ground, it would generate soundwaves that expanded outward until they refracted from the cavity's walls, changing the intonation of the waves and allowing her to estimate the size and shape of the space.

Twenty seconds passed.

Thirty.

Thirty-five.

The amplitude of the spikes shot up when the rock finally struck the ground, creating soundwaves that reverberated into the depths. The resultant refractory noises were chaotic and painted a picture not of a single cavern, but rather a network of interconnected spaces of indeterminate size and shape.

"You want me to throw another one?" Craig called.

"I'm pretty sure I got what I needed," she said. "You just focus on getting that drone ready to go."

"Aye-aye, *mon capitaine.*"

Dayna returned her attention to her computer. The program was taking its sweet time running through the calculations, almost as though the space was so vast that the soundwaves dissipated before reaching the end.

"I need to show you something," Sydney said. Dayna had been so caught up in her work that she hadn't heard the other woman approach. She nodded and followed the medical mycologist back to her setup. A lidless petri dish full of dirt rested beside a rectangular unit with an observation window and a fume hood. "This sample came from maybe a hundred feet down. If you look closely, you'll see little bits of rust-colored fuzz."

Dayna leaned closer to get a better look, but she didn't see anything out of the ordinary.

"Try this," Sydney said, offering a magnifying glass.

Dayna brought the lens right up to her face shield and studied the sample. Tiny clusters of reddish filaments resembling spiderwebs stood apart from the soil.

"What am I looking at?" she asked.

"Those fine strands are fungal hyphae. They help aerate the soil for plants and serve as a primary source of food for countless invertebrates. They're the first stage of visible growth from spores. Think of them like threads that clump together to form a mycelium, dozens of which combine to form a kind of root system that develops into a fruiting body, or what you think of as a mushroom."

"What's the significance?"

"Look at the ground around the crater. There's a reason nothing's growing there. You've seen the concentrations of chemicals in the soil. Elevated levels like that should kill pretty much every life form, or, at a minimum, severely restrict its proliferation." Sydney gestured toward the microwave-looking device on the tabletop. "Now look inside the incubator."

Dayna leaned closer to the viewport—

"Oh my God."

8

Rocky Mountain Arsenal

1966

"Its rate of proliferation is staggering," Dr. Thompson said through the speaker.

Randall leaned right up against the observation window of The Warren's sealed lab to get a better view of the rabbit on the dissection tray. Its front and hind legs had been stretched out and pinned to the black wax. The flesh had been parted straight up its spine, the skin and fur retracted, and the naked musculature exposed. Stalk-like growths protruded from the spinous processes of its vertebrae. The base of its skull had been opened to reveal its brain and cranial nerve bundles.

He pressed the button and spoke into the microphone so his chief scientist could hear him.

"It looks like it has already infiltrated the central nervous system."

"We theorize that it entered the circulatory system via the superficial capillaries and crossed the blood-brain barrier in the same manner it breaks through the exoskeleton of an insect," Thompson said. "There's a minimal amount of hemorrhaging and midline shift, but the greatest hematological difference appears to be in the total volume of residual blood, which we estimate to be roughly half that of a living specimen."

"There was no blood on the substrate."

"Precisely. Somehow, these two fungi appear to be working together to incorporate it into their shared biomass in much the same way that other multicellular species of fungi grow from corpses, accelerating the process of decomposition."

"Then how did it manage to infect the locusts in the first place?"

"Ophiocordyceps unilateralis is incredibly susceptible to infection from other fungi, which is why it doesn't simply wipe out entire ant species wherever it goes. That's nature's way of keeping its proliferation in check. To protect itself, the unilateralis engages in what's known as secondary metabolism, a process by which it stimulates the host to produce the antibacterial agents necessary to stave off pathogens during the fungus' reproductive cycle. That's why none of the other test batches survived. The locusts produced antibodies that caused the wheat stem rust to release deoxynivalenol in response to the threat, killing the unilateralis before it could assume command of the host's motor functions. The locusts that had *been bred for their aggressive response to predatory species added an element to the equation in the form of an avian blood source, a threat against which all three species — insect and fungi alike — were forced to work in tandem."*

Thompson used a pair forceps to lift off the crown in the rabbit's skull, which peeled away from the brain with long strands reminiscent of pinworms. The fungus had already taken root and was in the process of growing through the cranium.

"It's metabolizing the blood," Randall said.

"Our working hypothesis is that it's consuming some component of the blood to produce the antibodies necessary to circumvent the immune response and proliferate unchecked within the host's body, almost like a virus."

"To what end?"

"Any speculation at this point would be premature."

"I don't want speculation, Doctor. I want answers."

Randall glanced at the rabbit one last time before leaving the lab. He could have sworn there were even more filaments protruding from the muscles on either side of its spine than there'd been when he arrived.

"ARE you sure this is what they want?" Corporal Lyle Benjamin asked. "Because there's no going back from this. We've never decommissioned a well like this one. Hell, nothing like it has even existed before now. You're asking us to seal off a shaft through which we've forced volatile chemicals into porous rock where there wasn't space for them to begin with. Do you really expect them not to interact with

one another or the surrounding strata? And when they do, assuming they haven't already, where are those byproducts supposed to go?"

Randall looked up at the rigging of the derrick, which towered over them like a five-story spike driven into the earth. The chief engineer was right, of course, but he resented having his orders questioned; the uncertainty was the whole reason they were decommissioning the 12,045-foot-deep injection well in the first place.

The original plan had been to allow the chemicals to precipitate in open-air holding basins the size of small lakes. Unfortunately, the asphalt had dissolved and contaminated the groundwater to such an extent that farmers dozens of miles away were losing entire harvests. The backup plan of sealing the waste in drums and dumping it into the ocean had proven too costly, necessitating the alternative of injecting it so deep that it couldn't infiltrate the ground-water through the bedrock. The flaw was that the high pressure required to inject fluid into a space not designed to accommodate it had triggered a series of earthquakes — a regrettable outcome, to be sure, but nothing catastrophic. Or at least it hadn't been until the cause of the unprecedented seismic activity made the papers.

Honestly, Randall didn't care one way or the other. Production was his concern, not disposal, and he had so much on his plate today that he had neither the time nor the patience to hold the hand of an engineer who'd already received his orders from higher up the chain of command.

"Just get it done," he said.

"It's not as easy as plugging a hole. We have no idea how the concrete casings held up to the corrosive effects of the chemicals. We thought three concentric layers was overkill at the time, but we also thought the waste wouldn't be able to eat through half an inch of asphalt. It's possible that the pipe itself is the only thing holding the well together and once we remove it, the whole damn thing will collapse."

"Then leave the pipe."

"If we do, we risk the pressure building and creating a toxic geyser ten times the size of Old Faithful."

"Then take it out. What do you want me to say?"

"Here's the thing," Benjamin said. "The bottom seventy feet has no lining whatsoever. We've pumped more than a hundred million gallons of toxic chemicals into permeable Precambrian metamorphic rock. Lord only knows what effects they had on it. There could very well be a cavity eroded under half the state and we're about to destabilize the whole works."

Randall heard his name shouted from a distance and turned to see Thompson running across the field toward him. The production plants were little more than silhouettes against the plains behind him. He'd never seen the scientist in the sunlight before, let alone moving at a pace anywhere close to a jog. Something must have happened in the lab. Something of a sensitive nature that couldn't be broadcast across the open airwaves. It was time to end this conversation.

"You have your orders, Corporal. Tear the damn thing down."

Benjamin's eyes narrowed and his jaw muscles bulged.

"Yes, sir."

Randall turned his back on the engineer and struck off down the dirt road to meet Thompson. Benjamin immedi-

ately started barking orders behind him and the engines of demolition vehicles roared to life.

Thompson stopped a hundred yards away and doubled over to catch his breath. Randall closed the gap and pulled the scientist upright by the collar of his lab coat.

"What is it, Doctor?" he asked.

"There are no words to describe it. You have to see it to believe it."

"What in the name of God happened here?" Randall asked. "I saw them with my own eyes. Christ, I even held one. There's no doubt in my mind they were dead."

The rabbits had all moved to the front of their cages and pressed their foreheads against the mesh, their fur sticking out at odd angles. Fungal growths protruded from the bases of their skulls and the lengths of their spines like rows of antlers. A fuzz of hyphae covered their eyes, completely obscuring their vision, and yet Randall could feel the weight of their stares upon him.

"We theorize the fungi never actually killed the rabbits," Thompson said, "but rather suppressed their vital functions. They essentially created a state of deep hibernation, the physical characteristics of which match those of a moderate dose of deoxynivalenol."

"You're suggesting they can produce the toxin at will."

"Fungi don't have a 'will' any more than they have a brain to exert it, but it wouldn't be untrue to imply that the two species — graminis tritici and unilateralis — have formed something of a mutualistic relationship by which the

former produces the toxin in response to a threat to the latter, in this case the white blood cells of the host life form."

"Surely there's a way to manipulate that to work in our favor."

"You mean as an incapacitant?"

"We could win a war without excessive loss of life."

"Hoping for the fungi to pass from the locusts to the enemy is adding the very element of unpredictability we were seeking to avoid. Not to mention the fact that we know nothing about the physiological interactions of the fungal species inside the rabbit, let alone an infinitely more complex organism like man. This could be more than a mere fungal infection that their bodies can ultimately fight off; it could be actively killing them from the inside out. Or maybe any attempt to remove either species will cause the release of a lethal dose of the toxin. And if the two have somehow combined to form a single chimeric organism, then Lord only knows what it's capable of doing."

Thompson plucked one of the growths from the head of the nearest rabbit, which thrashed and hurled itself repeatedly against the wire mesh until its fur darkened with blood.

"Their growth rate is beyond anything we've ever seen," he said, turning it over and over in his gloved hand. *"An hour ago those protuberances were barely longer than the fur. Now they're close to three inches. Their life cycle hasn't merely been accelerated; it's been altered beyond our ability to form a predictive model. If it continues to metabolize the blood—"*

"The rabbit will just make more."

"That's not the point. Fungi don't grow indefinitely. Like I said, their sole purpose is to reproduce. Once that

happens, they no longer need the host. Biologically speaking, it will have outlived its usefulness. Like the ant that bites onto the leaf, the fungus will eventually consume it."

"Which would effectively make it the most lethal weapon in our arsenal," Randall said.

"But one outside of our control. You've seen what happened to these two simple species of fungus during the act of transmission from the locusts to the rabbits. There's no way to predict how they will respond to the human body. We have much more complicated immune and nervous systems, but we're no less susceptible to the effects of deoxynivalenol. I find it hard to believe the fungi could exert any influence over our actions like they do insects, but in sufficient quantity, they could produce deadly levels of toxins."

"Don't you think that's something we should look into?"

"Human testing? That's not a road I'm prepared to go down."

"What do you think it is we do here, Doctor? We don't cure diseases. We dream up ways of killing as many people as possible and hope to God we don't have to use them. But if — heaven forbid — we're forced to do so, we need to know exactly what to expect, for both our adversaries and our men on the battlefield."

"You see this tiny bulb here?" Thompson said, holding up the fungus for Randall to see. "This fruiting body holds thousands of microscopic spores that it will disperse in an explosive cloud. If they're able to enter the body through superficial capillaries protected by several layers of skin, they'll make short work of the bronchi in our lungs and the mucous membranes in our noses and mouths. We can't control their dispersion like chemical weapons. They don't

have half-lives like radiological isotopes. They can remain dormant for years. They can cross interspecific barriers. We could inadvertently eradicate all life forms on the planet."

The doctor was being melodramatic. Any one of the weapons at their disposal had the potential to wipe out all life on Earth. If they could eliminate the Communist threat without risking a single American life, then they at least needed to explore the possibility. The idea likely wouldn't work anyway, but if, by some slim chance, it could . . .

Randall imagined an invisible cloud of spores settling over Moscow.

"We need to try, Doctor."

"No," Thompson said. "What we need to do is proceed with the utmost caution. We could very well have created the means of our own extinction."

9

Rocky Mountain Arsenal National Wildlife Refuge
7:28 a.m.

A furry fungus grew around the edges of the viewport, like frost on a picture window. The petri dishes and shelves inside the incubator were positively covered with it. Whiplike stalks protruded from tests tubes, reaching toward the red and blue LED lights ringing the intake vent of the fume hood.

"I cultured the samples in those sterile agar trays less than twenty minutes ago," Sydney said. "Those test tubes are filled with two of the precursor chemicals we anticipated finding here: hydrofluoric acid and isopropylamine."

"The fungus is consuming the chemicals," Dayna said.

"It's worse than that . . . watch."

Dayna pressed her face shield right up against the incubator. She couldn't tell what she was . . . supposed . . . to. . .

One of the fruiting bodies closest to the light burst, releasing a swirling cloud of spores that sparkled in the purple glow. It dissipated like smoke from an extinguished candle, wispy tendrils fading into nothingness as the microscopic spores settled. A smudge formed on the inside of the viewport, through which a network of fine cracks spread.

"That observation window is made of half-inch-thick leaded acrylic," Sydney said. "You could hit it with a sledgehammer and still not cause the structural damage — negligible thought it might be — that you just watched those spores inflict all by themselves."

"How is that even possible?" Dayna whispered.

"I can't even begin to guess."

The smudge slowly thickened until it became a rust-colored biofilm reminiscent of lichen. A faint layer of fuzz formed before their eyes.

"The fungus is maturing at an unprecedented rate," Sydney said. "It's almost as though the chemicals have accelerated its entire life cycle, from spore to hypha to mycelium to fruiting body to spores again. If you look at the samples on the chemical mediums in the test tubes, they're growing at a much more rapid pace, but they're also dying faster. There has to be some kind of stabilizing environmental component we're missing."

"Like what?"

"Acceleration from germination to reproduction occurs in species under extreme existential pressure. It's an ingrained survival mechanism. Even human beings achieve reproductive potential at earlier ages in times of crisis, but such changes don't happen overnight, and they don't dramatically alter the nature of the species. Fungi are fairly resilient in the sense that they can thrive in complete darkness, acidic soil, and nearly anoxic conditions because they're able to synthesize the majority of the nutrients they need to live. There are, however, certain vitamins and minerals they need to obtain from their substrate that no amount of chemicals can provide. So while I believe this species has evolved to metabolize certain toxins, without the source of other critical forms of nutrition, it's essentially locked in reproductive panic mode while it searches for it."

"What could that be?"

"Most likely some form of organic matter. Most species flourish on damp detritus rife with decomposing plant and animal matter."

"Surely there's nothing like that down there."

"Something obviously is, but, for the life of me, I can't imagine what it might be." Sydney sighed and leaned against the tent post. "We've only just begun experimenting with fungi capable of synthesizing chemicals. There's a species called *Purpureocillium lilacinum* that's capable of living on undiluted glyphosate — the main component of the pesticide Roundup — and degrading its potency by as much as eighty percent, but considering all fungi are saprotrophs or symbionts — meaning they obtain their nutrients from either decaying organic matter or a living host — it still requires some other form of nutrition to survive."

"Then shouldn't this species be getting everything it needs from the soil around us?" Dayna asked.

"The fact that it's not already growing everywhere

suggests the chemical concentrations aren't high enough to trigger the accelerated reproductive rate. Or maybe there's enough organic matter to sustain a normal life cycle. Or it adapted to lower levels of oxygen, higher levels of acidity or pressure, or even a complete lack of sunlight down there during the last fifty years. This is simply a novel organism unlike any I've ever seen before."

"That's exciting, isn't it? You get to classify a brand-new species."

"It's not that simple," Sydney said. "This one demonstrates physical characteristics of numerous phylogenetic families, all of which are associated with potentially negative environmental concerns."

"Which is why they brought you here."

Sydney turned and looked Dayna dead in the eyes.

"Right . . . but how did they know? And who, exactly, are *they*?"

Dayna glanced at the sealed incubation box, where the fungus covered the inside of the container almost like coralline algae in a saltwater aquarium. She didn't have the slightest idea how to answer either question.

"When will you know what we're dealing with?" she asked.

"Its DNA should offer some insight. I'm running a sample through the genetic analyzer and microbial identification system now."

A buzzing sound drew Dayna's attention to the crater, where the drone lifted off from Craig's gloved hand. It streaked through the air, twisting and turning and performing all kinds of aerial acrobatics. With a scream, it abruptly plunged straight down, past the rim and into the shaft.

She recalled what Cassie had said on the phone and wondered what the "very powerful people" knew that she didn't. And why they hadn't told her from the start.

DAYNA WATCHED the drone's descent on a broadcast director monitor: a twenty-eight-inch screen built into the upper half of a military-grade plastic case, the lower half of which contained instrumentation and wireless network connections, like a great big industrial laptop. All four quadrants displayed a different live feed. The top two featured imagery from the drone's downward- and forward-facing cameras, while the bottom two showed the wire-frame raw footage from the LiDAR and a digital elevation map of the shaft, the distance from the surface climbing at a rapid click.

"Passing negative six thousand feet," Telford said. He sat at the folding table beside her, shifting uncomfortably inside his suit. The sun was barely above the horizon and already his face was red and beaded with sweat. "Can you slow it down a little? I want to get a better look at the strata."

"I'll die of boredom if I go any slower," Craig said from his perch at the crater's edge. He watched the small screen on the handheld console while manipulating the controls. "This gig was supposed to be a challenge. A kindergartner could do this."

"And without constantly whining like one," Stephens grumbled.

Dayna smirked and looked back at the chemical engineer, who watched the screen over her shoulder. He offered a half-smile for her benefit and returned his attention to the live feeds.

The lights mounted to the drone made the fumes rising from the darkness far below seem to shimmer. They barely limned the remains of the surrounding casing, revealing sections of concrete that appeared to disintegrate before her eyes. The underlying rock was visible in places, its surface pitted by erosion.

"With that much exposed sedimentary rock, it's a miracle the entire well didn't collapse years ago," Telford said.

"We might have been better off if it had," Dayna said. "Maybe then—"

She caught movement from the corner of her eye and glanced at her tablet. The infrasonic and seismographic readings, which resembled compressed EKG waves, had both spiked at once. Granted, it wasn't much of an uptick, but any anomaly was cause for concern.

"What's wrong?" Stephens asked.

"Probably nothing," she said, returning her attention to the drone footage.

As the quadcopter descended, the shaft's walls subtly widened and took on a reddish cast, almost as though . . .

She glanced at Sydney's incubator, then back again. There was no doubt in her mind that the same fungus was growing on the shale.

"Eight thousand feet," Telford said.

Another spike on Dayna's readings . . . slightly higher in amplitude . . . a faint vibration, one that produced sound in the infrasonic range. She studied the jagged lines scrolling past, watching for a recurrence.

"That biofilm growing on the rocks must be chemosynthetic," Stephens said. "Imagine how concentrated the fumes are down there. It would be like getting sprayed with pesticides twenty-four hours a day."

Sydney furrowed her brow and returned her attention to her genetic sequencer.

Dayna caught another simultaneous spike in the seismographic and infrasonic readings. While it was of similar amplitude to the preceding anomalies, it barely stood apart from the buzzing of the drone's propellers, the increasing reverberations from which exponentially amplified the sound.

"Ten thousand feet," Telford said.

"The echo of the drone's rotors is affecting my readings," she said. The background noise drowned out everything in the infrasonic range and rendered her seismograph essentially useless. "I've lost the anomaly."

She watched the drone's cameras as it rocketed straight down into the earth. The downward-facing light diffused into darkness deeper than any she'd ever seen, while the side beams failed to penetrate the shadows clinging to the eroded surface of the metamorphic rock.

"Eleven thousand," Telford said.

Dayna detected the faintest increase in seismic readings, barely larger than the vibrations of the propellers' soundwaves refracting from the surrounding stone.

"Wait . . . there it is again." Several more anomalies

appeared in rapid succession. "These vibrations aren't natural. There's no detectable rhythm or pattern. Something down there has to be causing them."

"You mean like an animal?" Telford asked. "Nothing could have survived falling two vertical miles. And there's not a single burrowing animal that could have tunneled that deep."

"Based on the levels of contamination we're detecting all the way up here," Stephens said, "I guarantee you there isn't a living being on this planet that could survive down there for any length of time."

Dayna scrutinized the live imagery from the drone as it passed through the end of the shaft. The walls on either side fell away, revealing a cavern so large that the lights merely dissipated into the darkness. The Army's engineers had expected the chemicals to disperse into the porous rock, not completely degrade its physical structure.

Again, the seismograph detected the faintest vibrations, as though some unknown mechanical force softly tapped the ground.

"I'm telling you . . . there's something down there."

"Twelve thousand," Telford said.

The ground materialized below the drone. It was pitted, like the surface of the moon, and riddled with fissures. Crystalline formations resembling thornbushes sparkled from the periphery, while quartzlike columns cast shadows sparkling with prismatic colors.

"It's how I imagine a forest on another planet," Stephens said.

Dayna could only shake her head in wonder. She

didn't know what she'd expected to find, but this was the furthest thing from it.

"Let's see what else is down there," she said.

"You don't have to tell me twice," Craig said.

The cameras swung wildly as the drone raced into the darkness.

"Slow down," Telford said for what had to be the hundredth time.

"The battery won't last forever," Craig said. "We're nearly to the point of no return already, so I'm trying to cover as much ground as possible before I have to turn around. That is, unless you want me to just keep going and let it crash when it runs out of juice."

"Might as well," Stephens said, looking up from his tablet, which displayed the chemical concentrations from the drone's photoionization detector. "Unless we can confirm the cavern's structural integrity and determine the source of that anomaly from up here, we're going to have to go down there anyway."

Dayna closed her eyes and focused on slowing her breathing. She'd realized as much the moment she'd detected the anomalous spikes, but hearing the words spoken aloud — and in such stark terms — drove home the reality of the situation in a manner that made her heart race.

"Keep scanning," she said, opening her eyes again. "For now, we just need to acquire as much data as we can."

She returned her attention to Telford's monitor, which

displayed the digital reconstruction of the cavern. While they'd been forced to trade resolution for speed, the imagery was more than sufficient to provide a virtual recreation of the vast space beneath their feet. The rocky walls appeared in shades of gray and kind of looked like pixilated storm clouds. As did the jagged stones breaching the milky-blue surface of the scattered puddles of standing fluid. Columns resembling broad charcoal-colored tree trunks supported the uneven ceiling, its surface spiked with long, pencil-thin stalactites. The forests of crystalline growths appeared deep blue, their intricate lattices resembling a cross between thornbushes with overly long spines and strangler fig vines attempting to claim the open air.

The inset box in the bottom right corner displayed a two-dimensional map of the cavern, which kind of reminded Dayna of a narrow lake filled with islands. A vertical yellow line marked the position of the three-dimensional imagery in relation to the overall scanned space. There were numerous branches the drone had yet to explore, but there was only so much time and the underground system seemed to go on forever.

Dayna glanced at her own monitor one last time, hoping for any reading to stand apart from the background noise, and headed over to check on Sydney, whose monitor displayed data she couldn't even begin to comprehend.

"What am I looking at?" she asked.

The medical mycologist glanced up at her and blinked several times, as though awakening from a deep sleep.

"This system extracts DNA from a sample, sequences its genome, and then compares it to a comprehensive database of every known species of bacterium and fungus. The fungus I collected from the well? It doesn't fully match any of them, but — as I suspected — it's genetically similar to two that never could have come into contact with one another in the natural world."

"What does that mean?"

"It means that whoever pulled the strings to get us all here knew the Army was experimenting with fungi, presumably with the intention of weaponizing them."

"Weaponizing? So you think they want you to figure out how to produce an antifungal agent to counteract it?"

"I'm worried they're hoping I'll confirm its efficacy."

Dayna glanced at the incubator, the observation window of which was covered with the reddish biofilm.

"You mean it could be dangerous?"

"Worse than that. It could very well be—"

"Did you see that?" Telford gasped.

"See what?" Craig asked.

Dayna rushed to the monitor displaying the live feeds from the drone's cameras, which relayed shadowed footage of earthen walls and strange speleothemic growths.

"I could have sworn I saw movement," Telford said.

"How many times do I have to say it?" Stephens asked. "There's no way any higher order of life could survive down there."

Dayna looked at her tablet just as a faint seismic spike separated from the background noise.

The drone's cameras abruptly swung, blurring the image of the cavern floor and projecting a shadow that looked like a grove of skeletal trees onto the wall. The live feeds went black first, followed by those displaying the

LiDAR imagery and the incoming data from the various sensors. Only Dayna's system remained active. Without the buzz of rotors, the infrasonic and seismic readings once more demonstrated simultaneous spikes, one after another, with no apparent pattern or rhythm.

There was no longer any doubt in her mind . . .

Something down there was definitely alive.

10

Denver International Airport
7:52 a.m.

The detonation of Randall's subterranean drone, beyond the westernmost runway and more than three hundred feet down, made the ground tremble. Rubble cascaded from the edges of the sinkhole, mere feet from where he stood. Dust billowed from the crevice way down at the bottom. He glanced at the aerial imagery from the Delta's drone, which hovered over the adjacent field. A lightning bolt-shaped section of earth had dropped several inches, but there didn't appear to be any damage to the tarmac. The tiny Semtex charge had worked as designed, producing a concussive blast large enough to destabilize the overlying rock without igniting the combustible chemicals . . . unlike Alpha's flamethrower.

He walked a circuit of the pit, spraying everything

within range with a thirty-foot stream of liquid fire. The earthen walls scorched, the train's exterior paint blistered, and its interior burned. By the time he was done, there would be no trace of the chemicals or the organism, or at least not enough for anyone to piece together an accurate picture of what had happened here. As far as anyone would ever know, the crash had caused an electrical fire that incinerated the bodies of all passengers, whose cremated remains — or some reasonable facsimile of them — would be released to their next of kin after the completion of a thorough investigation that would reveal nothing more than a tragic accident.

Of course, Malikov and her rapid response team would know better, but they wouldn't have enough evidence to prove they'd witnessed anything more nefarious than an ordinary government coverup, to which the general public had become so inured that no one would bat an eye.

The USGS team currently at the epicenter, however . . . they were going to have to be more carefully managed. Civilians weren't beholden to the same chain of command and cared nothing for the country's interests or the greater good. Worse, if they discovered the fungal agent and recognized its significance — or, heaven forbid, its potential — things would get a whole lot messier.

Randall and his unit needed to get over there and secure the site before that happened. He couldn't allow the organism to fall into the hands of the men he'd derailed his career to prevent from acquiring it in the first place, especially having now seen what it was capable of doing.

"Finish up down there," he said. "We move out in five minutes."

Alpha's response crackled from the inset speaker.

"Yes, sir."

Randall turned his back on the hole and strode toward the refrigerated truck, where his men loaded the portable isolation units onto shelves specially designed to accommodate them. Thanks to people like them, no one had any idea how often vehicles like this had been put to use.

Gamma glanced back at him, an uncharacteristically concerned expression on his face. The tech specialist said nothing that could potentially be overheard, but instead directed Randall's attention to the contractor's body with his eyes. Randall nodded his understanding. He climbed up into the truck beside his subordinate and scrutinized the remains through the transparent polycarbonate casing.

The fungal infection had advanced at such an astronomical rate that it caught him off guard. Where once nearly invisible hyphae had grown from the man's moist mucus membranes, there were now fruiting bodies. Slender stalks branched from the corners of his eyes and scaled his forehead, while others grew from his mouth in such a way as to pull the corners past his molars. Even more tendril-like growths protruded from his ears and the lacerations inflicted during the disaster. Were it not for the brownish-red coloration, Randall might not have recognized the wispy hyphae growing from seemingly every pore, creating a translucent fuzz on the man's exposed skin.

Gamma met his commanding officer's stare, then deliberately looked at the case itself. Randall leaned closer, but he still couldn't see what Gamma was trying to . . . show . . . him . . .

A fine dusting of particulate matter clung to the inside of the unit. Spores, he realized. The fungus had already reached sexual maturity, which meant it could be transmitted from one organism to the next without direct physical contact within a matter of hours, faster than he ever could have imagined possible. And the way it spread . . . it almost looked like fine fissures were forming in the reinforced polycarbonate surface.

Something even more frightening caught his attention, something that caused his heart to race and his breath to catch in his chest.

The faintest hint of condensation fogged a localized section of the capsule, just above the contractor's face. There, and then gone. Several seconds passed before it reappeared, only to dissipate once more.

The man was still breathing.

RANDALL WATCHED the refrigerated truck accelerate toward the outside world with a sinking sensation in the pit of his stomach. He was taking a tremendous risk by allowing the bodies to leave the premises, but there was simply no way around it at this juncture. At least he'd ensured there were fail-safes in place to prevent the organism from ever getting out of the containment units. The moment someone tried to open one, for any reason, all of the incendiary charges concealed in their casings would detonate at once, incinerating every last trace of the organism. Assuming he didn't remotely detonate them first. He needed to finish cleaning up the mess he'd made all those years ago before that happened. If anyone figured out that not only was the fungus viable, but that its capabilities also vastly exceeded their wildest expectations . . .

He suppressed the thought as the vehicle dispatched to transport his team to the former Rocky Mountain Arsenal backed into the recently vacated space. Delta threw open the rear doors of the Lenco BearCat for the others, who loaded their gear into the retrofitted SWAT vehicle as fast as they could. Randall looked around one last time to confirm they hadn't left anything behind that could connect them to the site and climbed up into the vehicle. He slammed the doors behind him and squeezed in beside Gamma on the bench seat as the truck started moving.

The driver on the other side of the partition didn't know the first thing about his passengers or their assignment. The men, however, knew exactly what they were doing. Beta swapped out the oxygen tanks in their primary life support subsystems, while his younger brother misted each of them with a gas that smelled so strongly of fruit that they would have been able to instantly tell if their suits had been compromised. Alpha checked their vital signs to confirm their physical readiness for the next phase of the operation, which fell squarely in Gamma's wheelhouse. He'd already tapped into the feeds from the FEMA mobile command center and the networked computers in the field.

"They've confirmed the deep injection well remains open a depth of twelve thousand and sixty feet," he said. "Drone footage shows near-complete deterioration of the concrete casing and considerable erosion of the surrounding strata. They've also used LiDAR to map a large portion of the subterranean space."

He passed Randall his tactical tablet, which revealed a vast cavity far larger than he'd anticipated. It was a miracle the damage underneath the airport had been confined to such a small area.

"It has to be the size of a parking garage," he said.

"Larger, I'm afraid. These interconnected spaces cover nearly two square miles of open space, and they've yet to officially map the end in any direction."

"What about the organism?"

Gamma hesitated.

"I applied an AI algorithm that transcribes radio communications and scrapes them for specific keywords." He extricated the tablet from Randall's grasp, tapped the screen a few times, and passed it back to him. "I'll let you read it for yourself."

Randall's stomach twisted in knots as he read the transcript.

1. this system extracts dna from a sample, sequences its genome, and then compares it to a comprehensive database of every known species of bacterium and fungus. The fungus i collected from the well?:: (0.4 secs) it doesn't fully match any of them, but — as i suspected — it's genetically similar to two that never could have come into contact with one another in the natural world.
2. what does that mean?

3. it means that whoever pulled the strings to get us all here knew the army was experimenting with fungi, presumably with the intention of weaponizing them.
4. weaponizing?:: (0.4 secs) so you think they want you to figure out how to produce an antifungal agent to counteract it?
5. i'm worried they're hoping i'll confirm its efficacy.
6. ((no voice 1.2 secs)) you mean it could be dangerous?
7. worse than that. it could very well be—
8. ((intr)) did you see that?
9. see what?
10. ((no voice 1.0 secs)) i could have sworn i saw movement.
11. how many times do i have to say it? there's no way any higher order of life could survive down there.

"For whatever reason, the drone appears to have stopped transmitting data after that," Gamma said.

"No one else sets foot on that property until we arrive," Randall said. "I don't want any information I haven't personally vetted getting in or out of there. Am I clear?"

"Yes, sir."

Beta opened a large case and started passing out specially designed flamethrowers, like the one Alpha had used inside the pit. Randall grabbed one, connected the hose to the valve on his PLiSS, and holstered it on the side.

The pressurized tank inside contained enough fuel for five minutes of continuous burn, although the combustible chemicals didn't need that much encouragement. Merely switching on the pilot light down there would ignite the trapped fumes, essentially turning the air to fire, but the billowing flames would quickly extinguish themselves. Any standing chemicals, however, would continue to burn until every last drop had been consumed or someone sealed off the shaft, halting the influx of oxygen from the surface.

Fortunately, their suits had been designed to withstand the heat. Their larger concern was further destabilizing a subterranean environment already on the brink of catastrophe, which meant they could only use the flamethrowers as a last resort. And if they did, they needed to be prepared to bring two vertical miles of solid rock down on their own heads.

Randall leaned back in his seat and stared blankly through the window behind Delta. The next-to-last line of the transcript — *I could have sworn I saw movement* — played over and over in his head as he relived the memory of condensation forming on the inside of the glass above the contractor's lips.

RANDALL WATCHED the world pass through a realm outside of time. He simultaneously existed in the past and present, seeing his surroundings both as they were and as they'd once been. A soccer stadium stood where the security gate once had. The specters of the red-and-white-checkered water tower and belching smokestacks lorded over rolling plains where there used to be processing plants, veritable cities employing thousands of dedicated workers, the majority of whom had presumably preceded him to the grave. Swatches of dead earth marked where buildings he could still clearly see had once serviced shipping fleets and railcars. Trees ringed lakes once so contaminated that nothing had grown from their shores, and spandex-clad bikers rode on paths beneath which he'd overseen the burial of countless barrels of toxic waste. There were even bison grazing way off in the distance, where once upon a time his men had detonated munitions.

This entire place was a living testament to the fact that the world he'd once known no longer existed. Soon, it would fade into the banks of memory. The thought saddened him. Not because he'd presided over some pivotal moment in history, but rather because as soon as humanity forgot the lessons learned here, it would once more be forced to call upon men like him to pull it back from the abyss.

"The cable reel handler will be here in fifteen minutes," Gamma said.

Randall nodded and shook off the nostalgia. He'd rejoin the past in due course, but for now, he needed to make sure it held no surprises that would come back to haunt him.

"Excellent," he said, banging on the side wall.

The driver slowed and pulled to the side of the road. Delta threw open the rear doors and hopped out. As arranged, he'd rendezvous with the construction vehicle and drive it the rest of the way to the decommissioned well. He fell away behind them as the BearCat accelerated across the grasslands. After several minutes, they veered east toward the FEMA Mobile Emergency Response Support Vehicle, although Randall would have recognized the location without it. In his mind, he could still see the aboveground rigging and support buildings . . . and recall how they'd smelled as they burned to the ground.

The moment the vehicle stopped, all four men piled out. Randall left the other three to unload the gear and strode straight through the weeds toward the gathered scientists, who looked curiously back at him from beneath their silly popup canopy, like they were enjoying a leisurely afternoon at a picnic. Perhaps no one had impressed upon them the direness of the situation and the need to sacrifice a few luxuries for expedience's sake.

He scanned for their communications frequency and took in everything around him as he approached. The infrasonic array and seismic detectors; the petite brunette evaluating the readings on her tablet. A portable monitor divided into quadrants featuring the various LiDAR data and reconstructions; the slender man working the console. The burly guy collecting chemical concentration data with a wand probe. A kid with messy hair attempting to restore communications to an obviously malfunctioning drone. And a woman, whose microbial identification system hummed as it ran through one sample after another, but it was her incubation chamber that caught his eye. Not just the fungal growth on the inner surface of the leaded acrylic window, but rather the fine network of fissures running through it.

"Who's in charge here?" he asked.

The brunette tentatively stepped forward.

"I am," she said. "Dr. Dayna—"

"Wrong," Randall said, looking from one confused face to the next. "From here on out, I'm in charge."

11

Rocky Mountain Arsenal National Wildlife Refuge
8:19 a.m.

"And just who the hell are you?" Dayna asked.

"General Jack Randall. United States Army CBRNE Enhanced Response Force. I'm here to make sure you do your jobs and ensure nothing happens to you in the process."

"Can you stop another earthquake? Because that's the only reason we'd need your protection."

"That's your job. Now, I suggest you ready yourselves to do it. A cable reel handler is currently en route to our location. As soon as it arrives, you'll be strapped into harnesses and lowered twelve thousand feet into the subterranean cavity, where you'll be tasked with completing your work as quickly as possible."

"Hold up," Dayna said. "I never called for a cable reel

handler. We haven't established if it's even safe for us to go down there."

"Millions of lives hang in the balance, Dr. Raines. Another earthquake could prove catastrophic."

"No one understands that better than I do, believe me, but we have to proceed with caution. Something down there is producing both seismic vibrations and sound in the infrasonic range, and until I have at least an idea of what it might be—"

"And just how do you propose figuring that out from up here?" Randall asked, tilting his head so the sun's reflection on his visor no longer concealed his face. Dayna flinched at the sight of his scarring. "I'm waiting."

"You don't need me," Craig said. "I just fly the drone."

"Which we will need you to continue doing," Randall said, staring daggers at the poor kid. "Correct me if I'm wrong, but you lost communication with the drone approximately twenty-five minutes ago, and no one else here has the requisite practical experience to restore it."

Dayna furrowed her brow with the realization that these men had access to their systems and communications. Again, she was reminded of Cassie's warning.

"Who *really* sent you?" she asked.

"The same people who sent you, Dr. Raines," Randall said, tilting his head so that the reflection of the rising sun once more veiled his expression.

"We're going to need more than that if you expect us to do anything you tell us."

"All you need to know is that no one alive understands what's down there better than I do."

A sudden realization struck Dayna.

"You were here."

"Then you know what that fungus is," Sydney said.

Randall looked through them as though they weren't even there, then turned on his heel and headed back toward his men.

"Ready your equipment for transport," he said. "And I suggest switching to a fresh oxygen tank. I'd hate for you to run out of air during the descent, because it's a long, long way down."

They all watched him walk away in stunned silence.

"He's right," Stephens said. "We should change our tanks while we can."

Dayna didn't like this — *all-consuming darkness, suffo-cating claustrophobia, Thunder's dying scream* — but Randall made a valid point: they weren't going to be able to find the answers they needed from up here.

"Don't we need some kind of special oxygen mix?" Craig asked. "I mean, that's what deep-sea divers use, and they don't go anywhere close to two miles down. And won't we get the bends on our way back up?"

"Think of this well like an elevator shaft in a really tall skyscraper," Telford said. "People work in mines deeper than this all the time. Believe it or not, if it weren't for the fumes, you wouldn't need to wear an oxygen mask at all. The increased pressure will make you feel heavier and tire faster, but beyond that, the most traumatic thing you'll experience is your ears popping on the way down. And you definitely won't get the bends." He chuckled and clapped Craig on the shoulder. "We're talking about just a little more pressure than you'd experience at the bottom of the deep end of a swimming pool."

"That can't possibly be right," Craig said, looking at each of them in turn. "Can it?"

Stephens shrugged. "Only one way to know for sure."

"Get all of your gear packed and ready to go first," Dayna said. "We need as much time to evaluate and stabilize the fault zone as we can possibly get."

"You can't seriously be thinking about following him down there," Sydney said.

"Honestly? The mere thought scares the hell out of me, but that's why we're here, isn't it? And much as I'm loath to admit it, having someone with us who knows what we're dealing with will be hugely beneficial."

"Assuming he actually shares that information," Telford said.

Dayna nibbled on the inside of her lip as she watched the old man rejoin his team. They appeared to be talking, which meant they were communicating on a separate frequency that only they could hear. It struck her that she'd be trusting them with her life, and if she was right about Randall's involvement here decades ago, then she needed to figure out precisely who she was dealing with.

"Go on ahead when you're finished," she said. "I'll be right behind you."

She packed up everything except her laptop and waited until the others were crossing the field to the FEMA trailer before opening the file containing the historical information about the Rocky Mountain Arsenal. The majority of the black-and-white pictures featured the exteriors of the buildings. A few showcased the facilities, but only a handful contained imagery of the scientists working inside them. It wasn't until she discovered an old congressional report titled "Logistics and Materiel Readiness: U.S. Army Armament, Munitions and Chemical Command (AMC-COM), Rocky Mountain Arsenal, Colorado" that she found what she was looking for. She scrolled through page after page of poorly reproduced photographs and heavily redacted documents until she suddenly stopped.

There he was. Randall looked like little more than a teenager, but his hawkish features were unmistakable. And completely unscarred. The photographer had captured him looking straight at the camera from behind a pair of men wearing lab coats and holding wire rabbit cages. His eyes seemed to stare right at her through the monitor. While his name had been blacked out, the rest of the caption had not. "Major [redacted], pictured here with two civilian scientists, has assumed full responsibility for the fire at the North Plants, which consumed millions of dollars' worth of materiel assets, erased countless years of [redacted] research, and claimed the lives of four men under his charge."

Dayna glanced up at the old man and found him looking back at her from across the distance. She lowered her gaze to the screen, read the report as fast as she could, and hurried to catch up with her teammates in the decontamination corridor.

DAYNA WATCHED the men in their space suits through the window of the mobile command center, mentally sifting through everything she'd just read while she switched out the oxygen tank on her back and donned her hazmat gear once more. It was a whole production made infinitely more difficult by the fact that it was still wet from the thorough soaking in the decontamination chamber and there were so many of them crammed into such a small space. Not to mention the tension hanging in the air between them.

"I don't like this," Sydney said.

"Neither do I," Stephens said, "but I don't see how we have much of a choice in the matter."

"Of course we have a choice!" Craig snapped. "We could just walk away and never look back. What are they going to do, arrest us? Imprison us? For what . . . not following the orders of someone we can't even be sure has the authority to give them? We're not even in the military, for Christ's sake!"

"But we do have a responsibility," Dayna said. She sighed and focused on keeping the dawning panic from creeping into her voice. "Look . . . none of you has to go down there if you don't want to. I won't think less of you if you don't. The aftershocks have diminished and the seismic readings suggest a measure of stability, but that could change at any minute. I need more data to generate a predictive model, and that takes time, which, unfortunately, is one thing we currently lack. All I know for sure is that if I do nothing and it costs millions of people their lives, I won't be able to live with myself."

Silence settled over the trailer. No one seemed to be capable of looking at anyone else. Water dripped from their suits and pattered the drain grates with a metronomic *plink . . . plink . . . plink.*

A beeping sound drew Dayna's attention to the

window, through which she watched a giant yellow construction vehicle back up to the crater. With a crane perched above its cab and a fifty-foot-long flatbed carrying giant spools of cable, it had to be one of the strangest looking vehicles she'd ever seen. It was hard to believe there was more than two continuous miles of braided wire coiled around those spools; harder still that she and the others were about to tether themselves to it and descend into the earth. While she'd known she might have to do so, the reality of watching the men uncoil it was something else entirely.

Her chest tightened and her heart raced. She couldn't seem to catch her breath.

Telford pulled her aside and met her stare. He raised the question with his eyebrows.

"I'm fine," she said. "Really."

To his credit, he said nothing. She didn't need to be reminded that she was about to stuff herself into a shaft barely wider than her shoulders and allow herself to be lowered into an enclosed space from which she couldn't escape on her own.

The thought struck her so hard that she started to hyperventilate. Jerking her arm from his grasp, she bounded out the door and willed her rising terror to subside. She could do this. She *had* to do this. There was no one else on the planet who could do what she could do. What she *needed* to do.

Swallowing a knot of fear, she lowered her head and struck off into the field.

DAYNA CHECKED the mess of tangled nylon and metal clamps tethering her harness to the cable for the thousandth time. What if the material tore or the carabiners broke? What if the steel clamp's teeth gave out or, heaven forbid, she accidentally squeezed the emergency release?

"Best to just keep your hands away from that lever altogether," the soldier the others called Alpha said. "I don't want to try to catch you."

He stepped right up to the edge of the shaft and, without so much as looking down, tucked his arms to his sides and stepped out over the nothingness.

"Lights and cameras on," he said through the speaker. "Status check."

"Cameras functional," Gamma said. "Integrating with drone and LiDAR imagery . . . now."

"Helmet-mounted display engaged. Imagery active."

All ten of them had dialed in to the same radio frequency, although the military men obviously utilized an additional private channel, as Dayna occasionally saw them communicating with each other when no voices were coming through her speaker.

Beta, the second man in line, waited for the cable to tighten before sitting down and dangling his legs over the nothingness.

"Look out below!" he said, pushing off and disappearing into the earth.

Dayna realized that the codenames assumed by the men under the general's charge not only marked their order of descent, but also served to conceal their identities from the scientific team and anyone who might intercept or preserve their radio communications. That Randall had used his real name sat just as poorly with her, as either he wasn't concerned about the potential consequences of his actions or he believed he had nothing to hide, which, as she'd recently learned, he most certainly did.

"We should have buttered ourselves up first," Beta said. "I feel like a gerbil in Richard Gere's—"

"Focus," Randall snapped. He turned to Dayna and her team while the remaining soldiers lowered their combined gear, secured to the cable in nylon-mesh nets, through the hole, one tightly packed bundle after another. "Remember, those tanks on your backs contained six hours of oxygen when you strapped them on, and you've already burned through nearly fifteen minutes of that just walking out here and getting into your harnesses. If you run out, there's no way to replenish it, at least not without taking off your suits and killing yourselves in the process. The descent will consume a full hour, and while the return trip won't take quite as long, we should reserve another hour to give ourselves time to decontaminate and get out of these suits, which means we have less than four hours to find and figure out how to stabilize that fault zone. Should we fail to do so, we'll be forced to return to the surface, reequip, and go back down again."

Dayna's heart beat so hard and fast that it felt like it might burst from her ribcage. Her proprietary algorithm required considerably more data to predict another earthquake, and even then, it wasn't an exact science. At best, her program could narrow the likelihood of seismic activity to a multi-hour window, but by the time it did so, they might already be too late.

"Set countdown for five hours and forty-five minutes," Randall said. "Sync on my mark. Three. . . two. . . one. . . "

The soldiers tapped the control pads on their forearms.

"How are the rest of us supposed to know how long we have left?" Craig asked.

"Do your jobs as fast as you can, and it won't be an issue."

The cable tightened, pulling Telford forward. He sat at the edge of the shaft, double-checked his harness, and grabbed onto the braided wire as they'd all been instructed. As he had the most experience evaluating the stability of mines, it made sense for him to be the first scientist to reach the bottom.

He took a deep breath, shifted his weight forward—

And then he was gone.

"Dr. Raines?" Randall prompted.

Dayna couldn't make herself take a single step closer. Her boots skidded on the gravel as the cable pulled her forward, twisting her sideways in the process.

"You have to sit down," Randall snapped.

She couldn't do it. Her body seemed to have a mind of its own, digging in with her heels like a stubborn mule.

"That cable will pull you down, whether you like it or not, so either do as I say or disengage the harness and get the hell out of there!"

The others' weight dragged her right to the precipice. She saw Telford maybe ten feet straight down. He seemed to take up the entire shaft, as though if it narrowed in the slightest, he'd become wedged in there like a cork in a bottle.

"Choose now, Dr. Raines!" Randall shouted. "Either

lower your legs into the shaft or use the emergency release!"

Dayna glanced to the south, toward the distant skyscrapers and the slowly dissipating cloud of smoke. Millions of people were counting on her. If she walked away now—

She lost her balance. One foot skidded sideways on the rubble, while the other came down on empty air.

"Cut her loose!" Randall shouted.

Gamma lunged for her from one side, while Delta slid down the loose rocks from the crater's lip. Jagged chunks of stone and concrete skittered past her and vanished into the darkness. Telford cried out in surprise.

Dayna's leg bent at an awkward angle. The harness pulled on her pelvis, amplifying the pain shooting all the way into her foot. If she didn't get that leg into the shaft right now, her hip was going to break. She screamed and drew her leg toward her chest—

And plummeted into the earth.

With a jerk, the harness brought her to an abrupt halt, her elbows and knees banging on the narrow walls. Voices burst from the speaker by her ear as everyone called to her at once, asking if she was all right or if she needed help or if they should reverse the cable and bring her back to the surface.

"I'm fine," she whispered.

The pulse rushing in her ears was so loud that she couldn't be certain she'd spoken out loud. She closed her eyes as tight as she could and flattened her arms against her sides so she couldn't feel the strata constricting around her.

"You're going to be okay," Telford's disembodied voice

said from beside her ear. "Concentrate on your breathing. In through your nose . . . out through your mouth. Think about anything other than your surroundings. Find something to occupy your mind. And just keep breathing."

"I can do this," she whispered.

The cable shook as Stephens slid into the chute above her, but the otherwise smooth descent continued. She forced herself to breathe — slowly, rhythmically — and channeled her mental energies into trying to understand something she'd read in the congressional report, namely how the man who'd been held accountable for the fatal fire at the North Plants had wound up in charge of the unit slowly sinking into the darkness with her.

12

Rocky Mountain Arsenal

1966

The setting sun cast Randall's shadow across the wavering grasses, through which a cool breeze rippled. It was strange not to see the massive derrick lording over the dark horizon, but, truth be told, he was happy to be rid of it. The earthquakes had been getting stronger with each passing year and it was only a matter of time before they ended up doing serious damage. Granted, Denver wasn't especially close to any major fault lines, but the fact that they'd been able to stimulate seismic activity as though it were troubled him.

He'd ultimately relented and taken the engineer's concerns to his commanding officer, who'd seen the benefits of maintaining the integrity of the well, if not the means of actively forcing fluid into it. None of them wanted the public relations nightmare of having millions of gallons of chemicals erupt from the earth or the entire base collapse into a toxic pit. The resolution had been to strip everything aboveground, from the generators and electric control house to the manifold and mast, leaving only a simple surface casing and blowout preventer, through which they could bleed the pressure. Eventually, they'd have to make a more permanent decision, but for now it bought them enough time to determine the best course of action.

Benjamin and his team were still out there, although they were about to lose the last of their light. Randall was just going to have to trust the Engineer Corps to work their magic because he already had more than he could handle on his own plate. With such a promising development in the biowarfare program, the brass cared about little else and expected another update once Thompson had a working theory regarding the fungal organism's life cycle and the exact means by which it triggered what they were calling the "resurrection response," a reaction they believed could be utilized under the right conditions to penetrate enemy lines inside the repatriated corpses of soldiers killed in battle.

Randall should have been more excited, he knew. Such unprecedented success would lead to rapid promotion and commendations galore, but Dr. Thompson's trepidation had become contagious. His gut was a seething ball of nerves that he couldn't calm, no matter how hard he tried.

He headed back inside and navigated the maze of corridors. The fresh air hadn't helped as much as he'd hoped it would. Thompson was still in his sealed lab, trying to keep up with the rapidly proliferating fungi. Even from the other side of the observation window, Randall could tell that the *growths on the rabbits had grown significantly. They now looked more like tree roots than antlers and covered the entirety of the animals' backs. The fruiting bodies were definitely more pronounced, too. If the chief scientist was right about their biological impetus, then it appeared as though it wouldn't be long before they achieved it.*

Thompson glanced up from his microscope and their eyes met through the glass. He looked like he hadn't slept in days.

Randall pressed the button to activate the inner speaker.

"How are you holding up in there, Doc?"

Thompson shrugged as though the question were of no consequence.

"The two fungal species appear to have been made for each other," he said. "It's almost as though they fit together like pieces of a puzzle. I've only just discovered that their spores adhere to form an aggregate. The graminis tritici *are a fraction of the size of the* unilateralis, *and cluster around it in much the same way metal filings cling to a magnet. Their bond is easily broken by adding water, but doing so produces a trace amount of an acid I have yet to qualify, one I speculate functions to wipe out white blood cells. I've never seen anything like it. It's almost as though they're metamorphosing into a single organism before my very eyes."*

"The brass only cares about whether or not we can control it."

Randall couldn't shake the feeling that the rabbits were watching him. They were still pressed against the wire walls of their cages, fungal protrusions poking out like porcupine quills.

"It's too soon to tell," Thompson said. "At this point, I

can't even be sure what the final product of their union will be."

"I need to throw them a bone. Give me something to work with."

"Tell them—"

The rabbits screamed in unison, a shrill sound that caused the speaker to crackle. Thompson whirled to face the cages. The fruiting bodies exploded as one, releasing a mist of spores that expanded outward like glittering red drapes blowing on the wind. They washed over him and accumulated on the inside of the window like a dusting of pollen.

Randall cautiously touched the glass. It was warm against his fingertips.

"You okay in there?" he asked.

The chief scientist turned around.

Randall staggered backward at the sight of him.

The lenses of Thompson's gas mask had shattered. Blood flowed freely from the skin around his eyes. He cried out and fell to his knees.

With a sharp crack, fissures spiderwebbed through the observation window.

Randall sprinted toward the emergency shutdown button. Slapped it. A klaxon blared. The overhead fixtures snapped off and the reserve lighting kicked on, casting a red glare over the entire facility. Electromagnetic doors closed with thudding sounds that reverberated from the hallways. Airflow through the ductwork ceased, but not quickly enough.

A fine scarlet mist shivered from the ceiling vents.

He grabbed an isolation suit, ducked under the chemical shower, and tugged the cord. Frigid water rained down upon *him, drenching him as he struggled into the protective gear. He seated a gas mask over his face and watched helplessly as the spores settled all around him.*

The observation window disintegrated, sending shards skittering across the floor. The same combination of enzymes and mechanical force the spores utilized to penetrate the exoskeletons of the insects must have worked every bit as well on the reinforced glass and Thompson's lenses.

There was no sign of movement through the empty frame. Only rows of dead rabbits staring back at him through hollow, skeletal sockets.

THE CHEMICAL SHOWER *might have saved Randall's life, but by the time he set off the fire alarm and triggered the building-wide sprinkler system, it was too late for the other scientists still in their labs. Spores had circulated through the air ducts and felled them in the midst of their work. Like Thompson's, their bodies demonstrated superficial lesions where the spores had eaten through their skin and infiltrated their circulatory systems. While he couldn't detect any appreciable signs of life, he knew better than to take their deaths for granted. If they exhibited the same resurrection response as the rabbits and the fungi subsumed their physical forms, then he was dealing with more than a mere infection. As the chief scientist had recently said, they were potentially dealing with the means of the extinction of their very species.*

Randall knew exactly what his commanding officer would say when he reported what had happened, which was why he wasn't about to tell him. At least not yet. This organism was beyond their ability to contain, let alone control. If a handful of locusts had been enough to begin a cycle deadly enough to kill everyone inside the building, then he didn't even want to imagine what could be accomplished with four human beings, whose bodies were currently in the early stages of fungal subsummation.

There was only one thing he could do, and it would likely derail his career. Maybe even more than that if anyone figured out he'd done so deliberately. As it was, he was taking a huge risk removing the bodies from the facility, but he couldn't allow the brass to get ahold of them.

He collected all four of the men and wrapped them individually in plastic tarps. The whole lot of rabbits fit into a fifth. He loaded them into the bed of a truck and drove out to where Benjamin's team had been mere hours earlier. He levered open the temporary iron hatch and stared down into the dark shaft. The chemical fumes emanating from the orifice made the air ripple.

The enormity of what he was about to do wasn't lost on him, but he couldn't afford to dwell on it for fear he might talk himself out of it. His plan was wrong on so many levels, and yet the consequences of doing the right thing could prove catastrophic. Thompson had recognized the dangers prior to his death and had planted the seeds of doubt in Randall, who believed in their mission to rid the world of the enemies of freedom and liberty, but not at the expense of all humanity.

The time had come to end this experiment once and for all.

Randall dragged the wrapped bodies from the Jeep and

forced them through the opening, which was barely wide enough to accommodate their width. He used a metal post from the demolished mast to tamp them down, until he was certain they'd fallen into the depths, where no one would ever think to look for them, let alone be able to recover them.

BY THE TIME *Randall returned to the main building, the pink stain of dawn had crept across the horizon. He'd had plenty of time to formulate a plan, which, if he was able to pull it off, would not only eradicate all evidence of the deadly organism he'd inadvertently helped create, but also potentially salvage his career. He might even come out of this unscathed. Professionally, anyway. Physically, this was going to hurt. A lot. And that was assuming he didn't kill himself in the process.*

With the interior of the facility drenched by the fire sprinklers, it would take more than a tank of petrol to do what needed to be done. Fortunately, there was a gas line in the lab and thousands of gallons of combustible precursor chemicals in storage, more than enough to turn the entire facility into a roaring inferno that would burn so hot and fast that there would be nothing left of it by the time the fire department arrived.

Randall strode from one lab to the next, sloshing chemicals onto countertops and desks, toppling full barrels onto floors, hosing down ceilings and walls. Even a superficial investigation would reveal that arson had been involved, but as long as four civilian scientists remained unaccounted for — whether their bodies had been incinerated in the blaze or they'd started the fire to cover up the theft of classified material and make it look *like they had — no one would suspect the commanding officer, a man who'd nearly died trying to save critical research.*

Nearly *being the operative word.*

By the time Randall opened the gas main, his eyes stung so badly that he could hardly keep them open. He went straight to the entomology lab and shattered the nearest aquarium, inside of which was one of the experimental groups that had successfully transmitted wheat stem rust but had proven resistant to cordyceps infection. The majority of the locusts had already succumbed to the fumes. He scooped up a fistful and hurried to the main entrance, where a lighter and a bottle of isopropyl alcohol waited.

There was no turning back now.

Maybe he should have just dropped a match into the well and blown the whole base to hell, but, despite having created an abomination of nature, he still had faith in what they were trying to do. Torching his career alongside the North Plants wouldn't accomplish anything. Other scientists would pick up right where his team left off, and the nightmare would begin anew. Someone needed to make sure that didn't happen. More importantly, someone needed to make sure that no one discovered what they'd achieved here.

Ever.

Randall doused himself with alcohol and waited for first shift to report. If he didn't time this just right, he'd be dead before anyone could help him. The moment headlights passed through the gate—

There.

He steadied his trembling hands and, clutching the locusts as tightly as he could, flicked the lighter—

Blinding lights flared from everywhere at once. Fire and smoke filled the air.

A scalding wind hurled him through the front door.

Darkness followed, bringing with it pain . . .

So much pain . . .

13

Rocky Mountain Arsenal National Wildlife Refuge
9:33 a.m.

Countdown to Commence Ascent: 4:20
Oxygen Remaining: 5:20

D ayna had lost all sense of space and time. It felt
like she'd been trapped in here forever, yet the
pain in her hip where her leg had twisted sideways was still fresh and raw. While they were only
descending at a rate of two miles an hour, she might as well
have been in freefall with the way her stomach seemed to
be lodged halfway up her throat. As long as she didn't
think about being trapped in here, she was able to stave off
the panic. If the much broader men and bundled supplies
below her didn't get stuck, then she was going to be just
fine. It helped that the soldier they'd left behind to man

the cable reel handler remained in constant communication.

"Passing eight thousand feet, sir."

"Acknowledged, Delta," Randall said.

Dayna finally summoned the courage to open her eyes—

And instantly regretted it.

With trembling fingers, she switched on the LED light clipped to her belt, which only made things worse. An intense white aura bloomed from her midsection, laying bare the eroded earth mere inches from her face. In that moment, she was again a teenager pinned beneath the rubble, unable to fill her lungs . . . to feel her legs . . . to tune out Thunder's awful screams . . .

She closed her eyes and tried to slow her breathing.

In-out. In-out.

In, out. In, out.

In . . . out. In . . . out.

She focused on the mere fact that she wasn't alone. The others were down here with her. Although she couldn't see them, she occasionally felt Alpha, Beta, and Telford jostle the cable below her, giving her time to mentally prepare for an impending narrowing of the shaft. Any kind of movement above her, however, practically slammed her from one wall to the other. She was slowly learning how to anticipate the jerking based on the timing of the others passing through the strictures above her — first Stephens, Sydney, and Craig, then Gamma and Randall, bringing up the rear.

Dayna was still surprised that the general hadn't

remained on the surface with Delta. He might have been in exceptionally good shape for his age, but that didn't mean there wasn't a greater chance of serious injury. He was taking an unnecessary risk that undoubtedly had something to do with what had happened at the North Plants half a century ago. The earthquakes and resultant decommissioning of the deep injection well had happened on his watch. So had the fire that killed four men under his charge and consumed facilities whose functions remained classified, even all these years later. Considering the Army had been in the process of transitioning from the production of chemical weapons of mass destruction to the development of biological agents, there was no way of knowing exactly what research they'd been conducting at the time, but given what Sydney had already found . . .

It struck her that Randall hadn't been surprised by the fungus' proliferation inside Sydney's incubation chamber, so either he didn't have the slightest idea what he was looking at, or he'd seen it before . . . perhaps even in one of the buildings that had burned to the ground. So why would the military keep around someone it obviously held responsible for the destruction of its facilities, let alone dispatch him to oversee the investigation into the earthquake unless . . .

The answer hit Dayna squarely in the gut.

Randall had already known exactly what they were going to find. The evidence of whatever the Army had been developing all those years ago had been incinerated in the fire, along with the scientists responsible for its creation, which meant that Randall was potentially the only living person who knew what this fungus was and, more importantly, what it was capable of doing.

The Army had kept him around all this time just in case something like this happened. If that fungal organism could still do what it had been designed to do . . .

The military wanted it back.

———

Randall dialed up the airflow from the slender oxygen tank on his back and yawned to alleviate the mounting pressure in his ears.

"Depth status," he said.

"Nearing twelve thousand feet," Delta replied.

"Copy. Slow descent by half."

"Slowing descent by half."

The fungal hyphae on the shaft wall, mere inches from his face, were now visible to the naked eye. Fuzzy reddish patches resembling dense networks of roots stood apart from the exposed rock. The intensifying fumes had to be responsible for sustaining some minimal level of growth, as he'd suspected after noticing the wild proliferation of fungi on the undiluted chemicals in Dr. Partridge's incubator.

"I can see the opening underneath me," Alpha said. "Maybe twenty feet down."

Randall concentrated on the live feed from Alpha's downward-facing camera, which his helmet-mounted display projected onto the transparent screen in front of his left eye. The disorienting view made him feel like he was suspended, upside down, from the end of the cable.

Alpha's light limned the rugged orifice and dissipated into the unfathomable darkness below. Ever so slowly, the shaft broadened, then faded away altogether, leaving Randall staring into a vast space of indeterminate size and shape.

The Army scientists had been wrong about the reaction of the metamorphic rock to the chemical waste. They'd been wrong about so much . . .

He tried not to think about the transcript of the USGS team's radio communications as the ground slowly emerged from the farthest reaches of the light. The rock had eroded into jagged terraces resembling giant mismatched paving stones, their surfaces coarse and pitted like the terrain on some faraway planet. Columnar formations appeared from the periphery, like monstrous sentries stepping from the shadows. Standing chemicals shimmered in the distance.

"The cavern appears to be composed primarily of quartzite and gneiss," Alpha said. "It looks almost sponge-like. In fact, it kind of resembles—"

"Lava rock," Randall finished for him. "Be careful transferring your weight. There's no way of knowing how stable it is."

"Copy," Alpha said. His beam constricted on the strange terrain as he descended. The camera nearly collided with the ground, so Randall switched to the tactical specialist's forward-facing camera feed.

A hint of slack rippled through the cable as Alpha touched down. He turned in a circle, the light mounted above his shoulder throwing shadows from briar-like crystalline formations.

"The substrate is exceedingly brittle," he said. "It

makes all kinds of crackling sounds when I move, but it seems stable enough. The pressure at this depth takes a little getting used to, though."

"I feel like I gained fifteen pounds on the way down," Beta said.

Randall changed the subject before he was forced to contemplate how the increased pressure would affect his aging body.

"Gamma, overlay LiDAR imagery," he said. "And Alpha . . . give me a broad sweep of the surrounding area."

"Yes, sir," both men said in unison.

Wire-frame data appeared, superimposed over the rock formations and cavern walls beyond the light's range. The camera slowly turned from left to right as Alpha surveyed the cavern, covering an area of easily a couple hundred square feet, showing Randall exactly what he expected to see. Or, more accurately, what he *didn't* see.

He allowed himself to breathe a sigh of relief.

There was no sign of the bodies he'd dumped down here decades ago.

"Aerial chemical concentrations are off the charts," Beta said. "We wouldn't last a full minute without these suits. And I wouldn't recommend striking a match."

"The fumes aren't the issue," Stephens said. "They'll burn off in a hurry, like hairspray in a lighter's flame. Any standing fluid, however, will continue to burn until every last drop has been consumed or we seal off the shaft."

"I'm less worried about flammability than structural integrity," Telford said. "There's a coal mine in Pennsylvania that's been actively burning for more than sixty years without significant geological degradation. My concern is that the residual chemicals will erode any fill substrate even faster than they did the metamorphic strata. We need to either pump them out or—"

"Leave the chemicals to me," Stephens said. "There has to be a way to neutralize them. You just make sure this place doesn't come down on our heads before I find it."

Randall tuned them out. He didn't care what they did or how they did it. They only had one shot at this, so they needed to make it count. If he so much as sensed that events were on the verge of spiraling out of control, he'd take matters into his own hands.

No matter the consequences.

DAYNA'S HEART beat faster and faster as she passed through the end of the shaft and into the vast domed space. She leaned her head just far enough forward that she could see her boots silhouetted against the diffuse glow below her. Telford slowly twirled in midair a dozen feet below her, helplessly awaiting his turn to land, while Alpha and Beta guided the netted equipment to the ground. Their lights did little to drive back the seemingly impenetrable shadows.

She relived the drone crash as she descended. Something had definitely struck it from above, and while it could have been debris falling from the destabilized roof, as everyone seemed to think, that explanation didn't justify the spikes in her infrasonic readings. Rocks falling from any distance would have created sounds much louder than those she'd been tracking. She could think of only one

thing capable of making such subtle sounds and vibrations: footsteps.

I could have sworn I saw movement.

The darkness seemed to come to life before her eyes.
She searched the shadows for the source of the anomaly,
knowing full well that nothing could have survived down
here for any length of time. Still, she couldn't shake the
feeling that they weren't alone.

Daggerlike stalactites protruded from the ceiling. They
way they'd grown — long, slender, and packed tightly
together — reminded her of icicles, glistening with chemical condensation. Honeycombed columns, some nearly
twenty feet tall, metered the cavern. That such a place
could even exist took her breath away, although not nearly
to the extent of the knowledge that this entire place was
one solid quake away from collapse.

"Magnificent," Telford said. He'd unfastened his
harness and kneeled on the ground, running his palms over
the choppy surface. "It almost feels like glass. And the
outermost layer is translucent."

He glanced up at Dayna and stepped aside to make
room for her to land. The moment her heels touched
down, she tore off her harness and collapsed to all fours,
her legs shaking so badly that she couldn't stand if she
tried. A sob of relief died on her lips when she noticed the
sharp edges of the terraced rock. If she'd torn her suit—

Gripped by panic, she struggled back to her feet and
inspected the fabric, pulling it this way and that until she
was certain, beyond all shadow of a doubt, that there
wasn't a single puncture. A breath she didn't even realize
she'd been holding burst from her lips. Everything was

going to be okay. She just needed to slow her breathing and focus on the task at hand.

The sooner they stabilized the fault zone and isolated the source of the anomalous readings, the sooner she'd be able to get out of here.

14

10:09 a.m.

Countdown to Commence Ascent: 3:44
Oxygen Remaining: 4:44

Randall scraped at the webwork of mycelia on the wall, which came away as a tangle of filaments on his fingertips. That the fumes alone couldn't sustain its growth cycle through sexual maturity was a blessing, or else they'd all be dead by now. No matter how long he lived, he'd never forget the moment the spores burst from the rabbits and shattered the lenses of Dr. Thompson's gas mask . . . or the chief civilian scientist's screams.

He glanced over his shoulder and found Dr. Partridge watching him. The medical mycologist caught him looking and returned her attention to the dense clump of mycelia she carefully tweezed from a crystalline formation. He waited until she returned to her battery-powered stereomicroscope before resuming his own investigation. She'd obviously figured out that the fungus had been engineered, but if she had even the slightest idea of what it could do, there was no chance in hell she'd still be down here.

Dr. Raines had set up another infrasonic array on the ground and affixed her seismic probes to the quartzite. She watched the readings on her tablet while she surveyed the surrounding area for the best locations to place additional sensing devices. Randall tried not to pressure her. First and foremost, he needed to know if there were any indications of impending seismic activity or, failing at that, if she was able to isolate the anomaly she'd detected from the surface. The idea of there being something capable of movement down here worried him, although not nearly as much as the thought of what it might be.

He passed Stephens — who chipped glassy chunks from the wall and placed them in an array of test tubes to determine the quartzite's reaction to various chemical neutralization agents — and approached Telford, sitting on the ground with his laptop on his thighs. The environmental engineer was so caught up in calculations Randall couldn't even begin to understand that he didn't notice the older man standing behind him. He finally glanced over his shoulder and shielded his eyes against general's shoulder-mounted light.

"Can you do it?" Randall asked.

"Without first confirming our ability to neutralize any residual chemicals, it's impossible to say exactly which fill agents—"

"Can. You. Do. It?"

Telford hesitated only briefly.

"If it can be done, I can do it."

"That's all I needed to know." Randall turned around and switched comm channels. "Gamma . . . I want you looking over their work to make sure there aren't any surprises."

"Yes, sir."

He switched back to the open channel and found Dr. Raines already talking.

"—not detecting any seismic activity."

Randall strode right up to her and tilted the tablet in her hands so he could see for himself.

"What about the anomaly?" he asked.

"There's too much background noise to be able to isolate it."

"Keep trying."

"Unless everyone stops moving and holds their breath—"

"You heard her," Randall snapped. "Everyone, freeze on my mark. Three. Two. One." The entire group stopped what they were doing and turned to face them. The readings in both the seismic and infrasonic ranges diminished dramatically. The jagged vertical lines scrolled past for five seconds . . . ten . . . fifteen. "Anything?"

Dr. Raines merely shook her head.

Randall rounded on Craig, who still stood right by the coiled cable, as though reluctant to take a single step away from his lone lifeline to the outer world, and pointed right at him when he spoke.

"You. With me."

"Me?" Craig said, pointing at his chest.

"That drone isn't going to fix itself. Where did it go down?"

"Roughly a mile due east of here."

"Alpha, you're with us."

Randall didn't wait for either man. He struck off away from the gathering, his light slashing through the darkness ahead of him.

DAYNA DIDN'T LIKE THIS.

Not one little bit.

Granted, she'd be able to detect any sort of imminent seismic activity before it became a problem — at least for the people aboveground — and preliminary readings suggested they were in at least a temporary window of inactivity, yet the unique nature of this situation introduced an element of unpredictability for which she couldn't entirely account. And it was rapidly becoming apparent that a single pairing of seismometers and infrasonic arrays wouldn't be sensitive enough to detect the anomaly while they were all clustered together, stomping and banging around. She was going to have to network additional remote sensing devices throughout the caverns — essentially creating one giant subterranean array capable of reinforcing and boosting their combined signals, like Wi-Fi extenders or 5G towers — and incorporate a mobile sensor of her own design if she hoped to detect subtle aberrations across a wide range of spectrums and filter out the background noise. Of course, that would also allow her to add a ton of data and really put her predictive algorithm to the test, but it would take time, and every passing second down here brought her closer to succumbing to the crippling claustrophobia she struggled to hold at bay.

She sighed and narrowly resisted the urge to lean against the wall. No matter how tired and overwhelmed she felt, the last thing she wanted to do was snag her suit on the eroded stone. While the portable stadium lights and the flow of oxygen from her mask helped stave off the worst of the effects, she couldn't help obsessing about the fact that she couldn't see the pressure gauge on her oxygen tank to know how much air she'd already used. Or, more importantly, how much she had left. She could only trust that the heavy cylinder on her back had contained a full six hours of air and pray they accomplished their mission within the four-hour window.

A glance at her tablet revealed they'd already been down here for more than twenty minutes and had nothing to show for it.

Her respirations accelerated as once more panic welled inside her. She needed to distract her mind, focus on anything other than the ticking clock, the cracks riddling the ceiling between the stalactites, and the countless tons of earth just waiting to crush them all.

Sydney leaned away from her microscope and rammed her fists into her visor, as though attempting to rub her eyes. She groaned in frustration.

"Are you all right?" Dayna asked.

The medical mycologist shook her head and leaned against a smooth section of the wall beside the flowstone shelf upon which her microscope rested.

"Just frustrated," she said. "You see all of those rootlike clusters of mycelia on the walls and ceiling? Rather than forming extensive underground lattices in the soil, like they would up top, they've adapted to growing directly on the quartzite."

"What's the significance?"

The soldier called Gamma tried to appear nonchalant as he crept close enough to observe.

"Mycelia grow in the dirt because that's where the nutrients are. Rotting leaves and detritus. Dead animals. That kind of thing. As long as there's a food source, they can theoretically live forever. These have adapted to growing without any appreciable source of nutrition beyond the stone itself."

"How do mushrooms eat rocks?" Stephens asked, glancing up from the readout on his portable GC-MS.

"They secrete digestive enzymes that break down large organic compounds into simpler molecules they're able to absorb through their hyphae. Those enzymes aren't acidic enough to eat through stone by themselves, but in conjunction with the chemicals already dissolving it, the fungi are obviously able to extract the trace amounts of bioavailable nitrogen, phosphorous, potassium, and magnesium contained within the quartzite. Beyond those minerals, all they really need to meet their basic nutritional demands is calcium—"

"The limestone and dolomite at this depth contain calcium carbonate," Telford interjected.

"And a source of protein and carbohydrates," Sydney said, finishing her thought. "Beyond the biomass of preceding generations of dead mycelia, I can't see anything capable of providing either. Where's the decaying organic matter?"

"You're saying that without it, the fungi should have died," Dayna said.

"Exactly."

"Can't they just release more spores?" Stephens asked.

"That's just it. They aren't receiving enough nutrition to reach their reproductive potential. Look around you . . . there isn't a single fruiting body. So if these mycelia aren't capable of living long enough to produce spores, then where did the spores from which they grew come from?"

Dayna furrowed her brow and turned in a circle. While there were countless weblike patches on the surrounding rock, there wasn't a single wiry protrusion like those she'd seen in the incubator.

She suddenly understood Sydney's frustration.

If the source of the spores responsible for continuously replenishing the mycelia wasn't in here, then where in the world was it? Decaying organic matter couldn't move . . .

Could it?

RANDALL SWEPT his light from one side of the cavern to the other, searching for any sign of the bodies he'd disposed of so long ago. There was no way their flesh and bones, let alone their clothing, could have survived decades of immersion in a toxic stew of corrosive chemicals, but he wasn't sure if eyeglasses and surgical fixation devices could. Not that such things could be traced back to their original owners. He'd know, however, and that would be more than enough to reopen those old wounds.

The cavern narrowed and the ground sloped upward as they continued east. Weathered ridges resembling stairs memorialized the high-water marks where the chemicals had stagnated for some length of time. It was astonishing how the combination of geologic forces and atmospheric pressure at this depth had forced the acidic fluid slowly toward the surface, almost like magma, rather than simply allowing it to eat deeper and deeper into the mantle until there was nothing left of it. That had never been in the cards, though. Even after devoting his entire life to the CBRNE Emergency Response Force, cleaning up messes like the one he'd made here in hopes of tipping the karmic scales in his favor, he'd known his day of reckoning would come.

He could only pray he didn't make things worse.

"That column looks familiar," Craig said. "It can't be much farther now."

"Watch your heads," Alpha said.

Randall raised his beam toward the spiked ceiling as they climbed. The stalactites were maybe six or seven feet above the point where the ground once more leveled off; high enough to avoid, but not so high that he and the others wouldn't need to be extremely careful.

"It should be right up ahead," Craig said. "I remember piloting the drone through here."

"Scout ahead and tell me what you find," Randall said.

Alpha took off without a word, his light bouncing as he advanced, creating long shadows that made the stalactites look like fangs. His beam suddenly swung down and pinned the earth.

"Got it," he said, rounding on his heel and momentarily blinding them.

Randall and Craig caught up with him and studied the quadcopter. One of its appendages had snapped off at the base, exposing the wiring inside. The LED spotlight had shattered, and the forward-facing camera had popped loose. A series of scratches marred the casing, as though it had been struck by something sharp.

"I can easily repair that broken arm," Craig said. He crouched and turned the drone over and over in his hands. "That light, however, is totally jacked. I'm going to have to replace the entire assembly. The good news is there's a spare in the case. The bad news is — see this crack on the lens right here? — the camera's beyond saving, and I don't remember seeing another one."

Randall was confident that Gamma would have a replacement, perhaps even an upgrade with night-vision and thermal imaging capabilities.

"Assuming I can get you another camera, how long before you can have it airborne again?" Randall asked.

"There's really no way of knowing until I start. It all depends on—"

"We've already burned through" — Randall glanced at the tiny digital countdown projected onto the corner of the transparent screen in front of his left eye — "ninety-eight minutes of our oxygen supply. That leaves us four hours and twenty-two minutes to return to the surface, and the pressure at this depth on both the tanks and our bodies introduces an element of unpredictability. Now, considering we've accomplished absolutely nothing so far, and that cable isn't pulling any of us out of here until we do, I suggest you hurry your ass back to the others and get to work."

Craig stared at him through wide, unblinking eyes.

"Now, Mr. Preston."

The pilot snatched up the drone and scampered back in the direction from which they'd come. Alpha hurried to catch up.

Randall lingered a moment longer, tracing his light over every square inch of the surrounding passage. There were no broken stalactites or divots in the ceiling marking where a chunk of debris had once been, nor was there any rubble on the ground.

In fact, there was no evidence of how the drone had been taken down at all.

15

10:42 a.m.

Countdown to Commence Ascent: 3:11
Oxygen Remaining: 4:11

Staking the geophones and digital accelerometers into solid rock had proven too difficult and time-consuming, forcing Dayna to adapt on the fly. She'd ended up removing the spikes and slathering some of Sydney's electrophoresis gel on the contacts to increase conductivity with the quartzite. Once she networked the devices with the additional seismometers and infrasonic arrays, she'd be able to detect even the slightest aberrations for miles in every direction. Plus, by integrating her mobile device into her remote sensing network, she'd be able to geolocate the source of any anomalous readings. More importantly, she'd be able to utilize her algorithm to generate the most accurate predictive model possible. If there was even the slightest chance of another earthquake, she'd know it soon enough.

Assuming she figured out how to filter out all of the background noise.

"Are the sensors picking up anything?" Stephens asked.

"The problem is they're picking up too much. This setup is so sensitive that it's detecting not only every footstep and voice down here, but also every subtle vibration passing through the ground above us. Every truck and construction vehicle. Every light rail car and airplane. All of that background noise needs to be subtracted from the data we want, and that takes time."

"And the end result?" Telford asked.

"A predictive model with incredible specificity. I'll not only be able to tell you if there's the potential for another earthquake; I'll be able to tell you when it will happen. Within a window of a few hours, anyway."

"Might have been useful to have something like that about twenty-four hours ago," Beta said.

Dayna kept forgetting that everyone within range could hear their conversations. Beta was so far across the cavern that he was little more than a dark silhouette against his spotlight. It shimmered on a pool of chemicals, before which Sydney crouched, studying the reddish fungal biofilm growing from the surface.

"The Global Seismographic Network utilizes systems similar to this one in densely populated regions with significant seismic activity," Dayna said. "Not in areas where there shouldn't be any."

While her statement wasn't entirely accurate, it served

to make her point. Even in a place like this, there were countless processes occurring deep within the Earth. Subtle shifting and movement at extreme depths created a constant stream of seismic ripples at any given time. Her job was to detect them, isolate them, and then interpret the patterns. It wasn't the activity itself she needed, but rather the time intervals between activities. Any change in those gaps indicated an element of instability, one that started the countdown to a seismic event. Unfortunately, all of those tasks and calculations took time, especially considering the limited processing power of her tablet.

"How long do you estimate this will take?" Gamma asked.

Dayna had been so wrapped up in what she was doing that she hadn't noticed him standing practically right behind her.

"At a guess? Maybe half an hour."

A light bloomed in the distance. Three silhouettes took form from the glow as they approached.

"See what you can do about expediting that timetable," Randall said.

Something about the way he said it made the hairs rise on the backs of her arms.

RANDALL COULDN'T TAKE his eyes off the scratches on the drone's casing. It looked as though they'd been inflicted by the tips of stalactites, only the angle was all wrong. They should have been parallel to the direction of travel, not at a thirty-degree angle to the forward-facing camera. The evidence simply didn't add up. He needed to see that footage again.

"Which one do you want first?" Gamma asked over the dedicated command channel.

"The live feed," Randall said, tearing his eyes from the quadcopter.

Gamma had found a relatively concealed spot away from the others and accessed the imagery from the drone on his tactical tablet. Randall kept his distance, so as not to draw attention to his tech specialist, who, with a tap of his gloved finger, projected the video onto the transparent screen in front of the general's left eye. As before, the drone streaked into the narrowing passage, the stalactites rendered indistinct blurs overhead. Seconds passed and then — *bang!* — the camera veered wildly and struck the ground.

"Replay it," Randall said. "Frame by frame."

The slower speed made everything appear fuzzy and grainy, but he could clearly see that the speleothems were at least a foot above the camera.

"It's coming up," Gamma said. "Right . . . now."

He paused playback just as the footage abruptly tilted, then backed up. One frame. Two.

"Stop," Randall said. There was something at the top of the screen, in the slender gap between stalactites, blurred by motion. "Can you enhance that?"

Gamma applied a filter and zoomed in on the object, which kind of resembled a short length of frayed rope, projecting at an oblique angle from behind a stalactite. Several of the sharp tips almost looked like thorns. He tried another filter and zoomed in again, but there still wasn't enough detail to tell exactly what it was.

"Damn it," Randall snapped. "Bring up the LiDAR."

The video vanished and a three-dimensional reconstruction of the cavern appeared on the small screen. Gamma scrolled through the imagery until he reached the point where the cavern tapered, roughly a hundred feet from where the drone had gone down. The wire frames were incomplete, lending the video a skeletal appearance.

"It takes time for the LiDAR to collect the data from the laser, interpret it, and apply the reconstruction algorithm, so most of the data gathered during the last few seconds was lost in the crash," Gamma said.

Randall nodded his understanding, but that didn't mean he had to like it.

"How close can you get to the moment of impact?"

Gamma scrolled ahead slowly, moving in fractional increments. The wires forming the frames grew sparser and sparser until the walls lacked any texture whatsoever and the stalactites—

"There!" Randall said. "Zoom in on that spot and rotate vertically ninety degrees."

Gamma did as he'd been ordered, and Randall found himself looking at the stalactites as though he were lying on his back. They were little more than dots with half-circles for their bases, with no apparent depth whatsoever, but there was more than enough detail for him to recognize that there was something up there that shouldn't have been, something that hadn't been there when he'd stood beneath that very spot.

I could have sworn I saw movement.

"What in God's name is that?" Gamma asked.

Randall shook his head as he stared at a wire-frame image. There was an oblong shape wedged between the stalactites, with something resembling a bird's foot projecting from it.

"I don't know, but we'd better figure it out in a hurry."

"DRUMROLL, PLEASE," Craig said.

"Just launch the infernal drone," Randall said.

"Sheesh. Just trying to lighten the mood around here a little."

"The drone, Mr. Preston."

The rotors ramped up with a buzz, raising the background noise levels on Dayna's tablet. Fortunately, she'd established a firm baseline, so all she had to do was subtract the corresponding seismic values and eliminate all additional noise between 175 and 450 Hertz. She could always add them back in later, but, for now, she'd be able to evaluate any subtle new sounds and vibrations in real time.

The drone rocketed away, its headlamp resembling a flare fired from a gun. Here, and then gone in the blink of an eye.

"Slow speed by three-quarters when you near the initial stricture," Randall said. "I want to see every little detail through that passage."

Craig drew a breath to respond, but wisely thought better of it and nodded instead.

Dayna glanced back and forth between the live footage on the suitcase monitor and the jagged waveforms on her tablet. The seismicity predictive model was still generating. Just when she thought it might have stalled at 92%, it changed to 93%. It wouldn't be much longer now.

The drone slowed as it passed through the narrowing. The stone walls and floor glistened with chemical condensation, while the tips of stalactites protruded from shadows seemingly impervious to the light. Randall watched the monitor like a hawk, searching for something. Dayna could only speculate as to what that was, but considering they'd detected a hint of movement during the previous flight, she had a pretty good idea.

The ceiling continued to lower as the passageway constricted. The drone couldn't have been more than a couple feet off the ground, and still it looked like the stalactites might clip its rotors. The LiDAR reconstruction followed, moving in blocky sections, lagging behind the live imagery by several seconds.

Dayna glanced at her tablet — 94% — then back at the upper right quadrant, just as the drone emerged from the tunnel. Jagged formations erupted from the darkness, appearing as if from nowhere. The camera jerked wildly as the drone slalomed through the crystalline forest, its headlamp sparkling from the razor-sharp protrusions.

"I never would have imagined that chemicals so deadly could create something so . . . beautiful," Stephens said.

Everyone watched in stunned silence as the drone slowed and weaved between the seemingly magical quartzite formations. They resembled the crystals Dayna had grown as a child, only much larger and far more intricate.

The shadows shifted in the bottom left corner of the

live feed. The movement was so subtle that she couldn't have been certain she'd seen anything at all. Until she glanced at her tablet. The readings had spiked several times in rapid succession, then abruptly stopped. She looked up and found Randall staring at her.

"You detected the anomaly," he said. It was a statement, not a question.

Before she could reply, Gamma grabbed the general by the arm and drew him away from the others. The two men struck off on their own, leaving everyone else staring at their backs and wondering what could possibly be more important than what they were doing now.

16

Washington, D.C.

1968

Randall had spent nearly a full year in the burn ward at Denver General Hospital, followed by another eight months bouncing from one rehabilitation facility to the next. He'd endured countless skin grafts — most of which had come from cadavers, as less than thirty percent of his body had been spared — and unrelenting agony while his cutaneous nerves regenerated. His muscles had atrophied to such an extent that he'd been forced to relearn basic skills like feeding himself and going to the bathroom on his own. He'd devoted hours every day to teaching himself how to walk again, just so he could be paraded before countless oversight committees, suffering one indignity after another, although today's spectacle had been the worst by far.

The Senate Real Estate and Military Construction Subcommittee was so lacking in prestige that only five senators had volunteered, and two hadn't even bothered to show up for his hearing. As the final stop on what he thought of as his Tour of Shame, it was his lot to explain the damage to the facilities, justify the cost of reconstruction, and theorize how best to prevent such a catastrophic failure from occurring again. Had he not been so close to the finish line, he would have told those stuffed shirts exactly what he thought of them, sitting behind that polished oak desk, looking down their noses at him, or, rather, at anything in the room other than him.

He loosened his collar as he exited the Russell Building, tucked his dress cap under his arm, and fished his keys from his pocket. At long last, his ordeal was over. His career, while damaged, remained largely intact. After a couple years of exemplary performance, he'd be able to transition into a role where he'd be able to make sure that nothing like what had happened at the RMA ever occurred again.

That thought gave him a small measure of comfort, fleeting though it was. For as confident as he felt about the chemicals dissolving every trace of the infected remains, he couldn't shake the feeling that he hadn't seen the last of them.

"Hold up!"

Randall turned around and found a man wearing a button-down and tie jogging toward him across the parking lot. His stomach sank at the sight of the junior senator from the good state of New Hampshire, whose name he'd already forgotten. Truth be told, he'd assumed the baby-faced kid with the messy hair and ill-fitted suit had been an aide until *he'd taken a seat at the table. He barely looked old enough to have graduated from whatever Ivy League university his great-grandparents had undoubtedly endowed.*

The senator caught up with him, took him by the arm, and doubled over to catch his breath.

"Whew," he said, panting. "I almost didn't get down here in time."

"I was just on my way—"

"We didn't get a chance to be properly introduced." He thrust his hand into Randall's chest like an appliance sales- man. "James Lowell. It's a pleasure to meet—"

"It's been a long day, Senator, as I'm sure you can appreciate—"

"Then I'll cut right to the chase," he said, letting his hand fall to his side. He took a step closer, invading Randall's personal space, and lowered his voice. "Maybe you have those slack-jawed imbeciles in there fooled, but I know better. You see, unlike my colleagues, I wasn't raised with a silver spoon in my mouth. I got my first job when I was ten years old: delivering papers for a dollar twenty-five a week. It took a full year of doing so — on foot and in the dark — to save up enough money for a bicycle. Do you know the first thing I learned? How to smell a dog turd from a mile away."

Randall held his ground. He refused to be backed down by any man, let alone some self-righteous punk who'd appeared so bored during his testimony that he hadn't opened his trap when he'd had the opportunity to do so.

"Are you accusing me of something, Senator?"

"No, sir," he said, cocking a half-smile. "In fact, quite the opposite. I'm commending you. More to the point, I'm

*going to make you an offer I have a hunch you won't be able
to refuse."*

RANDALL FOLLOWED *Lowell back into the Russell Senate
Office Building, only rather than returning to the Caucus
Room where the hearing had been held, they ducked down a
stairwell into the basement and followed the numbered
doors until they reached one marked by a fancy engraved
placard with the senator's name on it. Lowell struggled with
the lock, but finally led him into an office that looked like it
had been ransacked while the committee had been in session.*

*"You'll have to pardon the mess. Unlike some of my more
illustrious colleagues, I actually work in my office."*

*Randall merely surveyed the surprisingly utilitarian
space while Lowell shuffled around the piles of manila
folders on his desk. Once he found the stack he was looking
for, he took a seat and started leafing through the files,
burning through the last of Randall's patience.*

"What do you want from me, Senator?"

*"Sit, sit," Lowell said, gesturing to the chair opposite
him. "I'll be honest with you, Major. I didn't know what I
was getting myself into when I decided to run for office. It
just seemed like a logical choice after law school, but I quickly
learned that the law in theory and in practice are two
different animals."*

"What does that have to do with me?"

Lowell offered an amused smile.

*"My father was a newspaperman. I grew up believing
the world was black and white—that's a play on words,*

Major — but that's not the case at all, is it? The real story isn't told in words, but rather in the spaces between them. What isn't said, rather than what is. People only lie when their lips are moving, but they can't help telling the truth when they shut their mouths. Case in point? You, Major. You told my colleagues on the committee everything they needed to hear so they could wash their hands of a file they didn't even open, but me? I read the files and pay attention to the testimonies. More importantly, I listen to what people like you say . . . and what they don't."

Randall stared straight through the senator, refusing to rise to the bait.

"Relax, Major. I'm not impugning your character. If anything, I salute your willingness to fall on your sword in front of a few disinterested civilians, who likely should have been handing you a medal instead. Correct me if I'm wrong, but I believe you willingly subjected yourself to grievous bodily harm to save something from inside that building — something just barely important enough to justify risking your life in an attempt to recover — so that no one would wonder what you'd left behind that scared you so badly that you had to burn it to the ground in the first place."

The corners of Randall's vision throbbed with his racing heartbeat. It was all he could do to maintain a neutral expression.

Lowell grabbed the stack of files, walked around his desk, and took a seat beside Randall. When he spoke, it was in a voice barely above a whisper.

"Of all the committees and subcommittees, Real Estate and Military Construction is one of the least prestigious —

we rubber-stamp every capital investment and write off every financial loss — but for someone like me, who's accustomed to reading between the lines, it can be illuminating. For example, I'm sure you'd be surprised to learn that your story isn't as unique as you might think." He offered the folders to Randall, who met the senator's stare for several long moments before accepting them. "Go on. Open one."

Randall furrowed his brow as he perused the official typed summary and the enclosed photographs in the first. He set it aside and glanced at the next, and the next after that. When he finally looked up at Lowell, the senator wore a crooked smile on his face.

"See what I mean?"

"I NOTICED the similarities pretty much right away," Lowell said, tapping the folder in Randall's grasp, "but it wasn't until I got to digging around in the archives that I started to see the pattern."

Randall was so caught up in the file that he hardly heard a word the senator said.

"Over the course of the past twenty-five years, there have been twelve fires, seven explosions, and three catastrophic natural disasters at U.S. military installations around the world, every single one of which resulted in the loss of human life and the complete destruction of research facilities, without the slightest damage to the remainder of the base. Statistically speaking, I could see one or two. Heck, maybe even half a dozen. But twenty-five? That defies all probability. So I made it my mission to find out what was inside

those buildings, which turned out to be a whole lot harder than I thought, believe you me. You know how I finally started putting the pieces together?"

"By accessing the supply requisition forms," Randall said.

"Exactly. And do you know what I found? A curious amount of scientific equipment that had no business on those bases. I had to research the functions of most, but everything fell into place fairly quickly after that. It was really just a matter of securing personnel records, conducting interviews, and requisitioning photographic negatives and camera reels from the right long-term storage facilities and, voilà . . . you have what you see before you."

Randall sifted through files nearly identical to the one detailing the fire at the North Plants. All of the sensitive information had been scrubbed or redacted, but the amassed documentation painted a clear picture: his hadn't been the only classified bioengineering project to go south. Every last one of these folders contained a different failed attempt at weaponization, which someone like him had shut down in the most permanent manner possible. Unfortunately, the vast majority had died in the process, while the remainder had either committed suicide or vanished after testifying.

It was the photographs, however — which Lowell must have exerted an extreme amount of political pressure to acquire — that rendered him speechless. Images of bodies in dark buildings, sterile rooms, and open fields. Torn limb from limb. Attacked as though by wild animals. Burned. Exsanguinated. Twisted and deformed. Decomposing in bizarre patterns. The list went on and on, yet in each grainy black-and-white snapshot, he recognized the hallmarks of the same kind of experimentation he'd supervised.

"What do you want from me?" Randall asked.

"I'm gambling on you being the kind of man who recognizes that the risks of these projects vastly outweigh the rewards. Nuclear and chemical weapons are one thing, but this? Man was never meant to wield this kind of power. We're talking about playing God, Major. Can you imagine what would happen if our enemies acquired this research? Would Brezhnev or Mao share your qualms about using this . . . weaponry . . . even knowing the cost of doing so?" He paused. "Would we?"

Randall merely stared at the senator until he was able to formulate the words to speak.

"What exactly are you asking me to do?"

"I can't put an end to this kind of experimentation," Lowell said. "That genie's already out of the bottle. What I can do, however, is secure capital expenditures for discretionary projects within the existing military framework and pull a few strings to ensure that when things go wrong — which, invariably, they will — someone who understands the stakes is there to clean up the mess." He looked Randall dead in the eyes. "What I'm asking you to do, Major, is help me establish a rapid response unit capable of handling that eventuality."

17

Rocky Mountain Arsenal National Wildlife Refuge
11:03 a.m.

Countdown to Commence Ascent: 2:50
Oxygen Remaining: 3:50

"Where are they now?" Randall demanded.

"Buckley Space Force Base," Delta said, his voice crackling from the long-range comm channel. In addition to running ops topside, he'd been tasked with monitoring the remains recovered from the airport. "The embedded tracking device has been static for nearly an hour."

Randall's stomach sank. Buckley was right in the heart of Aurora, a suburb of four hundred thousand just east of downtown Denver.

"Can you pinpoint the location?"

"A hangar west of the main runway."

"They're preparing to move them out of state. Relay the imagery."

Gamma glanced over his shoulder to confirm no one was watching and propped his tactical tablet on an imperfection in the stone wall. Thumbnail images of the decedents, numbered one through twelve, filled the display. Gamma tapped the first, and a live feed of the contractor's face appeared on the tiny screen in front of Randall's left eye. The man had been closest to the point of dispersal, so his rate of infection had always been more advanced, but even with that knowledge, Randall had been unprepared for what he saw.

A reddish fuzz covered every inch of the man's skin, seemingly arising from his pores. The wiry hyphae growing from his mouth had crawled all the way up his cheeks and down his chin, peeling his lips so far back that the lower half of his face appeared skeletal. Tumbleweed-like protrusions pried open his nostrils and nearly concealed his ears, but it was his eyes . . . dear Lord . . . the cordyceps had retracted his lids to such an extent that the orbs seemed to merely rest in sockets far too large for them. Pinkish biofilm covered the sclera, save for tiny circular gaps over the pupils, which remained fixed and dilated.

Gamma swiped away the contractor's live feed and brought up the next victim, and the next after that. The pharmaceutical saleswoman, the baggage handler, the pilots and stewardesses . . . all of them exhibited nearly identical symptoms of acute fungal infection.

A voice from Randall's past rose unbidden, the ghostly words echoing inside his head.

You've seen what happened to these two simple species of

fungus during the act of transmission from the locusts to the rabbits. There's no way to predict how they will respond to the human body.

This was beyond anything they'd witnessed in the lab, beyond any theoretical worst-case scenario.

We have much more complicated immune and nervous systems, but we're no less susceptible to the effects of deoxynivalenol. I find it hard to believe the fungi could exert any influence over our actions like they do insects, but in sufficient quantity they could produce deadly levels of toxins.

Randall's heart beat faster and faster. He switched back to the camera in the contractor's patient isolation unit. It almost looked like the fungi had grown in the past few seconds. In fact, he could have sworn he detected several bulblike swellings near the tips.

This fruiting body holds thousands of microscopic spores that it will disperse in an explosive cloud. If they're able to enter the body through superficial capillaries protected by several layers of skin, they'll make short work of the bronchi in our lungs and the mucous membranes in our noses and mouths. We can't control their dispersion like chemical weapons. They don't have half-lives like radiological isotopes. They can remain dormant for years. They can cross interspecific barriers. We could inadvertently eradicate all life forms on the planet.

A tear crept from the corner of the man's eye and rolled down his temple.

We could very well have created the means of our own extinction.

Randall averted his gaze and stormed across the cavern.

"Don't take your eyes off those feeds, Delta," he said.

"Keep me apprised of every little development, no matter how trivial you think it might be."

He forced the images from his mind and focused on the anomalous readings and movement they'd detected deeper in the cavern. There was only one way to determine their source, although he had a sinking feeling that he already knew.

———

DAYNA WATCHED for any other signs of movement as the drone flew deeper and deeper into the subterranean warrens. Maybe she'd merely seen an optical illusion caused by light refracting from the curious crystalline speleothems — after all, there wasn't a higher order of life on this planet that could survive chemicals in such high concentrations, let alone in an environment bereft of food and water — yet still, she'd seen *something*, even if none of the others appeared to have noticed. The timing of the seismic and infrasonic spikes couldn't have been coincidental.

The maze of bramble-like formations ended as abruptly as it had begun, and the drone emerged into a cavern nearly as vast as this one, only the ceiling couldn't have been more than eight feet tall. A sea of chemical waste, marred by islands of dissolving stone, glimmered beneath stalactites connected by what at first looked like some kind of netting.

"Stop right there!" Sydney said.

She squeezed between Telford and Stephens and leaned closer to the monitor.

"It looks like a giant spider spun a web up there," Beta said.

"They're long strands of mycelia," Sydney whispered. She rounded on Craig, her eyes wild. "Zoom in on the ceiling. Please. I need a closer look."

"Your wish is my command," he said.

The drone abruptly stopped and raised its camera as close to straight up as it could get. Its light cast elongated shadows from the thick reddish strands onto the eroded rock underneath—

Dayna gasped.

Everyone turned and looked at her, but she couldn't tear her gaze from the monitor. A deep fissure cut through the cavern roof. One of the offset sides was markedly lower than the other. Rugged craters surrounded it, marking where entire clumps of stalactites had broken off and fallen into the pool. The combination of pressure and erosion, coupled with the sheer weight of the overlying strata, had created an artificial blind thrust fault, a diagonal fracture zone wherein one side sank faster than the other, exerting increasing force on the lower of the two. That pressure would continue to build, like compressing a spring, until the upper half slid past the lower, releasing all of that pressure in a violent upthrust that caused one side to erupt from the surface while the other suddenly dropped. It was the same kind of fault that ran under downtown Los Angeles, the kind responsible for the devastating 1994 Northridge and 2010 Haiti earthquakes.

The readings on Dayna's tablet spiked again, but she couldn't seem to look away from the video feed.

"Show me the chemicals," she whispered.

Craig aimed the camera down, revealing mounds of rubble and, beneath the murky liquid, a dark shadow spanning the width of the cavern that could very well be the same fault extending deeper into the Earth.

Dayna needed to evaluate it in person. It was only a matter of time before the western side collapsed and the eastern side rose with enough energy to tear straight through the ground for miles in every direction, swallowing houses, toppling skyscrapers, and claiming millions of lives. Unlike a tectonic fault, which extended for hundreds of miles into the crust, this one couldn't have been more than a few miles deep, making it dramatically more volatile.

But also more predictable.

She glanced at Telford, who furrowed his brow. The environmental engineer's eyes turned inward, then suddenly sought hers. He nodded slowly, as though reaching the same conclusion she had: if such a fault could be created, then, theoretically, it could also be uncreated.

On the screen, several rocks fell from the ceiling and splashed into the chemicals.

Dayna glanced at her tablet to compare the resultant seismic and infrasonic spikes to those of her anomaly, but something else caught her eye. Her predictive model's tracker had finally reached 100%. She opened the file and scanned through the data as quickly as possible.

The ground seemed to fall out from underneath her.

"What's wrong?" Sydney asked.

Randall snatched the tablet from her grasp, leaving her staring at her empty hands. Her voice seemed to come from somewhere far away when she spoke.

"There's going to be another earthquake."

———

"How long do we have?" Randall asked.

"There's an eighty-three-percent chance of an earthquake greater than five-point-two in magnitude within the next six to eight hours," Dr. Raines said.

"So there's a seventeen-percent chance that it won't happen at all."

"Or it could happen thirty seconds from now."

"That's not especially helpful."

"Countless variables, most of which are wildly independent of one another, go into the equation. We're relying on artificial intelligence to evaluate all of the combinations, project every possible outcome, and correlate them into a single model of statistical probability."

"Then you might as well be guessing."

"That's not what I'm saying at all. Seismologists at the University of Texas developed an AI algorithm capable of interpreting statistical anomalies in real-time. During its initial seven-month trial in China, it accurately predicted earthquakes seventy percent of the time." She switched screens and an amalgamation of data points beyond his interpretation appeared. "I piggybacked on their research and applied deep machine learning to create a new algorithm that could be applied to shallow, manmade earthquakes in areas with extensive commercial drilling operations."

"You're confident this prediction is accurate?"

"My program's been right ninety-two percent of the time," Dr. Raines said.

Randall clenched his jaw in frustration. He felt the passage of time bearing down on him. They had just over two and a half hours of oxygen left before they had to return to the surface and, if they failed to stabilize the fault zone before then, they wouldn't have enough time to reequip and try again. And that was assuming the impending earthquake didn't strike first. Plus, his age was increasingly becoming a factor, placing the entire mission at risk. The pressure and physical exertion were taking their toll faster than he'd anticipated, but he was the only one who could do this, and the consequences of failure would be catastrophic. If the fungal organism somehow reached the surface . . .

He suppressed the thought. There was simply no way he would allow that to happen.

"What if we backfilled the cavern?" he asked, rounding on Telford.

"It would likely stabilize the fault zone, but we don't have nearly enough time to neutralize the chemicals and move that much earth. There is, however, one way I think *might* work" — He took a deep breath and shared a knowing look with Dr. Raines — "but I can't say for sure. Not until I examine it in person."

"Then we're wasting time we don't have," Randall said. "Grab only what you can carry. We're moving out."

18

11:37 a.m.

Countdown to Commence Ascent: 2:16
Oxygen Remaining: 3:16

Dayna's chest heaved as she climbed the rugged ridges lining the steep slope to the passage where the drone had crashed. While she was by no means out of shape, the weight of her hard-shell cases, coupled with the pressure at this depth, exacted a steep physical toll. She didn't even want to think about what her heavy breathing was doing to her already diminishing oxygen supply. If she ran out before she was back inside the FEMA command center, she'd be forced to take off her mask and expose herself to chemicals designed to shred her lungs with a single breath, which, unfortunately, might be preferable to the fate awaiting her ahead.

Her heart raced at the thought of another earthquake

striking while they were still down here. Falling to her knees on the shivering earth while cracks raced through the ground around her . . . cradling her head in her arms as the ceiling disintegrated . . . gasping for air, every breath coming slower . . . and slower . . . until there was . . . no air left . . .

Dayna collapsed to her knees at the top of the hill. Her entire body trembled so badly that she couldn't seem to inhale . . . enough oxygen . . . to fill her lungs.

"We need to keep moving," Beta said as he crested the slope behind her.

"Give me . . . a second," she said, hoping he didn't hear the tremor in her voice or see how badly her hands shook. She pretended that she'd meant to stop and removed several geophones, digital accelerometers, and a small infrasonic array from the larger of the two cases. This was as good a place as any for her to set up additional sensing devices for her growing network.

Telford must have recognized that she was struggling. Without drawing attention to himself, he fell back, helped her connect the instruments to the power source and hustled her along to rejoin the others. He was kind enough not to say anything that might be overheard and simply offered a reassuring squeeze on the shoulder to let her know that everything was going to be all right. She nodded her thanks and turned away so he wouldn't see the tears on her cheeks.

"There's markedly less mycelial growth on the walls and ceiling in here," Sydney said. She crouched and inspected the ground. When she looked up, there was no mistaking the confusion on her face. "How far did you go last time you were here?"

"We found the drone just up ahead," Craig said. He walked in fits and starts, watching the small screen on his control console with one eye and the passage ahead with the other. They needed to map every square inch of that flooded cavern before they arrived. "Why?"

Sydney merely shook her head and resumed walking, reseating her overstuffed backpack every few steps. That she was still down here at all was a testament to either her courage or her professional curiosity. In her shoes, Dayna would have climbed straight up two vertical miles of cable to get out of here. Any of the others could have demanded their evacuation, yet still they trudged toward what could very well be their deaths, clinging to the hope that they could save millions of lives.

"Right over there," Craig said, stating the obvious.

Randall, Alpha, and Gamma encircled a swatch of stone ahead. All three shone their lights onto the ground between them, the amplified glow laying bare every mycelium and imperfection in the stone. Scratches marred the surface where the quadcopter had gone down, cutting through the patches of weblike growth, entire sections of which appeared to have been scuffed off or come away on someone's boots.

Dayna glanced at the ground behind her, where the fungal mat was now nearly nonexistent, and then at the tread of her boots. The implications crashed down on her like a tidal wave. She glanced first at the conspicuous areas of bare stone between the stalactites overhead, and then at the passageway ahead, where the soldiers' lights illuminated ground patchy with disturbed fungal growth.

She glanced back at Sydney, whose wide eyes suggested she'd come to the exact same conclusion.

"What's wrong?" Stephens asked.

Dayna could only shake her head.

Something was definitely down here with them.

She had to tell Randall. If an animal had somehow managed to survive . . .

Her thoughts dissipated when her eyes met his across the distance. He pressed his index finger to his visor over his respirator.

The ground fell out from underneath her.

He already knew.

———

RANDALL MOVED SLOWLY through the crystalline forest. While the translucent branches were more fragile than blown glass, they looked sharp enough to puncture even his reinforced suit. The civilians behind him needed to be even more cautious, which allowed him to get far enough ahead that he could covertly view the drone's camera feed.

"Bring up thermal imaging," he said over the command comm.

Gamma brought up the footage on his tablet and, with a tap of his finger, made it appear on Randall's helmet-mounted display. The tech specialist had offered Craig one of his cameras to replace the drone's damaged one, although he'd failed to share its additional capabilities.

The recorded playback rolled on the small transparent screen. While the cold stone surfaces remained black, the imperfections in the rock and the wicked tips of the stalactites appeared a deep shade of purple. Randall watched for a splash of color to betray the presence of a heat source above the ambient temperature. The telltale white glow of a being's mouth and eyes . . . the golden aura in its chest . . . the oranges and reds radiating outward into its arms and legs . . .

Several seconds passed as the drone weaved through the purple brambles.

Maroon flickered at the periphery.

"Stop," he said. "Zoom in right there."

Gamma focused on the vague purplish blur, nearly concealed by an earthen column.

"That color's way too dark for any living creature," he said. "Could be slightly warmer air rising from some kind of thermal vent."

Randall shook his head. This was right about the point during the flight when Dr. Raines's sensors had detected the anomaly.

"Keep going," he said.

Gamma resumed playback. The chemical lake appeared, its surface a shade of purple so dark it bordered on black. Above it, the fungal growths strung between the stalactites were a mere shade lighter. The drone abruptly stopped — as Dr. Partridge had commanded — and angled its camera upward—

"Pause it!" Randall snapped. Gamma tapped the screen, freezing the image. "Zoom in."

Something was definitely up there. A dark shade of

violet, nearly concealed by the interwoven network of indigo strands.

"Whatever it is," Gamma said, "it's not a living organism."

"What else could it be?"

"Any species, even hibernating mammals capable of sustaining such uniformly low body temperatures, still have to be able to breathe the air."

"Well, something took down that drone and scuffed up the ground back there," Randall said, picking his way toward the glimmering chemical reservoir, which finally appeared in the distance. "And there's only one way to figure out what it is."

DAYNA STARED across the glimmering pool of chemical waste in absolute awe. Their combined lights refracted from the surface in prismatic colors and created strange wavering illusions on the stalactites. The buzz of the drone's rotors emanated from somewhere on the far side, where the darkness had swallowed it whole.

"Do whatever you need to do," Randall said. "And be quick about it."

Telford glanced at Stephens.

"Are you sure this suit will hold up?"

"Assuming those chemicals aren't too deep."

"That's reassuring," Telford said, cautiously stepping into the shimmering fluid. He alternately shone his flashlight straight ahead and then up at the ceiling, mere feet above his head. The chemicals rose first over his feet, then his ankles. "The underlying quartzite is slick, but it seems solid enough."

His sloshing footsteps seemed to echo from everywhere at once. He passed several columns, the diffuse glow from his belt light revealing the vast networks of cracks riddling them. The chemicals crept up his shins, nearly to his knees. He had to be getting close.

"The drone's reached the end of the cavern," Craig said, the quadcopter's headlamp blurring across bare stone on his handheld monitor. "I'm turning around—"

"Not yet," Randall said. "You're missing something. Keep looking."

The certainty in the general's voice confirmed that he knew more than he was telling them. He shouldered past Craig and joined the other soldiers at the edge of the pool, where they watched Telford's silhouette shrink into the distance.

"You should be practically right underneath the fault," Beta said.

"Footing is becoming increasingly treacherous," Telford said. "The stone is cracked and uneven. Some sections are significantly lower than—"

With a surprised gasp, he vanished from sight. Here one moment, gone the next, his light snuffed out like a candle.

"Tim!" Stephens shouted.

Frantic breathing erupted from the speaker by Dayna's ear. Telford splashed back to the surface and swept his beam all around him in search of the shoreline. He lurched forward and fell to his hands and knees. Pushed himself up and staggered a few more feet. He flung the fluid from his arms and wiped it from his hood and chest.

"I found it," he said with a chuckle lacking any trace of humor. "There's considerable distraction of the eastern border of the fault line underfoot" — He aimed his light up at the stalactites — "which appears to be displaced in the opposite direction of fracture overhead. It's a miracle this place hasn't come down on our heads already."

"Can you stabilize it?" Randall asked.

Telford turned in a circle, his beam pinning one column after another. He shone it down into the chemicals and then back up at the ceiling again.

"I have a plan, but it's not without significant risk."

"What exactly are you proposing?" Stephens asked.

"Strategic implosion."

"You can't be serious."

"If we plant explosives in such a way as to collapse the cavern straight down and channel the shockwaves away from downtown, we should be able to realign the fault without triggering another earthquake. We'll need to figure out how to get a suitable amount of RDX down here—"

"I assume Semtex will work," Randall said. He glanced first at Alpha, who nodded and started jogging in the direction from which they'd come, and then at Dayna. "What's your assessment, Dr. Raines?"

"It's our only viable option in the time we have left. That being said, even if everything goes as planned, we'll still inflict significant geological damage to the two vertical miles of strata above us. And considering we haven't evaluated the full extent of this subterranean network" — She watched the general's face for even the slightest reaction to the contrary — "we have no idea how large it truly is. For all we know, it could run underneath the neighboring suburbs, or even the airport. We could inadvertently kill thousands of people."

"And what if everything *doesn't* go as planned?"

A preternatural silence settled over the cavern as all eyes turned toward Dayna.

"We could trigger the very event we're trying to avert," she said. "And cause the deaths of everyone within a ten-mile radius."

19

11:53 a.m.

Countdown to Commence Ascent: 2:00
Oxygen Remaining: 3:00

Randall slogged through the shallows, keeping one eye on the fungal growth overhead and the other on Telford, who plotted demolitions placement and ran through simulations on his tablet. If he made a mistake, they'd be responsible for one of the deadliest disasters in human history, but if they somehow pulled this off, they could eliminate the risk of another earthquake with minimal loss of life. Of course, they'd have to do something about the fungus first, as it had already demonstrated an uncanny knack for survival.

That it somehow thrived in the harshest environment on the planet was troubling, but not nearly as much as the fact that the earthquake had generated enough pressure to expel spores nearly all the way up the shaft and to a depth where they encountered insect life beneath the airport. Worse, its maturation rate was beyond anything he'd ever seen. He could only assume that the spider responsible for infecting the men and women on the train had been exposed prior to the earthquake and had simply seized the opportunity presented by the foundation's collapse, which meant they'd likely averted the catastrophic outbreak the arachnid might have caused had it reached the surface on its own, but even a single surviving spore could begin the nightmare anew.

It could lay dormant in the soil for Lord only knew how long, just waiting to infect a burrowing insect it could use to spread from one species to another, until it had sunken its hyphae into every terrestrial organism on the planet. And with as rapidly as it proliferated inside the victims in the patient isolation capsules — both living and deceased — there would be no hope of stopping it. If he didn't kill it — right here and now — then it *would* eventually find its way aboveground. And when it did, no one would be able to stop it.

He walked right to the edge of the fault and looked straight up. His powerful beam passed between the interwoven strands of mycelia, like sunlight through a dense forest canopy, and illuminated scratches and scuff marks in the biofilm. Or maybe he was merely seeing what he wanted to see. There'd been a faint heat signature on the video, though. *Something* had been up there . . . and it wasn't there now.

"There are holes in the ceiling," Craig said. "And there appears to be a recess above them."

"Get that drone up there," Randall said, splashing back toward dry land. "And relay live imagery directly to my in-helmet monitor."

Dark footage appeared on the tiny screen in front of his left eye as the drone rose past a thin layer of rock and entered a cavity that couldn't have been more than a couple feet high. The chemicals had eroded the rock into slender terraces, which the fluid appeared to have scaled as the pressure forced it upward. It didn't take very long for the drone to encounter a narrowing through which it couldn't pass, its light shining impotently up a shaft that extended well beyond its range.

"That's as far as she'll go," Craig said.

"Back out and try to find another egress," Randall said.

"I'll climb up there and widen that passage," Beta said. "There has to be another way through for such a significant amount of chemical waste to—"

"Get on it," Randall snapped, cutting him off. He glanced at the civilians on the shore, but none of them seemed to have noticed Beta's slipup. "I want to know the moment you break through."

Randall looked one last time at the scrapes in the biofilm overhead. It didn't matter whether or not anything had been up there, because when it came right down to it, everything burned.

DAYNA FINISHED SETTING up the last of her remote sensing arrays and assembling her mobile unit, which resembled a fat cane with eleven little legs, each of which housed a pair of infrasonic microphones, encircling the digital seismometer in its base. While it lacked the sensitivity of the fixed-position devices, it allowed her to incorporate the incoming data from a third, non-linear array to that of any two static arrays, giving her the ability to geolocate the source of even the most subtle infrasonic or seismic disturbance between the three points, like using cell towers to triangulate the origin of a call. Of course, the addition of so much data came at a cost. The detectors picked up so much background noise that she couldn't filter it all out, at least not without sacrificing the specificity she needed to detect any anomalous readings or accelerating seismic activity.

She resisted the urge to scream and hurl her tablet against the wall and instead spoke in the calmest voice she could muster.

"Everyone . . . I need you to freeze right where you are and hold your breath."

Conversations paused mid-sentence. The buzz of the distant drone ceased. The ripples caused by the men wading in the reservoir slowly dissipated. Ten seconds passed. Fifteen. Twenty. While there were no visible spikes in either the seismic or infrasonic readings, she was going to have to run the data through her algorithm to analyze it more carefully.

"Thank you," she whispered.

The noise resumed. She closed her eyes and took several long, steeling breaths.

Darkness. Dust filling her chest with every inhalation, clotting on her tongue. Cold stone pressing against her back.

Blood dripping from the lacerations on her forearms with a faint plat . . . plat . . . plat. *A horse screaming—*

Dayna's eyes snapped open. She couldn't allow the panic to overwhelm her. Not now. Not when so many people were counting on her.

Sydney looked up from her cellphone and blinked several times. She'd extricated a length of the mycelial webbing from the ceiling, cut it both crosswise and lengthwise, and stained the resultant samples. Her microscope had been too big and unwieldy to make the trek, so she'd utilized a clever digital lens that attached to the camera on her personal device. Its functionality was comparatively limited, but it presumably allowed her to see what she needed to see.

"That can't be right," she whispered.

Dayna applied the algorithm to her data and put the screen to sleep to conserve what little battery remained. She walked over to where Sydney kneeled on the ground, staring at her phone.

"What's wrong?"

"What does this look like to you?" Sydney asked.

Dayna carefully sat beside her and studied the small screen. At first glance, the magnified sample almost looked like a fatty ribeye steak. The magenta dye highlighted dozens of striated purple ribbons riddled with dark dots. Between them were several oblong shapes composed of numerous small lavender bulbs, each of which had a purple spot near the center. Transparent bubbles, compressed into sudsy masses, crowded them from all sides.

"This is a cross-sectional view of one of the dense

mycelial strands overhead," Sydney said. "Those grapelike clusters are individual hyphae woven into a single mycelium, running perpendicular to the slice. The purple strands are the exact same thing, only running parallel to it. The bubbles around them are haustoria: tiny appendages that grow from the mycelia of certain fungal plant parasites and function kind of like suction cups on a tentacle. They also produce enzymes that break down the tissue or substrate around them, rendering it into nutritional components small enough to pass through their cellular membranes. That's how the fungus has been able to both adhere to and assimilate minerals from the quartzite." She aligned the digital microscope lens with a different slide. "Now look at this."

Gamma sidled up behind them, his powerful beam momentarily washing out the screen.

Thick magenta bands comprised of numerous thinner strands stretched from one side of the image to the other, the spaces between them packed with haustoria bubbles. Each strand was composed of countless individual cells with kidney-shaped nuclei, arranged in single-file lines. Their surfaces appeared ribbed, almost like corduroy.

"It's been years since I took bio lab as an undergrad," Sydney said, "so correct me if I'm wrong . . . but doesn't that look a lot like skeletal muscle?"

Dayna couldn't seem to form a reply. That was exactly what it looked like.

Gamma crouched between them and tested the tensile strength of the remaining mycelial strand from which Sydney had taken the samples, pulling and twisting it between his gloved hands.

"It does look and feel like muscle," he said. Dayna peered back at him, curiosity crinkling her brow. "The hyphae forming the mycelia resemble individual muscle cells, right down to their nuclei; these striations resemble the myosin and actin filaments that help muscles elongate and contract; and those haustoria appear strikingly similar to endomysium: the bundles of nerves and blood vessels that surround individual muscle fibers and carry nutrients to the adjacent tissues. And the entire ropelike body—"

"Thallus," Sydney interjected.

"The entire thallus is seemingly encapsulated in a sheath of connective tissue."

Dayna shifted so she could clearly see soldier's face.

"What aren't you telling us?" she asked.

Gamma abruptly stood and shook his head, as though to clear his thoughts. His lips formed words she couldn't hear as he headed toward Randall.

Something was wrong. She didn't like this. Not at all.

Her tablet chimed to let her know the data was ready. She awakened the screen and instantly noticed numerous subtle anomalies similar to the one she'd been tracking, only these were of increasing amplitude and frequency, almost as though . . .

She closed her eyes and tried to remember exactly what the others had been doing when she'd called for them to hold still. None of them had been moving, yet these readings clearly indicated that someone — or rather *something* — had been.

RANDALL WATCHED Beta wade toward the far side of the chemical reservoir, Gamma's spectral voice reverberating inside his skull, uttering phrases that struck him like so many lashes.

"...resembles human muscle tissue...similar functionality...seemingly chimeric...interspecific aberration..."

Memories from a lifetime ago rose unbidden. He heard Dr. Thompson's voice — "...*it wouldn't be untrue to imply that the two species* — graminis tritici *and* unilateralis — *have formed something of a mutualistic relationship...*" — and saw rabbits he could have sworn were dead squeezing their little pink noses between their cage bars, their fur riddled with the very same wiry mycelia that now proliferated on the bodies inside the PIUs.

In the far distance, the darkness swallowed Beta's light.

Delta's animated voice burst from the speaker by Randall's ear, his words cutting in and out of the static.

"... not dead ... trying to get out ... relaying video feeds ..."

Live footage from the camera inside the baggage handler's capsule appeared on the screen in front of Randall's left eye. The long fungal growths protruding from his face concealed everything but his eyes and mouth. Teeth bared, he slammed his forehead into the outer shell — over and over again — spattering the surface with blood.

Delta switched from one feed to the next. The contractor ... the pilots and the stewardesses ... the pharmacy rep ... all of their faces contorted by spindly growths ... hurling themselves against their confines in a desperate, animalistic attempt to escape.

The blond woman suddenly froze, her eyes staring blankly into the camera.

Delta scrolled through the feeds, faster and faster. Every single one of the victims held perfectly still, as though waiting . . .

"Incinerate them," Randall said, his voice strangely foreign in his own ears.

A glittering haze erupted from the fungi obscuring the contractor's face. It swirled in the air above him like smoke and slowly accumulated on the inside of the capsule. The same thing happened inside all of the PIUs at once. Faint fissures, as delicate as spiderwebs, formed in the plexiglass, and quickly expanded into cracks.

"Now!" Randall shouted. "Do it now!"

The cracks spread through the capsules as though someone repeatedly struck them with a sledgehammer—

Blinding lights flared. Flames appeared. Men and women, their hair burning and their skin blistering, frantically beat at the glass—

And then the feeds went dark, leaving Randall once more staring blankly across the sea of chemicals.

"Chief!" Delta shouted. "Are you still there?"

Randall snapped to attention.

"Get me visual confirmation of complete incineration," he said, turning to Alpha, who'd only just returned with a pair of hard-shell cases. "How long will it take to plant those explosives?"

"An hour, tops."

"You have thirty minutes."

"Sir, if we're not precise—"

"I've given you a direct order."

"Yes, sir."

Randall turned around and nearly slammed into Dr. Raines.

"You need to see this," she said, proffering her tablet.

"I don't have time—" he started to say, but the words died on his lips. This was no mere anomaly she was tracking. The regularity . . . the pattern . . . he could almost feel the vibrations, hear the pattering sound in his head.

"Relaying aerial imagery," Delta said. An image of a burning hangar appeared, flames and churning black smoke gushing through the gaping holes in its aluminum roof. "Incineration confirmed."

"Are you even listening to me?" Dr. Raines asked.

Randall brushed past her and switched to the command channel.

"Beta," he snapped. "Acknowledge."

"I've cleared the obstruction, Chief. There's something up here. I think . . . you're going to want to see it for yourself."

Pulse thrumming, Randall splashed into the shallows and waded toward the far side of the reservoir.

20

12:21 p.m.

Countdown to Commence Ascent: 1:32
Oxygen Remaining: 2:32

Dayna narrowly resisted the urge to storm after Randall and give him a piece of her mind. She didn't appreciate being blown off like that, but it wasn't worth chasing him down and making a scene, not when their deadline to return to the surface was rapidly approaching and there was still so much left to do. Or at least not until she figured out what had caused the anomalous readings she'd detected while the others had been holding still, readings which, based on their seismic and acoustic qualities . . . their rhythm and repetition rate . . . their distinct patterns . . . left no doubt as to what they were: quadrupedal footsteps.

Something down here moved on four legs.

Whatever it was had presumably found its way underground in the aftermath of the earthquake, which meant there had to be some sort of opening to the surface they had yet . . . to . . . find . . .

Dayna furrowed her brow as she watched Randall slog through the knee-deep chemicals.

He already knew about the surface access, didn't he? That's why the soldiers had been so confident they'd find an egress at the far end of the cavern. What else did they know that they hadn't bothered to share?

She couldn't think about that now, not when there was so much riding on the success of their mission. When it came right down to it, it didn't matter what was in these caverns with them. Whether it was an animal from the wildlife preserve or a house pet from a neighboring suburb, it wouldn't survive for very long. Sure, there were feral dogs that had adapted to the obscene levels of radiation near Chernobyl and sea life that thrived in the toxic waters surrounding deep sea vents, but there was nothing capable of surviving exposure to chemical weapons for any length of time, especially something large enough for her equipment to detect its movements.

What did matter, however, was that any passage extending beyond the known cavern system introduced variables for which they couldn't account. The outward force of the detonation could propel chemicals through the uncharted network of cavities, accelerating erosion and creating the same kind of manmade fault responsible for their current predicament, or they could end up collapsing peripheral passageways running under highways and subdivisions, further destabilizing the surrounding strata.

Dayna was simply going to have to trust that Telford was the very best at what he did and carefully watch her readings for any changes in seismic activity. She grabbed her tablet and glanced one last time at Randall's distant light, just as it dissolved into the—

Darkness swallows her. Smothers her. Squeezes the air from her lungs.

Pain binds her to consciousness, her stinging lacerations announcing themselves with soft pattering sounds.

Rubble shifts above her and dirt rains onto her face.

She opens her mouth to cry out, but no sound emerges.

From somewhere far away, a horse screams—

The tablet fell from her hands and clattered to the ground.

"Dr. Raines?" Gamma said, gently resting his hand on her shoulder. "Are you okay?"

Dayna couldn't find the voice to respond. She merely nodded and stared at her blurry tablet through a sheen of tears.

RANDALL SLOSHED from the chemicals and leaned against a column until his legs stopped shaking. His body couldn't sustain this level of exertion for very much longer. He'd done everything in his power to keep himself in fighting shape, but there were physical realities of the aging process that simply wouldn't be denied. If he hadn't already known this would be his final assignment—

"Switching on helmet cam," Beta said.

Randall pushed off the column and joined Alpha

underneath the rocky orifice. Shadows played upon the ground between them as Beta squirmed higher into the eroded earth. A shaky image appeared on the lens in front of Randall's left eye.

"Are you seeing this?" Alpha whispered.

Randall could only nod. He didn't know what he'd expected to find up there, but this was just about the furthest thing from it. The fuzzy red biofilm gave way to a miniature forest of fungal appendages resembling antlers, some of which had to be nearly a foot long. Their swollen fruiting bodies glistened with chemical condensation.

"They feel spongy," Beta said, combing his fingers through them, "but with a surprising amount of tensile strength, almost like rubber."

A clump came away in his hand, revealing slender yellowish-brown crescents and—

Spores erupted from seemingly everywhere at once, overwhelming the camera with a smoky haze of shimmering particles. Beta tried to wave them away, but the swirling cloud reformed behind his hand.

"Did you see that?" he gasped. "There was something underneath them."

The camera lens clouded, then cracked, distorting the footage. Fissures rippled through the picture, which abruptly darkened with an electrical pop.

"The spores are adhering to my visor," Beta said, "like glitter on a stripper's—"

"Get out of there," Randall snapped.

"Let me see if I can collect a sample—"

"Now, Beta! That's an order!"

A sharp snapping sound burst from the speaker.

Beta shouted, his voice cracking in alarm.

Rocks rained from the hole, driving back Alpha and Randall. The shouting rose in volume and pitch as Beta careened from the hole and plummeted to the ground between them. His shoulder light burst with an explosion of plastic fragments. He pawed at his visor, screaming as a fine network of fissures formed.

"I can't get them off!" Beta screamed. "They're breaking the glass!"

Alpha threw himself onto the thrashing soldier, pinning him and scraping his visor with the sharp edge of his knife, leaving the spiderwebbed polycarbonate scratched so badly that it would be a miracle if Beta could see through it at all.

"You saw that, right?" Beta gasped. "What in God's name was that?"

"Gamma," Randall barked. "I need you to recover that footage."

"I'm on it, Chief."

Randall switched to the open comm channel.

"Mr. Preston, get that drone up there."

The quadcopter, perched on a nearby rock where the pilot had put it to sleep to conserve battery, came to life with a hum. A column of light shot from its tiny body as it rocketed past them and straight up into the earthen chute.

Beta tried to stand, but immediately collapsed to his knees. He looked up at Randall, who instinctively retreated a step. Rust-colored clusters of spores covered his suit, pinching the fabric, drawing it tight.

"It's my ankles," Beta said. "I think I busted them in the fall."

Randall glanced at Alpha to see if he'd noticed the spores, only to see the reddish dots adhering to the other man's suit, as well. While there were nowhere near as many, it was readily apparent they exerted some amount of manual force on the material.

"Help Beta to the other side. And tell Dr. Partridge I want to know exactly what's going on with those spores."

"Yes, sir," Alpha said.

He crouched, slung Beta over his shoulders in a fireman's carry, and waded back into the chemicals, leaving Randall staring up into the hole as the quadcopter's light dissipated into the higher reaches.

"Relay drone imagery to my screen," he said, following Alpha toward the silhouetted forms of Stephens and Telford, who carefully planted plastic explosives on the columns supporting the stalactite-riddled ceiling.

The jerky footage appeared before Randall's left eye, but he didn't even see it. He was too focused on the memory of the manila crescents beneath the fungi, and the horrific realization that he knew exactly what they were.

BETA SHOUTED SO LOUDLY that Dayna could hear him from halfway across the reservoir, even without a direct comm link. The sound cut right through her already shaky mental defenses. In that moment, they were Thunder's awful cries, dragging her back to a realm even darker than this one, a realm where only terror existed. And pain . . . so much pain.

Biting her lip to keep from sobbing, she stared down at

her tablet, lying cracked on the ground at her feet. The readings spiked, one after another. The shouting . . . the splashing . . . the stomping . . . all of the chaos concealed not only any subtle seismic activity, but also the source of the movement she'd detected mere minutes ago. Worse, much like a loud noise could start an avalanche, the sound-waves and vibrations could have already caused irreparable damage to the delicate subterranean environment and accelerated the timetable of the impending earthquake. She felt bad for Beta, who was obviously in a lot of pain, but she needed everyone to understand the gravity of the situation.

"Listen to me! Stop making so much noise or you'll bring this whole place down on our heads!"

She grabbed her tablet and started programming. The battery level was already down to twenty-four percent, most of which she'd drain gathering data and running it through her predictive algorithm again, so if she was going to try and locate whatever was down here with them, now was her only chance.

Beta stopped shouting, but he punctuated every step Alpha took with a muffled grunt. To the other soldier's credit, he did his best to minimize the splashing, even if the sound still echoed from seemingly everywhere at once. Dayna filtered out the corresponding values and set her predictive algorithm to run in the background, freeing up memory to see if she could isolate the source of the movement she'd detected before all of the chaos.

The progress bar slowly crept across the screen.

20% . . . 26% . . .

Alpha sloshed from the chemicals and collapsed onto

the ground, spilling Bata from his shoulders with an agonized shout. The way his boots pointed in completely different directions . . . there was no doubt that both bones in his lower legs were broken.

. . . 38% . . . 44% . . .

"Fight through the pain," Alpha snapped, his muffled voice emerging from the speaker inside Beta's helmet.

The wounded man merely bared his teeth in response, his face nearly concealed by the spiderwebbing fractures and scratches on his visor.

. . . 56% . . . 62% . . .

"Dr. Partridge," Alpha snapped. The sudden emergence of his voice beside Dayna's ear made her flinch. "I need you to examine his mask."

Sydney stepped past Dayna and crouched over Beta, who tried to hold still. She scraped some of the spores from the polycarbonate glass with a scalpel and carefully wiped them onto a viewing slide.

. . . 74% . . . 80% . . .

The medical mycologist scurried back to her equipment, dripped dye on the slide, and viewed the magnified image on her cell phone.

"I've never seen anything like this," she said. "They appear to be basidiospores, like those that develop during the final stage of the germination of a stem rust species, only they're septate, filiform, and bristled, like those of more aggressive parasitic species. But that's not the strangest part. They also contain spherical nuclei with distinct nucleoli, like you'd find in mammalian cells."

"What does that mean?" Randall asked as he slogged onto dry land.

. . . 92% . . . 98% . . .

"It means this species can theoretically germinate on any surface, parasitize any species, and insert its genetic code into a mammalian host's by essentially tricking the body into replicating the hybridized fungus' DNA as though it were its own native—"

Dayna's tablet chimed. She stepped away and tuned out everything but the acoustic waves on her handheld monitor. Subtracting the baseline noise and vibrations left her with relatively few spikes, each of which correspond to the voices and movements around her. If she'd correctly set the parameters and tolerances, however, any readings matching those she'd detected earlier should pop right off the—

Several spikes appeared.

Dayna turned in a circle. There was no sign of movement, yet the readings continued to appear. She grabbed her mobile array and struck off into the darkness, watching for any changes in the amplitude of the spikes to indicate their source was getting closer or farther away.

There was definitely an animal down here, and she was going to find it.

21

12:37 p.m.

Countdown to Commence Ascent: 1:16
Oxygen Remaining: 2:16

Randall stood behind Dr. Partridge, studying the magnified image on her cellphone over her shoulder. It had been a lifetime since he'd last seen the *Puccinia graminis tritici* and *Ophiocordyceps unilateralis* spores, but he'd never forget either as long as he lived. The way the wheat stem rust spores alternated form every other year, producing sexually dimorphic gametes one generation and reverting back to asexual reproduction the next, enabling it to survive on a secondary species while its primary host recovered from the previous year's infection . . . the way the cordyceps' acrospores burst from their fruiting bodies in swirling clouds capable of dispersing through air and water and any other medium with which they'd experimented . . . and the way the novel organism created by the hybridization of the two adhered to the locusts, released an acid that allowed it to infiltrate their carapaces, and assumed full control of their bodies within a matter of hours. But what he saw on the screen now? It was unlike any of them.

He recalled how the spores had cracked the lenses of Dr. Thompson's gas mask, but Beta's visor was made from space-age polycarbonate fibers capable of withstanding anything shy of a point-blank shot from a .45, and they'd cracked it as though it were no more substantial than the shell of a hummingbird's egg.

Crackling sounds emanated from Beta's helmet.

"How do we kill these spores?" Randall asked.

"First of all, fungal spores are practically indestructible," Dr. Partridge snapped. "Second, I don't have the slightest idea what we're actually dealing with. These spores have the characteristics of two distinct fungal species, plus a third that looks definitively mammalian in origin, which — I should add — is theoretically impossible. And finally, as you can clearly see from the biofilm on the walls, the mycelial strands above our heads, and, presumably, the fruiting bodies that produced these spores, this organism is capable of differentiation based on its environment, chemical concentrations, and potential food sources, in much the same way that stem cells can be used to regrow different parts of the human body." She looked Randall dead in the eyes, as though issuing a challenge. "So I suggest you tell me what it is we're actually dealing with so I can figure out how to *kill* it, as you so eloquently put it."

More crackling sounds drew Randall's attention to the fractured visor.

"We're dealing with a hybrid of *Puccinia graminis tritici* and *Ophiocordyceps unilateralis*," he said.

"Those two species shouldn't be capable of hybridization. The only way that could happen was if they were . . . " Dr. Partridge's voice trailed off. "You engineered them."

Randall said nothing.

"You wanted to weaponize the wheat stem rust using an insect vector. Hence, the cordyceps, but how did the hybrid develop mammalian stem cell—"

"Can you kill them or not?" Randall snapped.

"I'd need access to my equipment on the surface—"

"We can't go back up top. Not as long as these things—"

Beta's visor shattered. Polycarbonate fragments peppered his face. His eyes widened and a scream erupted from behind his oxygen mask. His skin first reddened, then blistered, then immediately started to peel. The blood vessels in his sclera ruptured, and a milky haze clouded his pupils. He clawed at his skin, his gloved fingertips tearing furrows in his cheeks. He bucked hard enough to knock Alpha onto his rear end, then fell still.

A hissing sound escaped from his regulator as his chest slowly deflated.

Randall merely stared at Beta's ruined face. It had all happened so fast . . .

His command instincts kicked in and he rounded on Alpha.

"Take care of the body," he snapped.

"What do you propose—?"

"I don't care what you do with it, as long as it doesn't return to the surface with us."

Randall glanced down at the body one final time and opened the long-range comm channel. Someone needed to tell Delta that his brother was dead.

DAYNA DIALED up the intensity on her belt light as she wandered away from the combined glow of the others' beams, stopping every twenty steps or so to allow her mobile array to gather data. The last thing she wanted to do was lose her bearings while tracking the anomaly, especially considering the constant din of voices increasingly gave way to static the farther away she got. She alternately watched the jagged sine waves on her tablet and took mental snapshots of her surroundings, committing every unique speleothem and shadowed enclave to memory. And it was a good thing she did, as every time she thought she was closing in on the source of the readings, she lost them again.

Several spikes streaked across her monitor as the crystalline forest materialized from the farthest reaches of the dim golden glow. Whatever she was following had definitely gone into the treacherous maze. She couldn't shake the feeling that they'd somehow switched roles, and instead of hunting it, it was luring her into the sharp formations.

Her tablet chimed, creating diminishing acoustic spikes as the sound echoed away into the depths.

She switched to the predictive algorithm and scrolled

through the data. A breath she hadn't even realized she'd been holding seeped from her chest. They'd finally caught a break. The seismic activity had intensified, but the window for the impending earthquake hadn't changed very much at all. Of course, that didn't mean they weren't still up against a ticking clock, but at least they didn't have to accelerate their timetable and risk making a mistake that could cost millions of people their lives.

Dayna closed the program just in time to watch the anomalous readings streak across the screen. The faint infrasonic and seismic spikes were of roughly the same amplitude as her own delicately placed footsteps, suggesting she was nearly right on top of whatever it was.

She unfastened her belt light and swept the beam across the bramble-like formations, throwing jagged shadows in every direction. Spikes rippled across the screen in rapid succession as something scampered away from her. She inched closer and crouched—

A small, dark shape darted through her peripheral vision.

Dayna quickly turned on her tablet's camera and set it for video mode. A poorly lit, grainy image appeared on the screen as she searched for the creature.

———

"RELAYING LIVE VIDEO FROM THE DRONE," Gamma said.

Blurry footage appeared before Randall's left eye. The dark passageway though the rock alternately widened and narrowed, steepened and leveled off. The biofilm on the walls became patchy and disappeared for long stretches at a time. While most of it retained its reddish hue, large swatches had faded to russet brown and turned to dust in the quadcopter's wake.

He switched to the open comm channel and walked right up behind the drone pilot.

"What are the drone's coordinates?"

Preston flinched and staggered backward.

"Jesus! You shouldn't sneak up on a guy like that. I nearly had a freaking heart attack and crashed the—"

"The coordinates, Mr. Preston."

"Just under half a mile east-northeast. Plus eight hundred feet in elevation."

Randall turned without another word and spoke over the command channel.

"Get me that LiDAR reconstruction. I want to know if there's any other possible point of egress."

"Yes, sir," Gamma said, hesitating. "How did Delta take the news?"

"Exactly as you'd expect. Now, get your head back in the game. Where's that imagery from Beta's feed?"

"I just need a few more minutes to isolate—"

"Where's Dr. Raines?" Randall snapped.

He turned in a circle, but he didn't see her anywhere. Where the hell had she gone? He tried hailing her on the open channel, but she didn't respond.

"She probably just wandered outside of short-range comms distance," Gamma said. "Do you want me to track her down?"

"You just get me that footage. I'll find her, and she'd better have a damn good explanation when I do."

Randall stormed off, leaving Telford and Stephens halfway across the chemical reservoir, Dr. Partridge quietly crying over her work, Gamma and Preston focused on their individual tasks, and Alpha discreetly weighing down Beta's remains beneath the murky fluid. Contrary to what he'd told Delta, his brother wouldn't be receiving a proper burial. Of course, if they'd further destabilized the cavern during the chaos, none of them would be.

Surely Dr. Raines would have told them if her program had shown increasing seismic activity. Of course, her obvious claustrophobia could have gotten the better of her and she'd made a mad dash for the only way out, but considering she couldn't climb two vertical miles of braided wire and she had no means of contacting Delta in the cable reel handler, it was safe to assume she was searching for her anomaly. And while a part of him hoped she'd finally identified it, the better part of him was terrified she'd done just that.

Randall recalled the final split-second of Beta's transmission — the fungi peeling away and revealing the yellowish-brown crescents — and suppressed an involuntary shiver. He needed to see it again before he alerted the others to the presence of something that couldn't possibly still be alive.

"Where's that infernal imagery from Beta's camera?" he snapped.

"Priming the footage as we speak," Gamma said.

A faint glow appeared in the distance. At first, Randall couldn't be sure he wasn't merely seeing his own beam reflected from the crystalline growths, but as he approached, Dr. Raines's silhouetted form slowly resolved from the aura. She held her belt light in one hand, slowly shining it from one side of the briar-like speleothems to the other, while she captured video on the tablet in the other.

"There you are," he said. "You need to respond to any and all direct communications—"

She whirled and pressed her index finger to her visor to silence him.

Randall nodded his understanding and proceeded at a measured pace, his pulse thrumming in anticipation.

Dr. Raines resumed sweeping her beam across the ground, illuminating the space below the sharp branches.

An image appeared before Randall's left eye. Beta's blurry hand concealed half of the frame, but there was no mistaking what he was looking at. The tatters of desiccated fur . . . the ridgeline of spinous processes . . . the parallel arches of—

"Are those ribs?" Gamma asked.

Randall was just about to answer when Dr. Raines's light reflected from two tiny red spheres.

22

12:53 p.m.

Countdown to Commence Ascent: 1:00
Oxygen Remaining: 2:00

The twin scarlet reflections vanished as though they'd never been there at all. Dayna swept her light through the maze of speleothems, casting wild, jagged shadows across the walls and ceiling, but there was no sign of movement.

"You saw that, right?" she asked, rounding on Randall.

His face had gone deathly pale behind his visor. He shook his head, but there was no doubt in her mind that he'd seen exactly what she had. In fact, his pallor suggested he'd recognized those twin red flashes for what they'd truly been . . .

Eyeshine.

Her beam had reflected from a small animal's *tapetum*

lucidum, the reflective layer of tissue behind the retina that amplified low levels of light so mammals could see at night. The anomaly she'd detected from the surface . . . she'd finally found it.

"Did you get a good look at it?" Randall asked. He shoved past her and entered the maze of sharp formations, his shoulder light peeling back the shadows before him. "It can't have gotten very far."

Dayna followed him. He was right: the animal was undoubtedly suffering the effects of the toxic fumes and probably already searching for a place to curl up and die.

She cautiously squeezed between the crystalline brambles, careful not to snag her hazmat suit on any of the pointed tips. Her beam cast shadows that seemed to slither away from her across the smooth surface. She knew that different species of animals produced different colors of eyeshine. Her ex-boyfriend's golden retriever's eyes had glowed gold in the moonlight, while her friend's cat's eyes had looked kind of orange, but this animal was significantly smaller than both. And its eyes had been almost teardrop shaped, as though set more on the sides of its head than the front, just like those of a deer or a horse—

A tsunami of memories crashes over her. Columns of light swirling with dust pass through the rubble. She tries to cry out, but there's no breath in her lungs. Her eyelids are so heavy that she can barely keep them open. She hears muffled voices, the clatter of rocks, sirens calling from far away. The pressure on her chest abates and a ferocious glow blinds her. Shadows converge upon her, dragging her from the earth and carrying her into the night, where parked cars aim their high beams at the ruined road from which the bed of her dad's pickup truck stands. The horse trailer lies on its side, crumpled behind it. Thunder's head protrudes from a ragged hole in the aluminum siding, the lacerations on his muzzle and neck glistening with blood, his lifeless eyes reflecting the headlights like two halves of a blue moon.

Dayna felt the warmth of tears on her cheeks, but she could no more wipe them away than she could slow the panicked beating of her heart. The urge to sprint to the cable overwhelmed her, but she couldn't even seem to make her legs—

A shadow slashed through her light.

She pinned it with her beam and prayed there was enough illumination for her camera to record what she saw. Wiry fungal growths protruded from the creature's hunched form as though countless sets of antlers had erupted from its skull and spine. Its patchy fur was desiccated, its exposed musculature a sickly shade of gray reminiscent of rotten meat. Strands of reddish mycelia covered the exposed tissue, wormlike stitches that appeared to hold the decomposing body together. Were it not for the tiny scarlet eyes and tattered ears, she never would have recognized that it was—

"A rabbit," she gasped.

At the sound of her voice, the creature vanished into the darkness once more.

———

THE GROUND SEEMED to drop out from underneath Randall. He remembered the rabbit lying seemingly dead on the examination tray, its body riddled with puncture wounds . . . the same animal hurling itself against its cage walls with all of the others . . . the whole lot of them abruptly falling still and filling the lab with a cloud of spores. And he recalled heaping their limp carcasses on a tarp and stuffing it down into the deep injection well all those years ago. That couldn't possibly have been one of those rabbits, could it? Surely even its bones would have decomposed by now, yet he'd seen the way the other rabbit's flesh had come away in Beta's grasp, the decaying musculature underneath it, the discolored bones . . .

The resurrection response.

If those rabbits had somehow survived, then was it possible that—?

Gamma's voice burst from his earpiece.

"You need to get back here, Chief."

"Give me a minute," Randall snapped, gripping the handle of his flamethrower. He forced his way deeper into the maze, swiveling from side to side. "There's something I need to take care of first."

"This can't wait." The way he said it prickled the fine hairs on Randall's neck. "Dr. Partridge discovered something you're going to want to see."

Randall growled in frustration. He squeezed from the narrow path between formations, grabbed Dr. Raines by the elbow, and dragged her along with him. She dug in her heels and jerked her arm from his grasp.

"I'm not going anywhere with you until you tell me what's going on."

"Fine. Stay here."

Randall strode away from her, not caring what she did. He had too many memories . . . too many emotions . .

. too many regrets . . . all colliding in his head. Why hadn't he just left the bodies to burn in the lab? Maybe the fungus would have been incinerated with the remains. He should have piled the dead in one room, doused them with every drop of accelerant he could find, and struck a match—

"You saw that rabbit," Dr. Raines said, stepping into his path and forcing him to stop. Her eyes searched his for the answers she somehow knew he possessed. "You saw the fungal growths on that rabbit. That's how the spores are spreading throughout the caverns and replenishing the biomass on the walls. And you knew it was down here. That's why you reached for your flamethrower as soon as you recognized it."

Randall shouldered passed her.

"In just under an hour," he said, "this place won't exist anymore and there'll be nothing left to worry about."

"So you *are* worried."

"Don't twist my words."

"Then talk to me. Tell me how in God's name a rabbit infected with the same fungal organism growing all around us is somehow alive down here."

"You don't have the security clearance—"

"Maybe not, but I do have a mouth, and I have no problem telling every news network what I saw."

Randall rounded on her and stepped into her personal space.

"Do you really think they'll allow that to happen? If they find out this organism survived, then every single one of us will vanish without a trace."

Understanding slowly dawned in her eyes.

"There you go," he said. "I figured you'd catch on sooner or later."

Randall strode away from her. He didn't care what she said or did. The only thing that mattered now was destroying this entire place before so much as a single spore got out.

DAYNA STOPPED dead in her tracks. The implications of Randall's words nearly knocked the wind out of her. She recalled what Cassie had said on the phone — *Some very powerful people have taken an acute interest in this situation, so be extremely careful* — and realized the truth of Randall's words. Her makeshift team hadn't been dispatched in an attempt to prevent another manmade earthquake; they were here to conceal an operation to recover the organism beneath a veil of scientific legitimacy. The people in power didn't care about millions of Denverites, generations of whom they'd already exposed to toxic chemicals from the Rocky Mountain Arsenal and nuclear waste from the Rocky Flats Plant. They wanted to secure the fungus, no matter the cost, and obliterate all traces of its existence, even if it meant collapsing the entire downtown area to do it.

She hurried to catch up with Randall.

"Who are *they*?"

"The government, the Pentagon, the military industrial complex. They're one and the same: mere toys in the sandbox of men who'd sooner destroy the world than give up even the tiniest fraction of their control over it. Do you think monsters like that care about the people living above us? They'll do anything to acquire that fungus. And if millions die in the process? Even better. The resultant fear only allows them to tighten their collective grip on power." He sighed and turned to face her. "You might not believe it, Dr. Raines, but you and I are on the same side."

"Really? Which side is that?"

"The side where we do what we came down here to do and get back to the surface in one piece."

He turned without another word and headed toward the others. His words echoed inside her head as she hurried to catch up with him. If the "very powerful people" who'd orchestrated their presence here were only interested in collecting an organism they believed had been destroyed in the fire at the Rocky Mountain Arsenal, an organism capable of frightening even a hardened soldier like Randall, then why in the world would he allow them to . . . have . . . it?

"The RMA didn't merely burn down under your command, did it?" Dayna said. "You started the fire yourself."

He kept walking as though he hadn't heard.

Dayna recalled the congressional report she'd read on the plane, which had recounted both the destruction of the lab facilities and the loss of life. If he'd truly set fire to his own base in an effort to destroy the fungus, then was he not willing to do the same thing down here, in a place where they were already surrounded by combustible chemicals? She'd seen how quickly he'd grabbed his flamethrower when the rabbit appeared. Had Gamma not called when he did . . .

"Did you know there were still men inside the lab when you started the fire?" she asked.

Randall flinched, but he continued looking straight ahead.

"There were no men inside the building."

"Yes, there were. I read the report—

"I would *never* do anything to harm the men under my charge."

"All evidence to the contrary aside?"

He faced her with fire in his eyes.

"None of those men died in the fire."

"Then did you kill them to make sure the fungus didn't get out?"

"Their bodies weren't even in—"

He bit off the words and clenched his fists in frustration.

"If they weren't in the lab when you burned it, then where . . . ?" Dayna closed her eyes and nodded to herself as she finally fit the pieces together. "The fire was a cover-up. The bodies were down here, weren't they? You came here to clean up the mess you made all those years ago. The people who sent us? They don't even know you're here, do they? Are you going to kill us like you did the others?"

When she opened her eyes, she found him staring past her, at something only he could see. He appeared diminished, as though burdened by some great weight he'd been carrying for too long. For the first time, he truly looked his age.

"I didn't kill those men, but I suppose I might as well have. Their safety was my responsibility. Not a single day goes by that I don't relive what happened to them and think about all of the things I could have done differently. *Should* have done differently. I've spent my entire life atoning for my failure . . . trying to make sure nothing like that ever happens again. That's why my men and I are here now. There's no way that organism will ever leave this place."

Dayna furrowed her brow and searched his face for the truth of his words.

"Then we're not on the same side," she said. "I'm here to prevent millions of people from dying."

"And I'm here to prevent an even worse catastrophe than that."

"Even if it means letting everyone above our heads die?"

He looked her dead in the eyes when he spoke.

"Even if it means killing them myself."

And with that, he strode away from her, leaving her staring at his back as his light faded into the distance.

23

1:12 p.m.

Countdown to Commence Ascent: 0:41
Oxygen Remaining: 1:41

Randall found Gamma kneeling beside Dr. Partridge, whose hands shook so badly she could barely load a slide under her digital microscope. His light threw her shadow across the ground in front of her as he approached. She let out a startled shriek and rounded on him, eyes wide with terror. He had to remind himself that he was dealing with civilians who'd likely never seen a dead body, let alone watched a man die before their very eyes.

"I'm sorry I startled you," he said. "What did you find?"

"The mycelia . . . they . . . " She closed her eyes, took a deep breath, and blew it out slowly to compose herself.

"You need to see for yourself. Hand me what's left of that strand over there."

Randall glanced at the footlong length of mycelium the medical mycologist had collected from the stalactites overhead, which lay maybe eighteen inches from her knee, well within her reach. He crouched and tried to scoop it up, but it clung to the bare rock. Adjusting his grip, he peeled it from the ground, creating threadlike strands that resembled cheese coming away with a slice of pizza.

"This species' growth rate is beyond anything I've ever seen," Dr. Partridge said. "Those hyphae you just saw regenerated within about ten minutes. And look closely at the ends. I severed them cleanly when I initially collected the sample."

Randall scrutinized first one end, then the other. They were bullet-shaped, with individual strands standing apart almost like frayed rope, and if he looked closely enough, he could still see the demarcations where she'd originally cut it. Both ends had grown nearly half an inch in under an hour.

"Now show him what you showed me," Gamma said, his tone of voice strangely flat, almost resigned.

Randall glanced from his tech specialist to the medical mycologist, who once more took a steadying breath.

"Over there," she said, gesturing toward the sparkling fragments of Beta's shattered visor. "You can see where . . . on the ground . . . where the . . . blood . . . "

Even from a dozen feet away, Randall could see the scarlet fuzz growing from the droplets and spatters. He thought of the ravaged bird carcasses on the substrate in the locusts' cage, the rabbits riddled with pinprick puncture wounds, the sickly gray flesh Beta had revealed when he peeled off a fistful of fruiting bodies . . .

"It's metabolizing the blood," he said, repeating the very words he'd spoken decades ago.

Dr. Thompson's haunting words arose from his subconscious, as though whispered in his ear: *Our working hypothesis is that it's consuming some component of the blood to produce the antibodies necessary to circumvent the immune response and proliferate unchecked within the host's body, almost like a virus.*

"Look at it under the microscope," Gamma said, nodding to Sydney's cellphone. She turned it so Randall could better see the slide she'd just loaded. Countless little pink bubbles filled the screen. Red blood cells. Filamentous structures clung to them, connecting them into a loosely tethered mass, like so many flies trapped in a spider's web.

"If you look closely, you can see where the hyphae have infiltrated the outer membranes of the RBCs without rupturing them," Dr. Partridge said. "Their relationship isn't entirely parasitic, but it isn't symbiotic either. It more closely resembles the way a virus binds to a host cell to evade the immune system and uses the cell's own ribosomes to manufacture more and more of the virus, keeping the host alive for as long as possible in the process."

"Why would it do that?" Gamma asked.

"I don't know. It's not like blood cells can survive for very long outside of the body, especially under these conditions, but inside the body . . . " She paused to gather her thoughts. "With such low oxygen concentrations down here, the body would be in a perpetual state of hypoxia, triggering an exponential increase in red blood cell production to keep up with the elevated demand for oxygen at the cellular level, creating an endless supply of nutrients for the fungi, which are obviously capable of assimilating the chemical byproducts . . . "

Dr. Partridge furrowed her brow and looked inward. Her lips moved with unvocalized thoughts.

"You said the mycelial strands resemble muscle tissue," Gamma said. "Are you suggesting possible interspecific hybridization?"

"Fungi are more closely related to animals than they are to plants. Even human beings, for all their complexity, share fifty percent of their DNA with fungi, which is why, believe it or not, the two species are susceptible to some of the same diseases. I suppose under ideal conditions and with the right technology, a complex holobiont, if not an actual hybrid, could be created. You'd just need the right mammalian species . . . "

"Like a rabbit?" Dr. Raines said, emerging from the shadows behind them.

––––––––––––

"WHAT DO you know that I don't?" Sydney asked.

Dayna stared daggers at Randall.

"Do you want to tell them or should I?"

Randall looked back at her, his face devoid of emotion.

"Dr. Raines found her anomaly," he said.

"There was a rabbit down here?" Gamma said. "And it was still alive?"

Dayna held up her tablet. She'd paused the recording just as the blurry rabbit bolted out from behind a jagged formation, its left eye a red streak across the darkness.

"That's what Beta saw before he—" Gamma's voice abruptly cut off midsentence, although Dayna was certain he continued talking. Once again, he and Randall communicated on a channel she couldn't hear, which only made her wonder—

"Where is Beta?" she asked, turning in a circle.

"He was just lying there," Sydney said. "His visor . . . it . . . it shattered . . . and he . . . and he . . . "

Dayna took in the polycarbonate shards and the patterns of crimson biofilm proliferating around them.

"He died?" she gasped.

"It was horrible," Sydney sobbed. "His eyes . . . they just . . . and he . . . he . . . "

Dayna found herself at a loss for words. How on earth could something like that have happened?

"That's what Beta saw before he . . . " she whispered, repeating the words Gamma had spoken after seeing her picture of the rabbit. How had he intended to finish that sentence? Before he climbed up into the chute? Before he fell and broke both ankles? She clearly remembered the fungal growths on the sickly rabbit's back, the swollen bulbs of their fruiting bodies. Is that what he'd seen before the cloud of spores burst in his face? The same rabbit . . .

Dayna felt a sinking feeling in the pit of her stomach as she turned on her tablet. She isolated the readings she'd used to locate the rabbit and stripped away all extraneous data. At roughly the same time Beta had climbed into the chute, her equipment had detected the rabbit behind her, not across the reservoir, which meant that if he'd truly seen a rabbit, not only did that mean there was there a second one down here, but its movements were beyond her sensing array's range. And if that were the case . . .

"Oh, God," she whispered.

She compared the rabbit's readings against those for the anomaly she'd detected from the surface. They didn't match. The amplitude . . . the patterns of movement . . . they weren't merely two different animals; they were two entirely different—

"What the hell is that?" Craig gasped.

Randall shouldered past Dayna and rushed to the drone pilot's side. She followed and squeezed in between them so she could see the monitor. The drone appeared to be in a space not much larger than it was. Biofilm covered the walls, tendril-like mycelia wavering in its rotor wash. One section appeared longer and of a slightly darker color than the others.

"Those are mature fruiting bodies," Sydney said. "See how they look coarser than the rest of the stroma. Most of them anyway. Others . . . "

If she finished her thought, Dayna didn't hear it. She was too focused on a strange gray swatch, and what almost looked like tiny bones—

The rabbit's eyes snapped open and its ears perked up. It had been so perfectly camouflaged against the wall that she hadn't even seen it. A shiver rippled through its body and a sparkling cloud rose into the air, swirling in the tumultuous air currents. A layer of what almost looked like frost appeared on the screen, growing increasingly opaque—

The lens shattered and the screen darkened.

"No, no, no," Craig shouted, drawing the attention of Alpha, Telford, and Stephens as they waded back toward them.

"Rewind the footage," Randall snapped. "Get me a clear view of that animal."

Dayna backed away from the others and glanced at her tablet. The readings showed both the anomaly she'd detected from the surface and the one that had turned out to be a rabbit. The former was once more active. The amplitude of the spikes was nearly off the charts, which meant . . .

She spun in a circle, searching the surrounding darkness for any sign of movement, but there wasn't anything there.

"What's wrong?" Sydney asked.

Dayna tuned her out and concentrated on the readings, which spiked over and over, their pattern resembling a racing heartbeat on an EKG. It had to be right on top of them. Where else could it be . . . ?

She stopped turning.

Her pulse rushed in her ears.

The world seemed to stand still as she slowly looked straight up.

———

RANDALL FOLLOWED Dr. Raines's stare to the stalactite-riddled ceiling, where he caught the faintest hint of movement, little more than a shifting of shadows above the mycelial web. He recalled the dark violet shape he'd seen on thermal imaging, pressed flat against the stone between stalactites. Was that what her readings had—?

A cloud of glittering spores burst from the gaps between fungal strands, swirling and churning as it descended.

"Move!" he shouted, shoving Preston into the chemicals and tackling Dr. Raines, who cried out as they rolled toward the cavern wall. Gamma streaked through his peripheral vision and threw himself on top of Dr. Partridge, leaving the other three scrambling for cover as the cloud settled. Alpha and Stephens dove into the chemicals, but Telford tripped over his own bulky boots and went down hard.

His eyes met Randall's across the distance as the spores settled onto him. A fine red patina formed on his yellow hazmat suit. He desperately tried to wipe off his face shield, his eyes widening as a fine network of fissures spiderwebbed—

The flimsy polycarbonate visor shattered.

Randall averted his eyes, but there was no escaping Telford's screams, which seemed to go on and on until, finally, with a whimper, the environmental engineer fell silent.

Dr. Raines sobbed and pushed Randall off of her, but he caught her by the shoulder before she could rush to Telford's aid.

Weeping blisters and tiny lacerations covered the poor man's exposed forehead and cheeks, and his eyes—

"Jesus," Randall gasped, shuddering off the image. He leaned back and swept his shoulder light through the mycelial strands, peeling back the darkness above them, searching for the source of the spores.

"Let go!" Dr. Raines shouted, jerking on her arm, but he held on tight.

"There's nothing you can do for him," he said, gesturing with his free hand toward the glimmering red dust still slowly settling to the ground around Telford's body. "You can't risk getting those spores on your suit."

She rolled over and shoved him.

"This is all your fault!" she screamed, pounding his chest with her fists.

Randall caught her by the wrists and looked her dead in the eyes.

"How did you know it was up there?"

"Let go of me!"

"Whatever did this is still up there, Dr. Raines," he said in the most patient voice he could muster.

Her shoulders rose as she drew a breath to speak, but no words came out. With a single nod, she stopped struggling and picked up her tablet.

Randall stood up and took in everyone around him at a glance: Gamma hauling Dr. Partridge to her feet as she stared in horror at the carnage; Craig crawling from the chemical reservoir; Alpha shoving Stephens through the shallows, giving Telford's remains a wide berth. He switched to the command channel to tune out the chaos.

"Demolitions status update."

"All munitions planted per specifications," Alpha said.

"Are you confident they'll work as intended and collapse this cavern straight down?"

"Assuming Telford knew what he was doing, but we can't really ask him now, can we?"

"Then we return to the surface. You take point." Randall switched to the open channel. "We're moving out. Everyone, fall in behind Alpha. Dr. Raines?"

"I'm working on it," she snapped.

"Work faster, dammit. Dr. Partridge—"

"We can't just leave him here like that," she sobbed.

"Gamma?" Randall said. The tech specialist wrapped his arms around Dr. Partridge and physically maneuvered her away from Telford's remains. "Stephens, Preston: stay right behind Gamma. I'll bring up the rear. I want everyone—"

A loud splashing sound echoed from the cavern behind him.

Randall's words died on his lips as he slowly turned around and looked at the chemical reservoir.

24

1:25 p.m.

Countdown to Commence Ascent: 0:28
Oxygen Remaining: 1:28

Dayna's pulse whooshed in her ears as she watched the distant ripples break against the crystalline columns and slowly roll to shore. She'd seen something. From the corner of her eye. She was sure of it. A shadow . . . nearly indistinguishable from the darkness . . . falling from the ceiling into the chemicals. Had a section of the earthen roof collapsed? If the degeneration of the fault zone was accelerating . . .

She glanced at her tablet and allowed a trapped breath to seep from her lips. The readings didn't reflect a sudden increase in seismic activity, but rather patterns of movement similar to those of the anomaly she'd identified from the surface, only slower and stealthier . . . almost as though whatever had been up there knew she could detect its presence. And now that it was immersed in the chemicals, if it could move without making contact with the ground, she wouldn't be able to sense it at all.

A chill rippled up her spine.

"What did you see?" Randall asked, snatching the tablet from her grasp.

"Something falling into the—"

"What did it look like?"

"I don't know. I didn't get a good look—"

"Did anyone see it?" he shouted, thrusting her tablet into her hands. "Anyone?"

Alpha took him by the elbow and stepped in front of him. Whatever the two were saying, Dayna couldn't hear it. Randall nodded and led Alpha around the dusting of spores surrounding Telford's body. The environmental engineer's blistered eyes seemed to stare past them and right at Dayna. His ruined face glistened with fresh blood, which continued to seep from countless lesions and lacerations. She recalled the kind smile he'd offered when she took the seat across the aisle from him on the plane, the concern he'd shown when she experienced the onslaught of claustrophobia while donning her hazmat suit, and the courage he'd demonstrated while wading into the chemicals to evaluate a fault that could have collapsed and killed them all at any moment.

"Everyone on me," Alpha said. "Don't fall behind."

Before Dayna even knew what she intended to do, she dropped her tablet, grabbed Telford's gloved hand, and started dragging him—

Randall swatted her wrists to release her grip and pulled her away from the body.

"What the hell is wrong with you?" he snapped.

"He risked his life to save everyone above us."

"Then he wouldn't want us to jeopardize them now." Dayna spun around and shoved Randall, but he held on even tighter and met her stare. "Don't let his sacrifice be in vain."

She looked down at Telford's face. The oxygen mask had fallen from his mouth and nose, revealing his bared teeth, memorializing his final moments of sheer agony. A furry red fuzz rimmed his gumline and ringed his nostrils.

Dayna's breath hitched in her chest. Randall was right: they couldn't allow the spores to reach the surface. She stopped struggling and reluctantly nodded. He let go of her wrists and took a step back.

She grabbed her tablet and mobile sensing device and hurried to catch up with the others. Several seconds passed before Randall fell in behind her, his spotlight hurling her shadow across the ground.

RANDALL ALTERNATED walking forward and backward, slashing his beam through the pitch black to make sure nothing was following them. The splashing sound had unnerved him, although not nearly as much as the fact that they were walking blindly into a veritable bottleneck where he'd already seen a rabbit. He couldn't shake the feeling that they were being herded, and he'd already seen just how stealthily these creatures could sneak up and disperse their spores without warning.

"Keep your eyes open, Alpha," he said, turning around once more. "Gamma: have you found another path back to the extraction point?"

"Negative," Gamma said. "I've identified several possible egresses on the LiDAR reconstruction, but the laser failed to penetrate any of them far enough to know for sure."

"Keep looking," Randall said. "Dr. Raines . . . are you picking up anything on your sensors?"

"Everyone freeze," she said, setting down her array and scrutinizing her tablet in the eerie green glow. Everyone held perfectly still while she waited for her program to run. Ten seconds passed. Fifteen. "Nothing."

"Pick up the pace," Randall said. His oxygen supply was already down to twenty-two percent, which meant the civilians in their vastly inferior suits had to be considerably lower than that.

Once more, he turned around and swept his beam along the ground, up one wall, across the stalactites, and back down the other. He tried not to think about how perfectly camouflaged the rabbit they'd seen on the drone footage had been, or how they never would have known it was there had it not opened its eyes. If there were others, and they were capable of holding that still, then the seven of them could find themselves completely surrounded—

"Nearing the bottleneck," Alpha said.

Randall dissected his memories of that fateful night all those years ago. He'd individually bundled and interred four of the men under his charge, men whose names he would never forget for as long as he lived — Doctors James Thompson, Calvin Waller, Angus Mann, and Jeremy Glade — but he couldn't remember how many rabbits he'd forced down the deep injection well. Twenty? Twenty-five? Had the cages been stacked five-by-four or five-by-five? Or had it been six-by-six? It was all a blur. The furry gray bodies, heaped in a tangle of limbs he could barely contain inside a single tarp, let alone lift into the truck. And considering two of them had been enough to take out Beta and Telford, he could only imagine what ten times that many could do.

Surely they hadn't all survived, but the fact that any of them had was more than enough to make him wonder if they hadn't been the only ones—

"Hold," Alpha whispered.

Everyone stopped at once. Without the sound of shuffling feet, a preternatural silence settled over the group.

"Dr. Raines?" Randall whispered.

A green glow blossomed from her tablet.

"Movement," Alpha whispered.

"I'm detecting it, too," Dr. Raines whispered. "The signal is consistent with the rabbit we saw — wait. There are multiple overlapping signatures. Some farther away than others."

"How far?" Alpha whispered.

"It's impossible to tell, but the rising amplitude of the spikes suggests they're getting closer."

"From which direction?" Randall asked, shining his beam into the darkness behind him.

"I don't know."

"How many sources?"

"At least two . . . maybe more. I can't . . . I just can't tell."

Dr. Partridge whimpered and dropped her microscope attachment. The clattering sound echoed away into the cavern.

"Talk to me, Alpha," Randall whispered.

"I can't see a blasted thing through all of these stalagmites."

"Gamma . . . tell me you found another way around."

"No, sir."

Randall's oxygen gauge dropped to twenty percent. He could positively feel time slipping away. And if he didn't detonate those explosives before the impending earthquake struck . . .

"Proceed with caution," he whispered.

———

ALPHA APPROACHED the jagged crystalline formations slowly, his spotlight creeping from left to right and back again. Sharp tips sparkled and rainbowlike refractions danced on the stalactites projecting from the cavern roof, mere feet overhead. The others fell into a single file line behind him. He glanced back at Dayna, who paused while she studied the incoming readings on her tablet, and then nodded for him to keep going.

From the middle of the pack, she watched him chart a winding course through the speleothems, alternately rising to his full height and crouching in an effort to better see his surroundings. Craig followed, far too closely, bumping into him from behind if he suddenly slowed his pace.

Stephens hung back so as not to risk doing the same, his flashlight never straying from the encroaching formations and the slick ground underfoot. Dayna kept one hand on his back and used him as a guide so she could concentrate on her tablet, leaving Gamma, Sydney, and Randall bringing up the rear, their beams slicing past her, animating the shadows.

Even with Alpha stopping every few seconds, she couldn't get solid readings from her sensing array, which simply hadn't been designed to be used on the fly. By the time she filtered out extraneous sounds and movement, too much time and distance had passed for the readings to be of any use. All the while, her battery drained — five percent . . . four percent . . . — and there was nothing she could do to stop it.

They were slowly running out of air, and every passing second brought them closer to the inevitable earthquake that would bury them alive.

She started to hyperventilate, her chest hitching with every rapid inhalation. The revelation that she was burning through her dwindling supply of oxygen faster only made it worse. She couldn't . . . focus . . . couldn't . . . make the ground hold still . . . the world stop . . . spinning . . .

Movement from the corner of her eye.

Dayna's rapid breathing abruptly ceased altogether. Her pulse thumped in her temples as she glanced down at the spikes streaking across her tablet.

Stephens stopped so suddenly that she stumbled into his back. She retreated a step and looked over his shoulder at Alpha, who stood maybe a dozen feet away, right at the point where the formations gave way to bare rock once more. A rabbit sat on the ground in front of him, its ears pinned back and its tiny red eyes reflecting his blinding spotlight. Its nose, held together by wormlike mycelia, twitched.

"I can reach it in time," he whispered. "Be ready to move when I tell you."

"Don't even think about it," Gamma whispered. "We'll find another way around."

"There isn't enough time," Alpha said, bending his knees.

Dayna realized with a start that he intended to throw himself onto the rabbit and shield them from the spores with his body.

The rabbit must have sensed it, too. It rose to its haunches, exposing sickly gray flesh held together by patches of fungal growth. A shiver rippled through its body as Alpha lunged, filling the air between them with a glimmering cloud of spores.

25

1:36 p.m.

Countdown to Commence Ascent: 0:17
Oxygen Remaining: 1:17

Screams erupted from the speaker by Randall's ear. Dr. Partridge spun and ran straight into him. He stepped aside and forced his way through the jagged formations, hoping to God the supposedly puncture-proof material held up. Silhouettes fled past him as he tried to get a better view without coming into contact with the swirling cloud, through which he could barely see Alpha, thrashing on the ground, trying to pin the rabbit underneath him, knowing full well that he was a dead man either way.

A crimson patina formed on the stalagmites, dulling their prismatic effect. If Alpha could hold on long enough for the rest of them to work their way around him—

The crystalline speleothems shattered, carpeting the earth with shards.

Alpha's cries rose to a fevered pitch as his visor did the same.

"Go!" he screamed, his voice degenerating into electrical noise.

Randall caught Dr. Raines by the arm.

"We have to keep going!" he yelled, but Preston barreled right through both of them, his eyes wide and his visor cracked.

Alpha gurgled and his body fell still. A pool of blood slowly spread from beneath his helmet. His body twitched — once, then again — and the rabbit squirmed out from underneath him, tearing a stripe of fungus from its spine in the process. Its scarlet eyes flashed as it rounded on Randall.

They were too late.

More formations shattered as the cloud of spores settled, destroying what little cover remained between them and the creature.

"Gamma!" he shouted, turning and shoving Dr. Raines ahead of him. "Find me another way around!"

They slalomed through the maze, their lights knifing violently through the darkness, concealing as much as they revealed.

"Get them off!" Preston shouted. "Get them off!"

There was too much chaos for Randall to formulate a plan. He needed to take charge of the situation before it spiraled completely out of control.

"Stay together," he barked. "Regroup once you're clear of the formations."

He was down two men, the drone was useless, and if they didn't reach the extraction point soon, they wouldn't have enough oxygen left to make the return trip to the surface. Worse, these creatures were far faster than they were and could be upon them without the slightest warning. If he was overcome by spores before he triggered the detonator—

Preston screamed and threw himself on the ground. He pawed at the spores on his visor, which only made it crack faster.

"Oh, God!" he screamed. "Make it stop!"

Randall grabbed a fistful of the drone pilot's suit and dragged him clear of the stalagmites, but there was nothing he could do for him.

"Please don't let me die," Preston whimpered. He clutched Randall's hand and looked him squarely in the eyes. His irises shivered and tears streamed down his cheeks. "Please, God . . . don't let . . . "

Preston's visor disintegrated, covering his face with polycarbonate fragments. Blisters formed on the delicate skin of his eyelids, lesions spread across his forehead, and a horrible cry burst from his chest. His hand slipped from Randall's grasp and fell to the ground.

And then he moved no more.

DAYNA STARED down at Craig's body in abject horror. Less than twelve hours ago, he'd been lounging on the plane without a care in the world, and now—

"Snap out of it," Randall said, tugging on her arm. "We need to keep moving."

She stumbled along behind him, her mind reeling. They'd lost two people in a matter of minutes, two people who'd died in just about the worst way she could possibly imagine, worse even than—

—the weight of the stone on her chest . . . the deep pinching sensation of broken ribs . . . makes it difficult to breathe. Dust coats her tongue, clogs her lungs, but she can't cough . . . can't move her torso in the slightest. Blood dribbles from the corner of her mouth and pools in her ear, muffling the sounds of the ground settling, the truck's engine dying, and Thunder screaming. Tears leak from her eyes as she looks through the dust swirling in the glow of the headlights and sees her parents. In that moment, she realizes they were the lucky ones; their deaths had come quickly, while hers would linger.

In a blind panic, she claws at the earth around her, tearing her fingernails and lacerating her fingertips. Dirt cascades onto her face, into her eyes, underneath her eyelids. Every movement comes at a cost. The rubble shifts and compresses her pelvis, increasing the pressure to the point that she fears the bones will break. The pain in her chest sharpens and blood creeps up her throat. If she continues to struggle, she'll only die faster, but the thought of holding still and accepting this fate feels like she's acquiescing to—

—being buried alive.

Gamma led the way, his shoulder-mounted light laying bare earthen columns attempting to hide in the utter blackness. Sydney struggled to keep pace, while Stephens fell farther and farther behind. He stumbled, lost his balance, and collapsed.

Randall caught up with him and rolled him onto his back. The chemical engineer's face was scarlet and beaded with sweat. Tiny blisters had risen from his forehead and cheek bones, and the blood vessels in the corner of his left eye had ruptured, flooding the sclera. He clutched a fistful of the fabric near his hip in one hand.

"How bad is it?" Randall asked.

"It's a tiny puncture," Stephens said, "but the damage has already been done."

Randall nodded.

"Gamma, find a secure position," he said, then turned to Dayna. "Help me get him up."

She felt sick to her stomach. Maybe if they got Stephens back to the surface quickly enough, there'd still be a chance of saving him, or perhaps—

She'd seen what had happened to the others, what the chemical fumes had done to them, how quickly they'd died, how painfully . . .

A sob shuddered from her chest as she helped Randall lift Stephens to his feet. The general slung the chemical engineer's arm over his shoulders and braced as much weight as he could bear, while she wrapped her arms around Stephens's waist and struggled to manage the rest.

They caught up with Gamma and Sydney at the base of a formation resembling a giant termite mound. He crouched over his tactical tablet, pinching and swiping at a three-dimensional model of the cavern system, while she leaned against the stone formation behind him.

"It targeted the dispersal of spores," she whispered. "Fungi can't do that . . . "

Randall shrugged out from beneath Stephens, who fell to the ground, clutching his compromised suit. Dayna crouched beside him and awakened her tablet.

"There," Gamma said, tapping his screen. He swiveled the device so the rest of them could see a digital recreation of a slender, rocky orifice, which only hinted at the depth of the tunnel inside. "I can't confirm it goes all the way through, but if you factor in the laser's angle of penetration and extrapolate the passage's course" — He zoomed out, swiped to the cavern into which they'd first descended, and zoomed in again — "there's a chance it connects to this outlet right here, albeit maybe a hundred feet down."

Spikes appeared on Dayna's tablet. One after another after another.

"A chance?" Randall said. "If we go in there and it's a dead end—"

"Guys," Dayna whispered. Everyone turned to face her, but she couldn't tear her eyes from her screen, where the amplitude of the spikes continued to rise. There were now so many distinct sources that it was nearly impossible to tell one from the next. "We're out of time."

RANDALL GLANCED from Gamma's tablet to Dr. Raines's and back again. He turned and looked into the shadows to his right, tucked around the corner from the bottleneck. If he angled his light, he could just make out an arched orifice above the surface of a standing pool of chemicals, maybe a couple hundred feet diagonally from the shoreline of the main reservoir. They'd have to lower themselves into the toxic stew to crawl through it, but with where Stephens's suit was compromised . . .

An expression of resignation settled on the chemical engineer's face as the reality of the situation sank in.

Randall swung his beam from the nearly invisible opening to the bottleneck—

Dozens of tiny red eyes reflected his light as the creatures raced through the crystalline forest.

Stephens grabbed him by the sleeve and pulled him closer. The chemical engineer's frightened eyes held his as he unholstered the flamethrower from the primary life support subsystem on the general's back.

"Make sure you aren't in standing fluid," he said. "The fumes will burn hot and fast, but your suits should protect you long enough. I'll buy you as much time as I can."

There was nothing Randall could say. He nodded and released the modular fuel unit from its housing. Stephens struggled to his feet and cradled it to his chest.

"What are you doing?" Dr. Partridge asked.

"Get going," Stephens said.

"We're not leaving—"

"Go!"

Eyeshine flashed in Randall's peripheral vision. The creatures fanned out as they neared the cavern. They were coordinating their movements, attempting to outflank them. If they cleared the bottleneck before he and the others reached the outlet, they'd be cut off—

"Get out of here!" Stephens shouted. He staggered

into open, his back to the reservoir, and took up position facing the oncoming creatures. Dropping the tank at his feet, he raised the nozzle.

Randall grabbed Dr. Raines by the hand and ran for the orifice. They splashed into the pool, churning up chemicals above their thighs. He tripped and went under. Pain flared in his knees, but he managed to crawl the rest of the way to the inlet. He ushered the others past him, one at a time, giving each of them a solid shove to hurry them along.

He was just about to follow when Stephens shouted, his voice reverberating from dark recesses that came to life with tiny red dots. Sensing their prey's vulnerability, the rabbits cautiously approached. The chemical engineer waited for them to get close enough that he'd be sure to take them with him when he ignited the pilot flame.

A dark form emerged from the chemicals behind him, so slowly that it hardly created a ripple, and rose to its full height.

Randall recalled the shape he'd seen clinging to the ceiling between the stalactites . . . the spores raining down on Telford . . . the splash he'd heard behind him.

The creature waded toward the shoreline behind Stephens, who didn't have the slightest idea that it was there. The way it moved . . . as though it possessed joints where others didn't . . . Randall would have recognized that gait anywhere, even after all these years and with its skeletal body bristling with wiry fungi . . .

Dr. Calvin Waller, the entomologist whose body he'd stuffed down the shaft.

"Stephens!" Randall shouted.

The chemical engineer turned around as Waller advanced, a cloud of spores erupting from his chest. Stephens bellowed and ignited the pilot light—

The air became fire, turning the two figures into silhouettes.

Randall dove through the opening and crawled for dear life.

With a roar, flames took root in the chemicals and raced past him into the depths.

26

1:45 p.m.

Countdown to Commence Ascent: 0:08
Oxygen Remaining: 1:08

A wall of heat buffeted Dayna from behind, hurling her from the chemicals and sending her tumbling across bare stone. Flames swallowed her, igniting the chemicals still covering her suit. She caught glimpses of the others through the fire: Gamma throwing himself on top of Sydney and shielding her with his body; Randall dragging himself through the flaming chemicals, his suit burning like a torch. She rolled over and grabbed his wrist, pulling him onto dry ground that somehow still burned. The heat passed through her protective suit as though it wasn't even there.

And then it was gone.

Smoke gushed from the blue flames rising from the

standing chemicals, but at least she no longer actively burned. She swatted at the dwindling fires clinging to her chest, scooted back against the stone wall, and wiped the black smudges from her visor. Heart pounding, chest heaving, she searched for the others, whose sweat-beaded faces slowly resolved from the smoke. Their suits were scorched, their visors carbon-scored, but they were still alive. Unlike Stephens—

Tears blurred her vision at the thought of the chemical engineer burning alive. She hung her head and started to cry—

"There's no time for that," Randall said, smothering the flames still burning on his boots. He wiped the soot from his spotlight, offered a curt nod of gratitude, and crawled past her. The smoke swallowed him almost immediately, leaving a diffuse glow for the rest of them to follow.

He was right, and she knew it. The sudden change in temperature and pressure had undoubtedly further destabilized the fault zone, and considering the entire chemical reservoir would burn until it had consumed every last molecule of oxygen, conditions would continue to degenerate rapidly. And there were still millions of unsuspecting people above their heads, their lives hanging in the balance.

Dayna cradled her bent sensor array and cracked tablet to her chest and crawled after Randall, whose silhouette alternately appeared and disappeared from the smoke. Sydney and Gamma squeezed through the narrowing behind her. The way their lights cast her shadow onto the smoke was disorienting. Worse, it lent substance to the air itself. She felt like she was being squeezed from all sides, slowly having the air forced from her lungs. A wave of panic rose inside her. She started to hyperventilate, which only amplified the panic. If she didn't slow her breathing, she would exhaust her dwindling oxygen supply too quickly.

She crawled faster, desperate to clear the smoke, to get out of this shrinking tunnel, which constricted like the throat of some great serpent—

Her oxygen tank struck the rock overhead. She screamed at the thought of being stuck in here, slowly running out of air while her body overheated, waiting for an earthquake to bring two vertical miles of stone down on her head or decomposing creatures bristling with fungi to find her—

A blinding light struck her right in the eyes. Randall emerged from the smoke and pressed his visor against hers.

"We can't afford to lose you right now," he said. "Focus on your breathing. In through your nose . . . out through your mouth. You can do this. In . . . out . . . Close your eyes and follow the sound of my voice. That's it. Keep crawling." He abruptly stopped, causing her to open her eyes, if only long enough to see that the tunnel ended right in front of him. "Something's blocking the way, but I think I can clear the obstruction." Dayna heard the screeching sound of stone on stone, followed by the clattering of smaller rocks striking the ground. Randall gave her hand a gentle squeeze and resumed crawling. "Everything's under control. You're almost there. Just a little farther."

She felt the walls recede and sensed a much larger space around her.

"Open your eyes," he said.

Dayna did as he asked . . .
And immediately wished that she hadn't.

IT LOOKED like millions of spiders had made themselves at home in the cavern. Weblike mycelia filled every available inch of space, from the ground underfoot to the stalactites mere inches above their heads. The columns and stalagmites were so densely covered that they were nearly indistinguishable from the spaces between them. There was so much fungal growth that it was impossible to estimate the size of the passage, let alone tell if it reached the other side.

Randall thrust his hands into the mess of gossamer strands and tore them apart. As he passed between them, the severed ends reached toward him, almost as though they'd become statically charged.

"Fungi react to changes in their environment," Dr. Partridge whispered, holding up her hand. The broken mycelia reached for it, while the intact webs bowed away from it, seemingly blown by a gentle breeze. "Their hyphae exhibit animal-like wound repair mechanisms and a type of membrane excitation that mimics the conduction of nerve impulses in the human heart. They react to restrictions in their physical space and alter their developmental patterns in response to interactions with other living beings. Studies have even shown signs of spatial recognition and learning, both of which are expressions of consciousness."

"You're suggesting that all of this is a singular organism capable of thought," Gamma said.

"Not in a traditional sense, but fungi use their root-like systems of mycelia, which can grow to hundreds of acres in size, to conduct impulses throughout their bodies, just like the neurons in our brains convey the electrical signals we interpret as thoughts. How else could a fungus like cordyceps influence the behavior of the insects it parasitizes? Its will, for lack of a better term, has to be stronger than its prey's survival instincts."

"And that's how it's controlling the rabbits? By interfacing directly with their brains?"

"More like their nervous systems as a whole."

"But if everything we see around us — the hyphal growths on the walls, the mycelial networks above the reservoir and in this cavern, and the mature fruiting bodies on the rabbits — are different phases in the life cycle of a single interconnected fungal species, and that species exhibits abilities associated with consciousness—"

"Then it knows we're here," Dr. Raines said, finishing his thought for him.

"Now's not the time for this," Randall snapped, tearing through the mycelial web even faster, heedless of the implications. The others understood what had happened to Stephens, but they hadn't *seen* it, hadn't watched a man who'd been dead for more than half a century rise from the chemicals, his entire skeletal body concealed beneath fungal protrusions. If there were others like him down here . . .

"Dr. Raines, check for seismic and infrasonic activity."

"Several of the mobile device's appendages are broken and there's no telling what kind of damage the fire did to the static arrays. Plus, there's only enough battery left to check one, maybe two more—"

"Now, Dr. Raines."

Randall pressed deeper into the cavern. If he couldn't find a way out of this godforsaken cave, then they'd be forced to waste precious time doubling back. And considering the chemicals through which they'd crawled were still actively burning and there was no way of knowing if any of the creatures had survived—

A faint glimmer caught his eye.

He tore through the mycelia at a frantic pace. A pool of chemicals appeared, maybe fifteen feet away. Another few swipes through the webbing, and the mouth of an orifice formed around it. If their theory was correct, the main cavern was a short distance away, but they'd be risking full immersion in—

"Freeze," Dr. Raines said.

Randall held perfectly still. The oxygen gauge at the corner of his peripheral vision dropped under fifteen percent, while the running clock below it counted all the way down.

00:00:03.

00:00:02.

00:00:01.

The readout turned red and started counting upward.

00:00:01.

00:00:02.

00:00:03.

They were out of time.

"Dr. Raines?" he asked.

"Hold on," she snapped. "It's almost . . . oh, God."

TINY SPIKES RACED across Dayna's tablet. Even more followed. Either she was detecting movement far away, or something moving slowly . . . stealthily . . . nearby.

She turned in a circle, sweeping her light through the surrounding mycelia.

Nothing.

A glance back down at her tablet revealed more spikes.

Larger spikes.

She flashed her beam across the jagged stalactites and the webbing connecting them.

Again, nothing.

Had the rabbits survived the ignition of the chemical fumes? Surely, no living being, let alone a fungus, could have withstood such extreme temperatures without protective gear. Yet still there was movement. Where was it?

She looked at her tablet. A final spike appeared on the screen right as the battery died. It had been considerably larger than the others.

Closer.

"What did you see?" Sydney asked.

Dayna ignored her and once more turned in circle. Something was in here with them. Several somethings, judging by the readings. Where were they?

"Come on," Randall said, grabbing her by the arm. She stopped to pick up her tablet and sensing array, but he pulled her along before she could. "Leave them. It's already too late."

Randall's words nearly knocked the wind out of her.

At any second, a cloud of spores could erupt from the darkness around them and there'd be nothing they could do to stop it.

Dayna followed Randall through the mycelia, the severed ends grasping at her as if to prevent her from escaping. She swung her beam through the surrounding darkness. Searching for movement. For eyeshine. For anything to betray the presence of the creatures she was certain were in here with her. They could be anywhere, blending into the fungi covering the walls . . . scurrying above the webbing overhead . . . hiding behind the massive stalagmites or—

Her beam struck what she'd thought was a pillar, only the dense mycelial webbing merely attenuated her light, revealing the dark shape bound inside it, suspended several feet above the ground. It wriggled and thrashed and clawed at its prison, like a moth trying to escape its cocoon. Skeletal fingers poked through and tore a hole in the crimson tangle. It thrust arms covered with fruiting bodies all the way through and squirmed until its face—

Dayna gasped.

It was a human being.

The man's lips had receded from his bared teeth. Fruiting bodies covered his face, like so many fingers trying to hide his hideous visage. His eyes appeared to have been stitched open, his orbits bulging as though ready to fall out. Fuzz covered the sclera, save for pupils so wide they nearly eclipsed the irises.

Sydney screamed at the sight.

Dayna whirled and grabbed her by the hand, but

before they could take a single step, she caught more movement from her peripheral vision.

Another human figure tore through its bindings, its mouth frozen in the same horrible rictus. It squeezed through the breach, thick strands of mycelia peeling away from the crown of its skull like so many EEG leads. Blood dripped from their severed ends, rolled down the creature's face, and outlined the ridges of its teeth, where the gray gums had given way to bare bone.

"Run!" Gamma shouted, shoving them from behind.

As if awakened by his cry, little red dots winked into being. Eyeshine. Reflective spheres appeared from seemingly everywhere at once. From within the densest webbing. The gaps between stalactites. Recesses so well hidden that she hadn't even sensed they were there.

"Hurry!" Randall shouted, beckoning them toward the pool.

He jumped in first, dove beneath the chemicals, and slithered through the narrow opening. There wasn't even enough space for him to raise his head above the surface. If the hazmat suits failed to withstand the increased pressure of total immersion, then she and Sydney wouldn't make it to the other side.

With a whispered prayer, Dayna threw herself into the chemicals and swam into the darkness.

27

1:58 p.m.

Oxygen Remaining: 0:55

Randall crawled for everything he was worth. He couldn't see a blasted thing through the murky chemicals, which reduced his light to a vague aura. His PLiSS caught on the ceiling. The walls constricted around his shoulders. He grabbed hold of any imperfection in the stone and pulled, but he couldn't . . . seem to . . . squeeze . . . through . . .

As the pressure mounted, a shout erupted from his lips—

He burst from the stricture and propelled himself in the opposite direction. His head breached the surface, followed by his shoulder light, its powerful beam shooting into another cavern riddled with mycelia. He dragged himself over the jagged edge and collapsed onto the eroded stone. The exertion had taken a steep toll. Every muscle ached and every joint felt as though there was ground glass between the bones. He labored to catch his breath while he took in his surroundings. Low ceiling. Sharp, icicle-like stalactites. Passages through the tangles of mycelia resembling funnels in a spider's web. Furry red growth on every surface. Mycelial tendrils snaking through it. Something sparkled in the corner of his eye. A belt buckle, partially concealed beneath accreted minerals.

The tunnel hadn't come out in the main cavern as they'd hoped, and he couldn't see another egress through the snarls of webbing.

They were in serious trouble.

Randall struggled to his hands and knees just as Dr. Raines appeared below him in the pool. He thrust his hands into the chemicals, grabbed her arm, and dragged her onto dry ground.

Her teary eyes were wide with panic, her body shaking so badly she couldn't even hold herself up. Tuning out her sobs, he reached back into the chemicals as soon as soon as Dr. Partridge emerged. She threw her arms around him and clung so tightly that she nearly pulled them both under. He helped her over the edge, and she scooted aside to make room for Gamma, whose submerged light limned the outlet of the tunnel. Seconds passed, yet the glow's intensity never changed. Had he gotten stuck?

Randall slid down into the chemicals and was just about to go under when Gamma spurted from the passage and nearly bowled him over.

"Did they follow you?" Randall snapped, hauling him to his feet.

"I don't know. I just dove in and started—"

Gamma went under with a splash, his light trailing him as he receded into the tunnel. Randall dove in after him and caught his rapidly retreating hand. Whatever held the tech specialist's legs jerked even harder, but Randall refused to let go. They abruptly stopped when Gamma's PLiSS got stuck in the narrowing.

Their eyes met in the combined glow of their beams, sediment and debris swirling through the murky chemicals between them.

"Let me go, Chief," Gamma said. His voice was calm, his expression serene. "Get those two out of here and do what needs to be done."

A sharp tug on his legs, and Gamma's face contorted with pain.

"I'm not leaving you behind," Randall said. He pulled even harder, but he lacked the leverage to dislodge the other man.

"Go!" Gamma shouted. "While you still—"

His eyes widened, and a scream erupted from the speaker by Randall's ear. A dark cloud of blood diffused into the fluid between them. Gamma thrashed from side to side, desperately trying to escape.

Randall was helpless but to watch as chemicals flooded into Gamma's helmet from inside his suit. They rose past his chin . . . his respirator . . . his eyes. His screams intensified as his skin blistered and dissolved, as his frightened eyes clouded and ruptured—

With an anguished shout, Randall released Gamma's limp hand and propelled himself backward into the pool once more.

DAYNA STARED down at the chemicals in abject horror. Gamma's final words . . . his tortured cries . . . the silence that followed . . .

Randall floated from the tunnel and splashed to the surface, his beam momentarily blinding her.

"Get to the extraction point!" He barely had the strength to drag himself over the edge and onto dry ground. "I'll radio ahead and have Delta . . . " His words trailed off as Gamma's body drifted into the pool and floated to the surface. He rose to his knees and looked Dayna dead in the eyes. "Run."

Dark shapes burst from the tunnel and streaked through the cloudy fluid.

Dayna dragged Randall to his feet and ran in the opposite direction, tearing through the mycelia. Sydney's belt light swung wildly as she ran, illuminating little more than the webbing surrounding her, the tattered ends of which streamed behind her.

Behind them, the creatures scurried onto dry land with rapid-fire clicking sounds.

Dayna screamed and pushed herself even harder, swatting blindly at the mycelia as she ran. Their footsteps echoed around them, their ragged breathing from the speakers providing a harsh counterpoint. She couldn't hear the creatures, couldn't tell where they were. This was where she would die. Down here in the darkness, buried beneath countless tons of rock.

An equine scream rose from her memory, and an anguished sob erupted from her chest—

The ground trembled and a roaring sound filled the air.

A tremor, she realized. She'd experienced similar events at dozens of fracking sites around the country. Sub 2.0 on the Richter scale. Nowhere near catastrophic levels, but a sign that the destabilization of the fault zone was accelerating. Even if they reached the cable in time, it would still take nearly an hour to reach the surface. An hour during which her oxygen supply would run out, assuming the shaft didn't collapse first.

Her vision sparkled. Oxygen deprivation. She was hyperventilating again, a condition exacerbated by the exertion. If she didn't . . . regain control . . . she was going to. . . black out.

She forced herself to breathe, to concentrate on anything other than slowly suffocating as air seeped from her lungs . . . as her bones first fractured, then shattered . . . as the pain mounted until she prayed for the end—

"Stay with me," Randall said, squeezing her hand.

"Over there!" Sydney shouted. Her light passed through the webbing and struck a ragged crevice at the base of a stone wall, where all of the funnels appeared to converge. Standing chemicals glimmered from its depths. She made a beeline toward it and turned to face them. Her eyes widened in alarm. "Hurry!"

Faint clattering sounds echoed from the cavern behind them. Growing louder by the second. Rhythmic, like footsteps. Dayna recalled the skeletal fingertips tearing through the mycelia . . . the clicking sounds of the creatures emerging from the pool . . . and gasped when the truth struck her.

The sound was exposed bones striking stone.

The creatures were right behind them.

"Go!" Randall shouted.

Sydney turned and was just about to crawl through the crevice when she suddenly stopped and raised her beam to the webbing overhead. Her light slowly defined the contours of the dark shape bound inside it.

A strikingly human shape.

Sydney screamed.

The creature opened its eyes.

EVEN AFTER ALL THESE YEARS, Randall recognized those eyes. They were the same eyes he'd seen in the lab every day for two years. The same eyes he'd looked into when the lenses of the gas mask shattered. The same eyes that had stared accusingly at him while he covered them with a tarp.

Dr. James Thompson.

His body had withered beneath the dense tangles of mycelia binding him to the eroded stone, while thicker strands connected his head to the converging funnels, from which all of the webbing originated. Much like the ant that crawled up the stem of a plant and succumbed to the fungus' will, his physical form had become completely subsumed. Mature fruiting bodies resembling cattails stood from his chest, their bulbous swellings positively engorged with spores.

The converging creatures stopped as one, their silhouettes clinging to the surrounding darkness. Thompson bared his teeth and tried to move, but unlike the others, there wasn't enough left of his physical form to do so. A hissing sound seeped from his chest and coalesced into what almost sounded like words.

"Ihhh eee."

A tear fell from the corner of Randall's eye.

Kill me.

His old friend was still alive in there.

Thompson's chest burst, filling the air overhead with a swirling cloud of spores. The creatures sprinted toward their lights with the rapid clattering of exposed phalanges striking bare quartzite.

Randall tackled Sydney and Dayna into the crevice. They splashed into the chemicals and slid across the slick bottom—

The ground abruptly fell out from underneath them.

They plummeted into the darkness in a tangle of limbs, striking speleothems and outcroppings as they fell. Their beams reflected from the glistening stone walls and the standing chemicals rushing to meet them—

The impact with the surface knocked the wind out of Randall. He gasped for air as he tumbled through the murky fluid, unsure of even which way was up. The mount for his shoulder light broke, leaving the lens dangling by its cables, its flickering glow diffusing around him. The weight of one of the scientists drove him to the slippery bottom. He propelled himself upward and emerged from a pool that couldn't have been more than five feet deep.

Clicking sounds echoed from the eroded chute above him.

"Where's Sydney?" Dr. Raines shouted, bursting from the chemicals beside him.

A boot struck Randall squarely in the lower back. He caught Dr. Partridge's leg, turned her around, and hauled her upright. Her panicked sobs echoed in his helmet as he dragged her into the shallows and away from the rising sound of clattering bones. Terraced flowstone formations led straight up the face of a sheer cliff, over the crest of which a steady stream of toxins trickled. The surface glimmered as though coated with a layer of black ice.

"Start climbing," he said, boosting Dr. Partridge onto a ledge. "They're right behind us."

The dissolved minerals were even slicker than they looked, but the three of them were out of options. They climbed as fast as humanly possible, one slippery ledge after another. The sounds of pursuit grew louder by the second, eclipsing even the amplified sounds of their heavy breathing. By the time they reached the top, the clicking noises were practically right on top of them.

Randall crawled over the ledge and slid face-first into another pool. His strength was spent, his body rapidly failing him. He could barely raise his head high enough to see dry land, let alone drag himself to it. His broken light dangled against his chest, its glow limning the surrounding cavern and reflecting from the distant cable, its braided wires glimmering with the promise of salvation.

He switched to the long-range communications channel.

"Delta, respond." The sudden drain on his battery caused the light to dim. "I repeat, Delta—"

"What the hell's going on down there, Chief? I haven't heard—"

"Listen to me, dammit. We're coming in hot. The moment I give the order, you reel in that line as fast as it will go."

"Yes, sir."

Randall switched back to the open channel.

"Do you remember how to attach your harnesses?"

"Yes, but—" Dr. Raines started to say, but he cut her off.

"As soon as you've done so, I'll give the order to raise you to the surface."

"What about you?" Dr. Partridge asked.

"I need to finish what I started," he said, struggling to his feet.

Behind him, the first shadow materialized from the darkness.

28

2:06 p.m.

Oxygen Remaining: 0:47

Randall pressed an object into Dayna's palm.

"Wait as long as you possibly can," he said. "But make sure you do it before it's too late."

A stub antenna protruded from the top of the small box cradled in her palm. Three LED lights graced its face: two green and one red.

"Press the button on the side first, then flip open the trigger guard," Randall said.

"And then?"

"Hope to God you're clear of the blast when you press the button." He shoved her to get her moving. "Go!"

Dayna ran as fast as the cumbersome hazmat suit would allow. Every muscle in her body cried out from the high-pressure exertion, especially with the weight of the tank on her back, yet she pushed through it, her eyes fixed on the distant cable. It alternately appeared and disappeared in Sydney's light, which failed to illuminate much of anything beyond the chemical veins between the paving stone-like rocks. The seismic monitors and infrasonic arrays materialized from the peripheral glow, followed by the crates and equipment they'd left behind mere hours ago.

There had been nine of them when they'd set out in search of the fault zone, completely unprepared for the horrors that awaited them in the depths of the eroded earth, and now—

The ground trembled. Harder this time.

Dayna stumbled and fell, taking Sydney down with her. Panic rippled through her at the prospect of having torn her suit, but she couldn't afford to slow down for a single second. Not while those creatures were coming up fast behind them.

She risked a glance over her shoulder. Randall limped after them, the darkness behind him seemingly boiling with shadows. He waved for her to keep going as he fell farther and farther behind, the broken light hanging from his shoulder swinging like a lantern.

Sydney reached the harnesses first. Her hands shook so badly that she struggled to step into the straps and attach the series of metal clips and clamps to a loop of the coiled cable. Her eyes widened as she looked past Dayna.

"Hurry!"

Dayna slipped on the harness and cinched it tight. It took several tries to fasten it to the cable with one hand, but she refused to set down the detonator for even a single second. If the creatures reached her before she rose into the shaft . . .

Randall staggered after them. He fell, pushed himself to his feet, and managed a few unsteady steps before falling again. His eyes met Dayna's across the distance.

"Hold on tight," he said.

The coiled wire beside her suddenly started to unravel as the cable raced upward into the chute.

Sydney gasped as the creatures materialized in the glow of Randall's light. Desiccated beings covered with fungal growths, their bared teeth and recessed eyes the only remotely human things about them. Rabbits darted in and out of the shadows, their eyes flashing red—

With a jolt, the cable yanked Dayna off her feet. The harness bit into her thighs, and the whiplash nearly knocked her hood right off her head. She swung sideways, jerking wildly as the ground fell away below her. Her stomach sank into her gut as she started to rise even faster.

Sydney shrieked. Dayna could barely see her, maybe a dozen feet straight down, clinging to her clamp for dear life.

The cable rocketed straight up toward the eroded ceiling and the narrow orifice—

Dayna leaned forward and wrapped her arms and legs around the cable just as she passed through the stricture and the walls constricted around her.

———

RANDALL'S LEGS GAVE OUT. He managed a couple stumbling strides before collapsing with a resounding snap. Something had broken. Either his kneecaps or his femur. Maybe his hip. It didn't matter now. Nothing mattered beyond finally cleaning up the mess he'd made more than half a century ago.

Shadows converged upon him with the clicking of bare bones and claws striking quartzite. They moved like liquid through the darkness. On the ground. The walls. Even the domed roof high overhead, their sharp digits latching onto imperfections and crevices in the stone.

Clutching his thigh, he rolled over and watched Dr. Partridge rise into the shaft. The last of the adrenaline that had sustained his aging body fled him as the end of the cable unraveled and rocketed skyward.

For the first time, he truly felt the weight of his years.

Randall turned to face the consequences of his failure. His heart sank at the sight of the ruby reflections of rabbits' eyes and the desiccated forms of the men he'd left for dead as they converged. Their lipless, bared teeth . . . their shrunken, jaundiced eyes . . . the fungal growths proliferating wildly from their seemingly mummified skin.

He had to wait until they were right on top of him. There could be no doubt that he was taking every last one of them with him. He needed to see the end with his own eyes.

Even if it was the last thing he saw.

"Come on . . . " he whispered, clutching his broken light in his fist. One sharp tug and—

The creatures approaching on the ground abruptly stopped, while those scuttling across the ceiling kept going.

Something was wrong.

"What are you waiting for?" he shouted.

Several silhouettes slowly separated from the darkness beyond the light's glow, drawing contrast as they neared.

Randall's heart sank as the closest stepped into the light . . . white protective suit, distended by chemicals . . . a fringe of broken polycarbonate glass, framing the gaping hole in the helmet where the visor had once been. The face inside was suppurated and raw, the skin stitched together with faint mycelial sutures, and the eyes . . .

Dear Lord, its eyes . . .

"The resurrection response," he whispered.

The creature that had once been Beta merely bared its teeth in response.

Others staggered into the glow behind him, as though having only recently learned to walk. Bloodstained hazmat suits . . . ruined faces . . . hideous rictus grins . . .

Randall took one final deep breath . . .

And yanked — hard — on the broken light.

Complete and utter darkness descended with the clattering of bones.

Randall cast aside the lens and fumbled with the severed power cable. He pinched a wire in each gloved hand. Pulled them apart to separate them. Touched one frayed end to the other—

A spark of light revealed the withered, infected scientists. Heads thrown back. Arms extended. Spores erupting from the overgrowth on their chests—

With a roar, the chemical fumes ignited. The air turned to fire, burning hot and fast. Through his cracking visor, Randall caught a glimpse of the figures around him going up in flames, the drenched forms of the men he'd led to their deaths becoming torches, and blazing shapes streaking across the ceiling toward the shaft.

His visor shattered, and his screams echoed deeper into the earth.

RANDALL'S CRIES exploded from the speaker beside Dayna's ear, with Sydney's hot on their heels. Fire funneled straight up the well. A fist of heat closed around her, squeezing the sweat from her skin and charring the visor of her hazmat suit. A scream burst from her lips as she glanced down the burning shaft, where Sydney was little more than a silhouette at the heart of the flames.

The burning sensation abruptly ceased as the fireball streaked up toward the surface, leaving their suits and the surrounding walls blackened.

Randall fell silent, leaving an oppressive silence marred by Sydney's gentle crying. Dayna closed her eyes and let her tears drain down her cheeks. Randall had sacrificed himself to buy them time to escape. Surely the creatures couldn't have survived—

Sydney screamed.

Dayna opened her eyes and found herself looking straight down at a flaming rabbit scurrying up the eroded stone. Sydney's cries rose an octave as she kicked at the creature, connecting over and over until—

A crimson cloud exploded from the rabbit and swirled around Sydney's flailing legs. She shielded her face in a desperate attempt to protect her visor from the spores, which rose up to her waist, clinging to her suit.

The entire Earth shuddered.

An earthquake, maybe 2.5 on the Richter scale.

Dayna clung to the cable as it flung her from side to side, bludgeoning her against the walls. She bit her tongue, nipping off a scream. Rubble crumbled from the walls and rained down the well, striking her head and shoulders. Stars flashed before her eyes, and she tasted blood in the back of her throat. She struggled to remain conscious while she watched Sydney, thrashing helplessly below her. There was nothing she could do for the medical mycologist. Not without disengaging her clamp and sliding down—

A stone struck her shoulder, sending shooting pain all the way into her fingertips. Its weight burrowed into her flesh, a jagged edge digging into the point where bone met bone, eliciting a stabbing sensation with every jostle of the cable.

Sydney's screams grew frantic. The rabbit moved through the dense cloud, little more than a vague skeletal shape. It hopped from the wall to her legs and scurried higher—

Dayna groaned as she dragged the rock off her shoulder and cradled it to her chest. She waited for the cable to swing her over the rabbit . . . and let it go.

The stone plummeted past her legs and struck the rabbit squarely in the head, sending it careening into the depths.

Several seconds passed before a clattering sound echoed from the darkness.

"Are you okay?" Dayna asked.

"I think so. I mean . . . I can feel the fabric tightening on my legs, but I don't think any spores got on my visor."

She looked up at Dayna, tears of relief in her eyes.

The dissipating spores billowed below her. A dark shape emerged, scuttling up the wall in halting, jerky movements. Thick ebon smoke rose from the dwindling flames on its head and shoulders. Its skin was blackened and burned, its bared teeth thick with soot, its milky eyes ruptured. Patches of wiry fungal growth clung to its chest, its throat, and the underside of its chin, as though it had flattened itself to the wall as the fireball rocketed skyward.

Sydney must have recognized the panic on Dayna's face. She looked down just as the creature grabbed her legs and scurried up her back. Kicking and screaming, she tried to shake the monstrosity, but its skeletal fingertips latched onto her suit, embedding themselves in the material. It tore off her belt, sending the light careening down the shaft.

"Help me!" Sydney screamed, her eyes meeting Dayna's. "Don't let me die down here."

The creature leaned back, exposing the bristling red protrusions running from its groin all the way up to its mandible.

"No!" Dayna screamed, but there was nothing she could do to stop it.

Spores ruptured from seemingly every branchlike fruiting body at once, filling the entire width of the shaft. Sydney momentarily vanished into the scarlet smoke. When she reemerged, her face was concealed by the accumulation of spores on her visor. She sobbed and begged for her life as she tried to scrape them off—

Sydney's visor shattered. Her eyes widened in alarm. The skin on her exposed forehead and cheeks reddened and blistered. The vessels in her eyes ruptured and her irises clouded. Seizures wracked her form. Her screams rose to a trilling crescendo, then slowly faded to a soft gurgle.

A delicate hiss of escaping air trickled from Dayna's speaker.

And then there was no sound at all.

29

2:25 p.m.

Oxygen Remaining: 0:28

Dayna hung her head as she ascended, the biofilm-coated walls blurring past in her teary vision. The silence was a physical entity, smothering, suffocating. Her belt light flickered, then died. She gasped at the sudden darkness, from deep inside of which she heard Thunder's dying scream.

Panic set in. She rocked back and looked up. There was no light. No way out. Only thousands of feet of utter blackness. The same blackness she'd experienced beneath the ground so many years ago . . . the same blackness that would be waiting for her at the moment of her—

A dim glow burst from her light. It flickered and dimmed, but it remained on. Heart hammering, she shouted into the microphone, hoping to God she was finally within range of the surface. Her voice echoed from the speaker inside Sydney's ruined hood.

Dayna glanced at the woman's lifeless body. Blood dribbled down her hazmat suit, the crimson fluid drawing lines through the lingering soot. It traced the contours of her shoulder and trickled onto the creature's hand, which clutched her suit in a death grip, its skeletal fingertips—

Twitched.

Dayna cried out.

The index finger had moved. She was certain of it.

Her light flickered again. She screamed in surprise, her voice echoing in the brief interlude of darkness.

The creature's fist tightened, creating new folds in the fabric. Was rigor mortis setting in? Were the fungi's final chemical signals passing through the dead being's nervous system?

Randall had made the ultimate sacrifice so she could detonate the explosives and ensure the organism never reached the outside world. He'd known what would happen if it did, yet here she was, towing it right up to the surface with her, and there was nothing she could do about it. No way to cut the cable or—

Dayna's light flickered and went dark.

"No, no, no," she whispered, slapping the lens over and over. "Please, God—"

The light came on once more, its dim glow stretching down the well. Sydney's body hung suspended at the outermost reaches of the illumination, while the creature—

Had it moved? Its hand was in a different place. Higher on Sydney's chest, closer to her hood.

Dayna watched for any hint of movement, any sign that the horrific burned thing was somehow still—

Her light brightened, dimmed, then abruptly died.

The darkness coiled around her, constricting tighter and tighter until she couldn't breathe. She gave in to the panic. Repeatedly slapping the light. Banging her knees against the walls. Striking her toes and heels, her oxygen tank rebounding from the stone with hollow clanging sounds that reminded her of just how little air remained.

Her beam snapped on again.

She sobbed in relief and once more glanced down—

The creature had crawled over Sydney's body and now clung to the cable with both gnarled hands, staring up at her through ruined eyes. It slowly opened his mouth, revealing the tendril-like fungal growths protruding from the back of its throat.

Dayna screamed and looked up. She was still too far away from the surface to see so much as a hint of daylight.

Below her, the creature started to climb, its exposed bones and tendons clicking on the braided wire.

Her light flickered and died, only this time, no matter how many times or how hard she struck the lens, it remained dead.

DAYNA COULDN'T EVEN DRAW enough breath to scream. It was so dark that she couldn't see the walls passing mere inches in front of her face. The only sound was the clicking and scratching of bones on metal. Coming up fast. If she allowed the creature to reach her . . .

to get close enough to shatter her visor with its spores . . .
then she would die like all of the others. Skin blistering,
blood vessels rupturing, body contorting. There'd be no
one left to detonate the explosives before the impending
earthquake killed millions of innocent people. And worse,
there'd be nothing to stop the fungal organism from
reaching the outside world. With the entire city reeling
from the natural disaster, it would spread like wildfire.

Clack-clack-clack-clack!

Dayna clutched the detonator so tightly that she feared
it might break.

She didn't want to die. Not down here. Not like this.
But if she didn't flip the switch now, then she might not be
able to do it at all.

Tears streaming down her cheeks, she pressed the
button on the side of the box. A tiny green light blossomed
from her hand.

Clack-clack-clack-clack!

A thought struck her so hard that she sobbed out
loud. What if the explosion failed to seal the deep injection
well? Would the cable drag the creature's body all the way
to the surface? Or if the shaft did collapse, would it be
possible to recover its remains? Could the spores still
somehow find a way out on their own? The fungus Sydney
had originally scraped from the inner wall had been barely
a hundred feet down. What if it was already—?

The incubator.

There were samples flourishing on the media in Sydney's
sterile chamber. Nobody up there had any idea what it was
capable of doing. If anyone opened it, they'd unleash hell

upon an unsuspecting world. And heaven forbid the "very powerful people" Cassie had warned her about got their hands on a weapon beyond their ability to control.

She couldn't die down here or there would be no one left to destroy it.

Clack-clack-clack-clack!

The creature was right below her. So close she could feel the vibrations traveling through the steel. She kicked blindly, but her feet connected with only open air.

A bony hand caught her boot. She felt the sharp fingertips, even through the thick rubber, and screamed.

The clicking ceased as the monster caught her suit with its other hand and transferred its full weight to her leg.

If it climbed any higher . . .

Dayna flipped open the trigger guard and the second green light blossomed, revealing the cadaverous, charred beast clinging to her suit. It reared back and opened its jaws, wiry tendrils protruding from between its blackened teeth.

She couldn't allow it to release its spores before she pressed the trigger, nor could she risk its infected body finding its way topside. Either way, this was where she would die. Down here in the darkness, her worst nightmare come true.

An equine scream rose from her subconscious.

A roaring sound eclipsed it. The entire shaft shook, slamming her against the walls.

Another earthquake. Stronger this time. 3.0, maybe 3.1.

The creature clutched the material even tighter as it crawled up her legs.

Stones rained down on Dayna, striking her head and shoulders, clanging from her oxygen tank.

It was now or never.

She slid her thumb onto the button and—

"Wait," she whispered.

Maybe there was still a way . . .

With her free hand, she fumbled with the cable latch until she found the handbrake. She met the creature's dead stare in the wan green glow, secured her grip on the detonator, and squeezed the release.

Dayna plummeted straight down into the darkness, clinging to the clamp in one hand and the detonator in the other. The creature scrabbled at her legs in a desperate attempt to secure purchase. Its decaying fingers raked her thighs through the thick Tyvek—

She struck Sydney's body going faster than anticipated, but, as she'd hoped, it arrested her fall. The force of the impact dislodged the creature. It fell several feet farther before grabbing onto Sydney's isolation suit, buying Dayna just enough time to reattach her clamp to the cable and engage the brake.

She kicked at Sydney's clamp, over and over, as the creature scurried up the dead woman's back. With a scream, Dayna kicked one last time, as hard as she possibly could. The creature lunged—

Sydney's brake released.

Time seemed to stand still as the medical mycologist fell, her ragdoll form rebounding from the unforgiving walls. Spores burst from the creature's mouth. Its fingers grazed Dayna's boot as it vanished into the swirling red cloud.

And then it was gone.

DAYNA ASCENDED in complete and utter silence. She'd listened for the sound of bodies hitting the ground thousands of feet down until long after they should have impacted. On a rational level, she knew the cavern was too far away for any noise to reach her, but considering there was nothing remotely rational about this situation, she half expected to hear the clamor of skeletal fingertips striking stone as the creature scuttled back up the shaft.

She'd released the side button on the detonator to make sure the lights didn't drain its battery, but she kept her thumb right beside it, just in case she needed to trigger the device in a hurry. There hadn't been any seismic activity since the last tremor, but that didn't mean a cataclysmic earthquake couldn't strike at any moment. Right now, she was weighing her own life against those of the three million people overhead, hoping to God she reached the surface before she was forced to detonate the explosives, knowing full well that by doing so she could be damning them all, but if Sydney's incubator fell into the wrong hands . . .

She continually whispered into her comm link, praying to finally be within range of the surface, yet not even static replied.

The atmospheric pressure slowly lessened with every rapid vertical foot of ascension, although somehow her chest felt heavier, even as her head grew lighter. It wasn't until her vision started sparkling that she realized what was happening.

She was running out of air.

The thought sent lightning bolts of terror shooting through her entire body. Her worst fear was about to be realized. The darkness. The inability to breathe. The slow suffocation, all the while fully cognizant of everything that was happening to her. It was the same nightmare from which she awakened in a cold sweat every night, only the screams reverberating from the darkness weren't those of her long-dead horse.

They were hers.

Dayna needed to calm down. Slow her respirations. She was burning through what little oxygen remained far too quickly.

The flow of cool air from her regulator slowed to a trickle, then ceased altogether.

She forced down the panic and looked straight up the well. Was it a little lighter above her, or was it just her imagination? How long had she been rising? She was definitely climbing faster than she'd descended. It had taken a full hour to reach the bottom, so it wouldn't take nearly that long to make the return trip, but she didn't have the slightest idea how long it had been since she'd abandoned Randall to his fate.

The darkness became watery, as though she were swimming in tar. The sparkles became firecrackers. Her chest hitched with every desperate inhalation. It was only a matter of time before she lost consciousness. When that happened, the detonator would fall from her grasp and

Delta would be left to reel her lifeless body back into the sunlight, assuming an earthquake didn't turn the entire area into a giant crater first.

Dayna couldn't let that happen.

Her breathing grew ragged. It felt like she was trying to suck air through a wet blanket. She tried to dislodge her respirator from her mouth and nose, to glean what little oxygen remained trapped inside her suit, but she couldn't manipulate it through the hood. Her lungs felt compressed, as though only the tiniest portion still inflated, and even then with warm air that she'd already breathed before.

"Help," she gasped, but there was no response.

She had to trigger the explosives before she blacked out, or all was lost. She could only pray that whoever found the incubator destroyed the fungi inside. Maybe there was still hope. If she was in communications range and anyone up there could hear her . . .

"Kill . . . it . . . " she rasped, draining the last of the air from her lungs. "Don't . . . let . . . "

Reddish blebs expanded against the darkness.

This was the end.

Dayna pressed the side button on the detonator, then opened the trigger guard. Twin green lights faded in and out of her vision. She slid her thumb onto the button and pressed down. A red light blossomed, followed by a resounding thud. The entire Earth shook. A golden light materialized beneath her feet and a wall of superheated air raced up the collapsing well. Flames swallowed her and launched her straight up toward the surface—

Darkness.

30

2:52 p.m.

High-pitched ringing summoned Dayna from unconsciousness. Pain followed. Sharp, unrelenting. Her chest shuddered and a sob rose to her lips, which only amplified the agony.

A voice called to her from someplace far away, its words tinny, like a mosquito's whine.

Darkness.

She was only vaguely aware of the fists gripping the fabric on her shoulders, the coarse ground raking her back. Her eyes parted, but she saw only a dark silhouette through the churning smoke. Blood trickled down the back of her throat. The pressure in her chest . . . like a stone, crushing her. She clung to the realization that she was still alive—

Darkness.

A man's voice, too loud in her ears. His arms, tight

around her chest. Fluid, pattering her suit and visor. A sliver of light, a glimpse of inflatable walls and high-pressure nozzles. Her body, convulsing as it frantically tried to draw air—

Darkness.

Bouncing. The fleeting impression of someone carrying her. The roiling sky passing overhead, followed by a door frame, an interior ceiling. Blunt impact to her back and the base of her skull. A ghostly white shape leaning over her, slipping in and out of the growing darkness. Shouting, from a million miles away.

" . . . with me, dammit! Stay . . . "

Darkness.

Air rushed into her lungs. Cold and sharp. Breaking the seal in her chest, bringing with it pain beyond anything she'd ever experienced. Her chest heaved with every desperate gasp. The darkness gave way to swirling colors, and finally to the form of a man in a spacesuit. Leaning over her. He collapsed to his haunches and removed his helmet, revealing a sweat-beaded face that she didn't immediately recognize. His words floated around her, as though trying to take solid form.

" . . . happened to the others? . . . any of them survive?"

Tears streamed from Dayna's eyes as the reality of the situation came crashing down on her. She was surrounded by scientific equipment, racks overflowing with supplies, empty stalls where hazmat suits had once hung. The Mobile Emergency Response Support Vehicle. She was inside the FEMA command center.

More and more people crowded around her, asking

questions she couldn't answer, using words she couldn't understand.

She rolled over and cried out. Every bruise . . . every broken bone . . . announcing itself with fiery torment. Pain cut through the confusion of thoughts, binding her to the moment.

Her hood lay beside her amid the comm link's cables. Her respirator dangled from the collar of her hazmat suit, which had been cut off and cast aside. There was an acute ache in the center of her chest. Had the man — Delta . . . his name was Delta — given her compressions?

She tried to stand. Collapsed. Struggled to all fours and waited for the dizziness to abate. Found her feet and staggered to the window, but she couldn't see anything at all through the smoke.

"Did it . . . ?" she croaked. It felt like her words had been dipped in acid. She swallowed and tried again. "Did it work?"

"You need to lie down," Delta said. "There's nothing you—"

Dayna brushed past him and grabbed a fresh hazmat suit from the hanger in one of the stalls. Memories of everything she'd endured, everything she'd survived, cascaded over her. The creatures. The spores. All of the suffering and death. It couldn't be for nothing. She needed to be sure . . .

"Help me," she sobbed. "Please."

Delta nodded and assisted her with the cumbersome suit.

THE AIR WAS SO thick with dust and smoke that she couldn't see more than a few feet in any direction. Entire sections of the road and the surrounding fields had collapsed, creating veritable canyons where once there'd been vast stretches of weathered asphalt and barren prairie. The FEMA Rapid Response Team had been lucky they'd parked their command center where they had, as it couldn't have been more than five feet from the abrupt ledge where the earth had swallowed everything in front of it, including a police cruiser, whose lights flashed impotently thirty feet down, diffusing into the pall.

Men in yellow hazmat suits appeared like specters from the haze, stirring the dust with their waving wands, only to disappear into it once more. The levels of airborne toxins had risen exponentially. Fortunately, they'd evacuated the surrounding neighborhoods while she was underground, although it remained to be seen just how far the contamination had spread. No one could tell her the extent of the damage or even wager a guess as to the number of casualties. There was simply too much chaos and too little information available. She continually glanced to the south, hoping for a glimpse of the downtown skyline, but she couldn't even see the running lights of the helicopters circling seemingly right above her head.

Her seismic and infrasonic arrays had registered a magnitude 5.9 event on the Richter scale before going offline, which should have been enough to collapse the entire downtown area if Telford's calculations had been wrong. Or maybe even if they hadn't. It came down to whether or not he'd successfully directed the propagation of seismic waves from the explosion through the surrounding strata and away from the population centers. All she could do was listen to the distant wail of sirens and pray.

Where once an eight-foot-wide pit had marked the outlet of the deep injection well, a veritable crater now extended well beyond her range of sight to the east. Chemicals expelled from the depths still burned on upthrust slabs of granite and schist. The cable real handler stood from the rubble at a forty-five-degree angle, its entire rear half swallowed by the collapsing ground, which had taken all of the equipment they'd left on the surface with it.

Dayna pulled Delta close and looked him directly in the eyes when she spoke.

"There's an incubation box somewhere in this mess. I need your help finding it. We have to destroy it before anyone else knows it's here."

"What's in it?" Delta asked.

"The reason Randall gave his life to make sure I got out alive."

Delta's eyes hardened. He offered a single nod and picked his way down the rugged slope, his shoulder light sweeping through the haze.

Dayna desperately tried to remember where Sydney's gear had been before they descended, although nothing looked remotely like it had mere hours ago. It had been maybe twenty-five feet to the southwest of the well, where she'd set it up on a folding table next to her microbial identification system, underneath a popup—

"Over there," she said, pointing at a tatter of neon green fabric waving on the breeze.

She scrambled downhill and started rolling aside rocks. Delta joined her, and together they moved enough rubble to reveal the remains of the popup canopy tent. Sydney's equipment lay broken beneath it. Either the continued expulsion of spores or the violent burial had shattered the leaded acrylic observation window, scattering its contents everywhere. While the vast majority of the specimens appeared to have been incinerated when the fireball ignited the fumes in the air and the chemicals from which they grew, a mycelial fuzz had already taken root on the surrounding rocks. A handful of tendril-like fruiting bodies protruded from the crevices. If she didn't destroy them before they released their spores—

"Dr. Raines!" a woman called, her voice erupting from Dayna's speaker. She glanced up toward the rim, where several figures in hazmat suits materialized from the dust. "My name is Lieutenant Colonel Tanja Malikov. I'm the Medical Element Commander of the Colorado Chemical Biological Rapid Response Team. I need a few minutes of your time."

Dayna looked at Delta, her eyes wide with panic.

"Go," he said. "I've got everything under control here."

She couldn't tear her eyes away from his. If he didn't immediately destroy the organism, or if it somehow fell into the wrong hands . . .

He nodded solemnly. His entire team had died down there. His *brother* had died down there. She had to trust that he understood what was at stake.

Dayna turned her back on Delta and crawled up the slope toward the waiting phalanx of emergency military personnel. She was nearly to the top when she heard a pilot light ignite and felt the heat of flames on her back.

Voices burst from her speaker as Malikov and her men shouted for Delta to extinguish his flamethrower before he burned down the entire state.

Dayna just kept walking toward the command trailer, a faint smile settling upon her lips.

———

MALIKOV'S DEBRIEFING had lasted somewhere between an eternity and forever. Dayna hadn't been prepared for such an intense interrogation, but she'd answered every question honestly. Or at least as honestly as she could. The truth was she couldn't even think about what had happened down there without starting to go into shock. She didn't know how she'd ever come to grips with the horrific deaths of eight people, let alone rationalize any of the seemingly impossible things she'd seen. How was she supposed to explain decomposing rabbits animated by some sort of fungal hive mind or human beings preserved in a state of suspended animation while a chimeric organism slowly consumed them and spread its brainlike mycelial network throughout the caverns?

For now, it was enough that the Medical Element Commander of the Colorado Chemical Biological Rapid Response Team believed the accelerating seismic activity had forced the premature detonation of the explosives and Dayna had been lucky to survive, a fact memorialized by closed-circuit footage capturing a churning flume of fire hurling her limp form fifty feet into the air. Let them assume the others' bodies had either been incinerated or plummeted into the depths, where all evidence to the contrary was buried beneath two vertical miles of compressed earth. More importantly, let the families of the deceased believe they'd died quickly and mercifully.

Delta had been long gone by the time she emerged from the command trailer, leaving fiery destruction in his wake. Surely nothing could have survived the towering flames she'd seen through the window during her interrogation, but with the rubble still burning, she couldn't get close enough to confirm it with her own eyes. She recalled Telford's story about the Pennsylvania coal mine that had been burning for sixty years and wondered how long hundreds of millions of gallons of volatile chemicals would fuel this blaze. Not that she cared. As long as she knew that nothing in those caverns could have possibly survived, she would be able to sleep at night.

Just not for a while.

She had a feeling it wouldn't be Thunder's screams awakening her at night anymore. Even now, she could still hear Sydney's final whimper, Randall's dying shout, and the clatter of exposed bones striking stone. And it would be a long time before they faded from memory.

Assuming they ever did.

31

Rocky Mountain Metropolitan Airport
8:00 a.m.

One Day Later...

Delta entered the remote hangar through the service tunnel, as instructed. Despite wearing his tactical isolation suit, he didn't feel protected in the slightest. Not with the airtight canister stowed in the side compartment of his PLiSS. He might not have witnessed in person what the organism contained within it was capable of doing, but the men it had killed at the bottom of that well hadn't been slackers by any stretch of the imagination. Especially his big brother, with whose death he had yet to come to grips, and likely never would.

The men waiting for him outside the open door of the C-21 Learjet wore gear just like his. Even the elderly man, leaning heavily on his cane, who needed no introduction.

James Lowell's illustrious career had run the gamut from senator to secretary of defense, and everything in between, yet Delta knew him from his role in the creation and oversight of the U.S. Army CBRNE Enhanced Response Force.

Lowell dismissed his entourage with a subtle wave and gingerly made his way toward Delta with an echoing *tap... tap... tap*. His voice emerged from the speaker by Delta's ear.

"Did you retrieve the specimen?"

Delta merely nodded. As ordered, he'd collected a sample of the crimson biofilm from the rubble, flash frozen it in liquid nitrogen, and preserved it within the vacuum chamber of the stainless-steel container.

"What will you do with it?" he asked.

"The same thing we've done with all of the others," Lowell said. "Figure out every possible way of neutralizing it."

Delta hesitated only briefly before removing the canister from his PLiSS and handing it to Lowell.

"You should be especially careful with this one."

"We're especially careful with *all of them*."

Delta glanced past Lowell as the pilot started the engine of the sleek military passenger jet. The old man's retinue flanked the lowered stairs, waiting patiently for him to conclude his business.

"So what happens now?" Delta asked.

"Have you considered my offer?"

"Do I have a choice?"

Lowell's eyes softened. He understood the gravity of what he was asking.

"Of course you have a choice."

"Even after everything I've seen?" Delta asked.

"Especially after everything you've seen."

"So how does this work?"

"You take time to grieve," Lowell said. "And when you're ready, there will be a stack of personnel jackets and incident files waiting on your desk. After that, it's up to you."

Delta watched the hangar door slowly rise, admitting a cloud of dust that would take days to settle. The old man might have offered him the illusion of choice, but when it came right down to it, there really wasn't much of one at all. Without men like him and those whose bodies were buried two miles down, there would be no one standing between the monsters intent on destroying the world and the unsuspecting public, who didn't have the slightest clue about the perils they faced on a daily basis.

Delta offered a single nod.

Lowell clapped him on the shoulder and struck off toward the plane. He stopped on the top step and looked back at Delta.

"Take all the time you need . . . Chief."

And with that, he vanished into the interior. His men followed and closed the door behind him. The twin turbofan engines ramped up with a high-pitched whine as the plane taxied onto the runway, leaving the new Commander of CERF watching its navigation lights vanish into the settling dust and wondering what in the name of God he'd just done.

Denver International Airport
9:25 a.m.

DAYNA PRESSED her forehead against the window as the charter plane rose sharply into the air. She tried not to think about being summoned to appear in a closed-door hearing before a national emergency response panel chaired by a former senator and secretary of defense named James Lowell, Director of the U.S. Army's CBRNE Enhanced Response Force and Randall's immediate superior, when she landed in D.C. and merely watched Denver International Airport fall away below her. Emergency vehicles and news vans flooded the parking lots and crowded the runways of the concourse farthest from the terminal. Long lines of bumper-to-bumper traffic extended in both directions, all the way to the point where Peña Road abruptly terminated in a newly formed chasm.

While the dust hadn't cleared, it had thinned enough to see the damage she'd caused. The plains to the west of the airport had become a shallow canyon, one roughly the same depth and shape as the collapsed cavern system far below, with side ravines branching in seemingly every direction. An entire fleet of FEMA Mobile Emergency Response Support Vehicles had descended upon the rim, disgorging a veritable army of hazmat-clad scientists into the rubble in hopes of containing the aerial spread of chemicals and toxic fumes vented from the depths by the explosion.

Helicopters circled downtown, their winking red and green lights diffusing into the pall, through which she marveled at the skyscrapers still standing. Ambulances and fire trucks sped through the surrounding neighborhoods, entire swaths of which had collapsed. Ruptured water mains sprayed into the air. Sunken foundations cradled the ruins of wood-framed homes. The rooftops of vehicles glinted from sinkholes in residential streets. National Guardsmen and Search and Rescue personnel combed through the wreckage, collecting the dead and evacuating the injured to hastily erected emergency shelters throughout the city.

None of the nearby seismic monitoring stations had detected so much as a single tremor since the explosion, and while authorities were still adding to the growing number of casualties, the total so far was only in the thirties. Property damage, however, would likely be in the tens of billions. The detonation had produced seismic waves strong enough to level suburbs like Northfield and Montbello, whose names would be immortalized during the coming news cycles, but they'd left Park Hill and the entirety of Denver proper standing. Granted, it would take months to repair the damage to I-70, bringing commercial shipping to a grinding halt, and maybe even longer to recapture the zoo animals that had escaped from their fallen enclosures, but life would eventually return to normal, which seemed a fitting tribute to the brave men and women who'd lost their lives at the bottom of the deep injection well. Millions of people, who would never know how close they came to dying, were still alive because of them.

She was still alive.

Maybe she would never fully vanquish the demons that had plagued her since her parents' deaths, but she had accomplished what she'd originally set out to do. Manmade earthquakes would never catch anyone by surprise again. Her predictive algorithm had proven its efficacy in the field, and under the most difficult of conditions. In the process, however, she'd discovered that mankind was capable of far worse crimes against nature. She'd seen the horrors that sprung from the twisted minds of deranged men, horrors capable of inflicting far worse damage than any number of earthquakes. Someone needed to make sure that nothing like what she'd seen down there ever happened again.

As the only survivor, it fell to her.

Whether she liked it or not.

So bring on Lowell and his national emergency response panel. If they wanted to know what *really* happened down there, then by God she would tell them. It was high time that someone stood up to these "very powerful people" and put an end to this kind of biological experimentation. Let them hold her up to ridicule or make her their scapegoat for the disaster. Let the military try to recover the ashes of the bioweapon she'd incinerated and buried two miles down. None of that mattered now.

She was going to do what was right.

Regardless of the consequences.

Federal Emergency Management Agency Headquarters
Washington, D.C.
4:05 p.m.

LOWELL STUDIED Dr. Raines from his chair at the head of the conference table. American and FEMA flags stood to either side of him, while the agency's logo and mission statement adorned the wall at his back. The seismologist, sitting a dozen feet away at the foot, visibly dismissed the handful of stuffed suits and empty chairs along both sides and stared directly at him. Her defiant expression told him that she knew about the experimentation at the RMA all those years ago and understood exactly what she'd seen at the bottom of the well. Even better, she was prepared to go to war over it.

He smiled, laced his arthritic fingers on the tabletop, and leaned closer to his microphone.

"Thank you for coming, Dr. Raines. My name is James Lowell and I'm—"

"I know exactly who you are," she said. Her eyes narrowed and her lips tightened across her teeth. "You knew what was down there, didn't you? Before you even contacted the USGS. You knew what was down there and you sent us anyway."

Lowell arched an eyebrow, leaned back in his seat, and waited for her to proceed. Her unflinching stare locked onto his.

"Eight people died down there. In the worst possible ways. Forty-three more lost their lives because of the explosion that *we* caused. Had Tim's calculations been off, we'd be mourning millions more. And for what? So that you and the military could get your hands on what was down there? Even Randall knew that if you did—"

Lowell held up his hand to silence her. He nodded first to the men on his left, then to the men on his right. All five collected their briefcases, straightened their jackets, and, without a word, filed out of the room. As soon as he and Dr. Raines were alone, he switched off the recording and rose from his chair. Her eyes never left his as he hobbled around the table with a *tap . . . tap . . . tap* of his cane and took the seat next to hers.

"I first met General Randall at a hearing not unlike this one," he said, sighing and loosening his tie. "Of course, he wasn't nearly as forthcoming — or confrontational — as you, Dr. Raines. He'd suffered through countless painful surgeries and months of grueling physical rehabilitation, just so he could fall on his sword in front of one useless subcommittee after another. But I had his number from the get-go. I knew what he'd done. More importantly, I knew *why*. So, to make a long story short, we put our heads together and we've been working together, for a common cause, ever since. And while he could be a prickly bastard, he was also my friend." A nostalgic smile settled on his face, but it vanished as quickly as it appeared. "Tell me how he *really* died. I need to know."

Dr. Raines stared at him for a long moment, as though gauging his sincerity. When she finally spoke, it was in a voice barely above a whisper.

"He ignited the fumes to buy Sydney and me time to escape."

"Fire?" It was all Lowell could do to keep from

laughing and crying at the same time. "You have to admire his commitment, if not his creativity."

A faint smile traced Dr. Raines's lips.

"You remind me of him, you know," Lowell said. "He was little more than a kid when we met, yet even then he'd understood that there were some boxes that should never be opened. He'd been willing to throw away his career — heck, his very life — for the greater good." He leaned forward and looked Dr. Raines dead in the eyes. "Correct me if I'm wrong, but I have a hunch you're willing to do the same."

EPILOGUE

Alexandria, Virginia

Tap . . . tap . . . tap.

Dayna followed Lowell from the guard station into a white-paneled hallway, her head on a swivel. From the outside, the former canning factory had looked abandoned, at least until she'd noticed the security fencing and cameras, while the inside reminded her of a business suite. Framed pictures of uniformed men and women with flat eyes and serious faces adorned the walls. Tiny golden placards identified them by both their real and code names. It wasn't until she reached the end of the hallway and recognized the men who'd died at the bottom of the well that she realized this was a memorial to the officers lost in the field.

Lowell stopped before a vault door and looked directly at a digital screen, upon which his face appeared next to a scan of both irises. With a thud of disengaging electromagnetic locks and a hydraulic hiss, the two-foot-thick slab of reinforced metal receded into the wall, admitting them into a passthrough chamber with security cameras mounted above chemical, biological, and radiological contaminant detectors and another digital scanner. The old man placed his palm flat against it and spoke his name aloud. A detailed map of the blood vessels in his hand appeared beside a spectrogram of his voice. The outer door slowly closed, the inner door opened, and the metronomic tapping of Lowell's cane resumed.

Tap . . . tap . . . tap.

Dayna experienced a sensation of dislocation, as though she'd stepped through an invisible veil separating the world she knew from one beyond her ability to comprehend. She noticed Lowell covertly studying her from the corner of his eye and tried to mask the expression of utter disbelief on her face.

"It's a lot to take in at once," Lowell said. "I'd love to say you'll get used to it, but no one ever does."

Climate-controlled cases metered the vast space. The artifacts preserved inside were unlike any she'd ever seen before. Animalian and humanoid skulls — plus seemingly random combinations of the two — with deformities ranging from elongated and flattened craniums to obscenely long tusks and fangs. Skeletal appendages with too many and too few digits, claws and barbed knuckles, paws and hooves. Mutated insects with pincers and wings and stingers where there should have been none. Desiccated plant species that nature alone could never have spawned.

"Even after all these years, these things scare the living

hell out of me," he said. "I can't walk through here without remembering every detail of the field operations responsible for their collection, or the men we lost in the process. I think that's part of the reason I've kept going for as long as I have, but even I can't do this forever."

Dayna opened her mouth to speak, but no sound came out. Even after everything she'd endured, and despite Lowell's best efforts to prepare her, she couldn't seem to wrap her brain around what she was seeing.

"I went to D.C. as a wide-eyed kid convinced I could fix the system, but I quickly learned that man is a creature of entropy. All he does is break things. There's only picking up the pieces and trying to put them back together again. Thanks to some powerful, likeminded men within the system, that's what Randall and I did here. And what I hope you and the new commander will continue to do when I'm gone. I hesitate to think what will happen if you don't."

He led her from the museum-like space into a long rectangular room illuminated by blacklights. Bubbling fluid chambers preserved terrifying hybridized species that should never have been able to exist, most of which looked like they'd merely fallen asleep, while glass freezer units, frosted with ice, displayed stainless-steel containers housing Lord only knew what kinds of nightmares. Doors on either side gave way to sterile corridors where coiled oxygen tubes dangled from the ceiling and isolation suits hung from the walls.

Tap . . . tap . . . tap.

The final room appeared to be a command center of sorts. Video screens displaying various maps, satellite imagery, photographs, and documents dominated the walls. Various workstations had been set up around the room, several of which appeared to have been recently cleared of personal belongings. Lowell stopped before the nearest and awakened the screen. A long list of coded file-names appeared, each and every one of them labeled *ACTIVE*.

"These files contain flagged information from covert research operations around the world. And just like the creatures preserved out there, every single one of them has a story to tell. Our job is to determine if the experimentation poses an imminent threat and, if it does, how best to eliminate it, yet no matter how many files we clear, they just keep on coming. Faster and faster with every passing year. It's thankless, demoralizing work, and once you start down this road, there's no turning back. Are you sure that's what you want?"

Dayna felt a sinking feeling in the pit of her stomach. She wanted no part of this, but if she didn't do it, who would? The words were out of her mouth before she even knew what she intended to say.

"Where should I start?"

AUTHOR'S NOTE

Spores has had a long, winding journey from inception to publication. In either 2004 or 2005 — holy cow, has it really been two decades? — fellow author Brian Knight and I decided to write a novel together. We came up with the idea of using *Ophiocordyceps unilateralis* to control some kind of primitive protohuman species. (That's how I remember it, anyway; as we've already established, a lot of years have passed since then.) We only wrote a few chapters before realizing that neither of us was the collaborating kind. Some authors can pull it off, but I'm not one of them. Thus, the book was scrapped and, as it's wont to do, time moved on.

Until 2016 or so, when author and editor extraordinaire Lee Murray invited me to write a story for a book called *Hellhole: An Anthology of Subterranean Terror*. I'd just finished writing (as Michael Laurence) the second book in *The Extinction Agenda* series, *The Annihilation Protocol*, and had spent a ton of time learning about the sordid history of the Rocky Mountain Arsenal. I'd utilized the chemical warfare program, but it was still driving me crazy that I'd somehow failed to use the deep injection well. Of course, a novelette about a hellhole gave me the perfect opportunity to do so, and "A Plague of Locusts" was published alongside stories from Sean Ellis and Jonathan Maberry. The book even went on to be nominated for a Bram Stoker Award in 2018.

My initial plan was to release the story as a standalone eBook, but as I was rereading it, I realized that there was so much more story to tell. While the idea of simply expanding it to novel length held a certain appeal, I decided to write a different storyline featuring an entirely new set of characters and even higher stakes. Enter Dr. Dayna Raines and her merry band of scientists (and Craig). Randall and crew survived the cut, although their backstory, much like the fungal chimera and its hosts, took on a life of its own and led me on the journey you just finished.

I hope you enjoyed *Spores* and take a chance on some of the other books from my catalog, where you'll find more adventure, science, history, and nightmarish creatures. Feel free to check out my website and drop me a line while you're there.

ABOUT THE AUTHOR

MICHAEL McBRIDE was born in Colorado Springs, Colorado to an engineer and a teacher, who kindled his passions for science and history. He holds multiple advanced certifications in medical imaging and worked as an x-ray/CT/MRI technologist before achieving his life-long dream of becoming a full-time author. He lives in the Lakes Region of New Hampshire with his wife, kids, and a couple of crazy Labrador Retrievers.

Printed in Great Britain
by Amazon